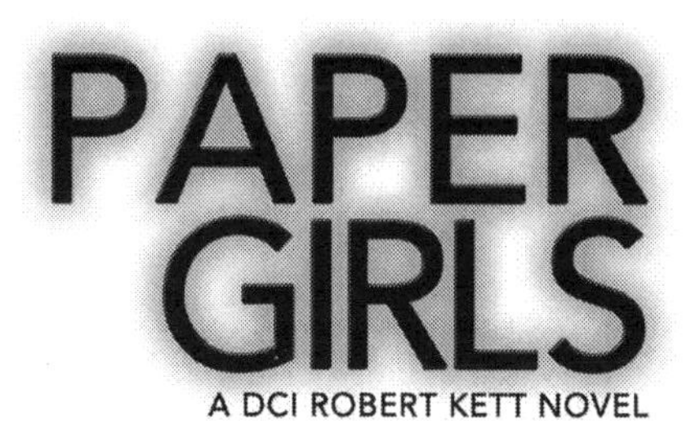

PAPER GIRLS

A DCI ROBERT KETT NOVEL

ALEX SMITH

RELENTLESS MEDIA

PAPER GIRLS
Published Worldwide by Relentless Media.
This edition published in 2019.

ISBN: 978-1-913877-00-2

www.alexsmithbooks.com
www.relentless.media

ALSO BY ALEX SMITH FROM RELENTLESS MEDIA

The DCI Robert Kett Thrillers

Paper Girls

Bad Dog

Three Little Pigs

Whip Crack

Run Rabbit Run

Cry Baby: A Novella

The Softley Softley Thrillers

The Harder They Fall

Hard Luck House (Coming Soon)

Other Books

Six Days, Six Hours, Six Minutes

*For my own equally wonderful,
equally annoying daughters.
Love you!*

PROLOGUE

Tuesday

Everybody remembered the rain. They remembered it because the days had been flawless, and the heat had been almost unbearable. The streets had been too hot to walk on so the kids had been out in force on two wheels, bikes thrumming on the shimmering tarmac, their laughter carrying in the way laughter only really carries in summer.

Then, out of nowhere, the skies had darkened like a bruise and split wide open. It had happened so suddenly that even the weather reporters had been taken by surprise, almost apologetic on their midday catch-ups. The storm had been supposed to miss the east, they said, it should have been scooped out across the coast where the North Sea would pummel it into nothing. Instead it had cast its sights on Norfolk and struck with a fury that made windows rattle and trees bend backwards. Not a soul had been out that day, not unless they had no choice. The city was a gallery of ghostly faces who watched the downpour through their fogged-up windows.

Everybody remembered the rain, afterwards. It's what they said in every statement, and on every broadcast. *She shouldn't have been working. Her mother must have been crazy to let her out. The rain was so strong it must have washed her out to sea.*

Everybody remembered the rain. The rain that kept the city indoors.

Not a soul had been out that day, not a soul apart from that one poor girl.

And the man who took her away.

"MUM, PLEASE!"

At eleven, going on twelve, Maisie Malone was too old for foot stamping, but she'd clean run out of options. She'd tried arguing her case a hundred different ways, to the point where her mum had actually put her fingers in her ears, dancing from foot to foot while yelling, "*Lalala.*" She'd tried shutting herself in her room but her mum had threatened to take away her phone. She'd tried the same old threat that she always used, to run away and never come back. But mum had just shrugged and called her bluff, because the whole point of the stupid argument was that Maisie didn't *want* to go outside. So where was she going to run to? The cupboard under the sink?

Other than stamping her foot on the worn living room carpet, what else could she do?

"Just look, mum, it's pouring!"

It really was. It had switched from sunshine to monsoon

in a heartbeat, the rain coming down so hard that there was a river of it running down the hill.

"I know what rain looks like, Maisie," said her mum, walking out of their tiny kitchen in her dressing gown and PJs—even though it had gone noon. She had a soft pack of Mayfairs in her hand and the same yellow disposable lighter she must have owned for as long as Maisie had been alive. "I also know it can't hurt you. Not unless you're a Gremlin."

She looked Maisie up and down.

"Actually, maybe you *are* a Gremlin. That would explain a lot of things."

"Mum!"

She wanted to scream the house down, but there was nothing guaranteed to make mum lose her rag like a tantrum. Her phone was a brand-new iPhone 7—well, brand new to her, mum had got it off Facebook marketplace for cheap because it had a scratch on the screen—and she'd already lost it once for refusing to help hoover up. She couldn't risk losing it again, not now that she'd finally figured out how to install the Minecraft app.

"Look, I'll do it tomorrow," she pleaded. "Mr Walker's never even bothered if we're late."

"Yes, he is," mum said, lighting up a cigarette. Maisie waved the smoke out of her face, glaring hard. "And it's not even him, it's his customers. They expect their papers on time. No point getting them a week after the news, is there? It won't be news then. It will be *olds*."

She laughed at her own joke and Maisie grunted.

"It's the free paper," she moaned. "Nobody even reads it."

Her mum inhaled deeply, holding the smoke in her lungs. She turned around to breathe it back into the kitchen —the only place she was really supposed to spark up—but it still went everywhere, so strong that it made Maisie's head ring. Every wall in the house was yellow, and she wondered if her lungs were the same.

"Maisie, what did I say to you yesterday?" her mum said, her calmness infuriating.

Maisie shrugged, but she remembered all too well.

"I said you needed to do your rounds, didn't I? I said if you leave it until tomorrow then you'll regret it. And here we are, a quarter past three on a Tuesday afternoon, and do you regret it? Yes. You wanted the job, you wanted the extra money. Nobody forced you to do it, and if you want to quit, you can call Mr Walker right now."

Maisie stamped her foot again, but all it succeeded in doing was plastering a smug grin on her mum's fat, yellow face. For a moment she half thought about doing exactly that, calling Mr Walker and telling him to stick his job where the sun didn't shine. But he paid her three pounds an hour, and the tenner it got her every week helped pay for all the stuff that mum's benefits couldn't stretch to.

Not to mention the extra money she got for selling the *other* things.

Besides, mum was right, it was only rain.

She sighed, looking at the door.

"Please?" she tried, one more time.

She was surprised to feel her mum's arm around her, pulling tight, the cigarette held high above her head so it wouldn't burn her eye out.

"I'm proud of you, Lazy-Maisie," her mum said. "You're growing up fast, you're becoming such a big girl."

She let go, then slapped her on the bum.

"Go on, get it over and done with. I'll bung some fishfingers in the oven and we can have sandwiches the second you get in. Yeah?"

Maisie blew another sigh through her lips.

"Fine."

IT WASN'T EVEN that bad, after the first few seconds. It wasn't cold rain, there was an almost pleasant warmth to it, like standing in the shower. It was as powerful as a shower too, more so maybe, compared to their own one with its limescale crust and its pitiful flow. Once the shock of being hit in the face by a thousand angry droplets had passed, Maisie almost enjoyed the feel of it.

The ride through the estate was almost all downhill, but she kept one hand locked on the brakes to stop her wheels from sliding all over the place. The water streamed into the drains, pooling so deep in places that there were little whirlpools. Every time she steered through a puddle she sent sheets of water over the empty pavements and she almost laughed at the thought of drenching imaginary people—her mum being right at the top of that list. The newspaper bag was a tonne weight on her shoulder but she was used to it, and she took it easy around the corners so that it wouldn't drag her over.

Every now and then a car would pass, moving almost in slow motion, headlights blazing even though it was the middle of the day. A couple of people waved to her, a couple more pointed and laughed. One old woman even rolled down her window and asked her if she wanted a lift home. She didn't reply, she knew better than to talk to strangers—even kind ones in flowery frocks. She just stood on her pedals and fought her way up the hill on the other side of the estate until she wheezed into the first little cul-de-sac that made up her route.

It was deserted, like some kind of zombie apocalypse had hit—which wasn't too weird a thought, really, given that everyone who lived around here was about a hundred years old and moved like the undead. She parked her bike outside the first bungalow and wrestled with the gate. Then she ran into the driving rain, so fast that she slipped on the cobbles and flew into the door. Her knuckles cracked against the wood and she brought them to her lips, wincing as the pain pulsed through her hand. The newspaper was drenched the second she pulled it from her bag, but she managed to push it through the stubborn letterbox, poking the last corner in with her finger until it snapped free and dropped.

It took her less than eight minutes to do the first side of the road, a little longer to do the opposite because Number 4 had a mean old dog and she was always terrified it was going to bite off her thumb. Grabbing her bike, she wheeled down the main road and into the next cul-de-sac, which was almost identical to the last. She spotted a few crinkled faces behind the net curtains and offered them unenthusiastic waves. If they waved back, she didn't see. The rain poured into her eyes, turning the world into a kaleidoscope of blurred shapes and colours.

She finished the street then took refuge in a bus shelter, pulling the sodden hair from her face and blowing the raindrops from her lips. The downpour drummed its fingers against the roof, dropped mercilessly onto the street, locking her inside a cage of glass and falling water. Drying her hands as best she could, she yanked the phone from her jeans, her heart tripping over itself as she noticed how wet the screen was. It still worked, though, telling her that half an hour had passed since she'd left home. Again, that brief thought tickled her brain: she could call Mr Walker now, quit this stupid job, dump the papers here then go home.

But if she did that then she lost her Saturday rouna. The one that took her to the heath. The one that *really* made the money. Twenty quid some days.

She shook her head, pushing the phone into the waterproof newspaper bag to keep it safe. She only had three streets left to go, and it wasn't like she could get any wetter.

Bracing herself, she stepped out into the rain and crossed the deserted street, the water coming up to her ankles and filling her trainers from top to bottom. She squelched to the first bungalow, her feet ridiculously heavy, and rested her bike against the crumbling brick wall. She was halfway up the path, a paper in her hand, when she paused.

The front door was open. Not just a crack, either, it was *wide* open. From where she was standing, Maisie could see water pooling on the hallway carpet, droplets hitting the top of a walnut phone table. It was ridiculously dark inside, and when she glanced at the two large front windows—one a living room, presumably, the other the bedroom—she saw that the heavy curtains were pulled tight.

She took another couple of steps, the newspaper already limp. Something was going off in her head—not a noise, exactly, more a *feeling*. It was an alarm, instinctive, unmistakable. There was something off about this house. Something *wrong*. She smudged the water from her eyes, noticing how painful it was to blink. Behind her, the street stood silent and still, almost like a cardboard theatre set. Nothing felt quite real beneath the fury of the storm, as if it might start to fold and crumble. The house just waited.

It's only a house, she told herself. And just like that, the feeling went. Any longer and the newspaper would dissolve, so she ran to the front door and threw it inside, getting ready to bolt back to the street.

stopped her. A voice from inside. Thin, reedy,
e.

”

It was as though the day had filled her with rainwater and then frozen her solid. For an awful moment, Maisie couldn't even move. She took a step back, her skin tingling, her scalp shrinking so fast she wondered if her hair would drop out.

"Please?" the voice said. It sounded old, *ancient*.

All of a sudden, Maisie felt terrible for even thinking about leaving. Maybe somebody had fallen over and couldn't get up? Old folks were always having accidents and breaking themselves, she knew that from watching Casualty with her mum.

"Um..." she said, her voice hiding in her throat. "Hello? Do you need help? I've, uh, I've got a phone."

She reached into the newspaper bag, fumbling for it. There was no reply from inside the house—at least none that she could hear over the pounding rain—and she walked to the door, craning in, not quite willing to put any of herself closer than it needed to be. There was a weird smell from inside, stronger even than the rain-churned earth. It was a rotten smell, like when they didn't put the bin out in the middle of summer, but there was something medicinal about it too, something that reminded her of hospitals. It caught in her throat.

"Hello?" she called, louder this time. It was impossible to see anything in there, there just wasn't enough light in the day. The world might have ended halfway down that corridor. "I'll call an ambulance, hang on."

Nothing.

She found her phone, almost whooping with triumph. Her hands were shaking, her thumb too wet to unlock it.

"Give me a second," she said, typing in her passcode. "It will be okay."

Still no reply.

"Come on, dammit," she growled at her phone. It finally unlocked, and she glanced at the copper number screwed to the side of the door, trying to remember what flower this cul-de-sac was named after. Geranium Close? Gerbera Close? She was so flustered that for a moment she couldn't even remember the number for 999.

It's 999, you idiot!

She dialled it, holding the phone to her ear and listening to it ring.

Come on, hurry up.

There was no movement inside the house, just a deep, heavy, silent darkness that made her tummy feel funny. She stared into it, trying to make sense of anything there, trying to find a contour or edge or outline that would ground her.

There, wasn't that something? A deeper shadow amongst the gloom? Tall, thin. A clock, perhaps? A coat stand? She focussed on it as the phone rang, and rang, and—

The shape moved, it moved *fast*. Maisie had the sudden sense of a train punching its way through a tunnel, a rush of darkness so swift and so sudden that the scream burned itself out of her before she even knew it was coming. That wall of shadow rushed towards her, filling the doorway, and a hand clamped itself over her jaw.

The phone clicked, a tiny voice asked her what the emergency was, but she couldn't answer.

Another hand grabbed her hair, twisting her head and wrenching her inside. And hidden by the thunder of the rain, Maisie's world went black.

CHAPTER ONE

Wednesday

"Are we nearly there yet?"

It took every ounce of patience that Robert Kett had left not to slam his foot on the brake and run, screaming, out of the car. To be fair, he'd been feeling like this for the last three hours, ever since the ten-year-old, pigeon-shit-green Volvo had pulled away from their house in Stepney and begun the infuriating drive north-east. Two of the three kids in the back had asked this question every ten minutes. The third was only eighteen months old, too young to speak in full sentences, but her relentless screaming had more than made up for it.

Outside, the world was on fire. The freak summer storm yesterday seemed to have sucked every drop of moisture from the sky, and the sun set about its work with a hammer. It filled Kett's windscreen like liquid and turned the tarmac to a shimmering mirage. He'd been squinting so hard, and for so long, that it felt like the front of his head had been compressed in a vice.

"Dad? Are we?"

He cleared the lorry and pulled back into the left-hand lane of the A11 before glancing in the rear-view mirror. Alice frowned back at him, her jaw bulging as she chewed a piece of gum that had lasted the entire journey. A white van overtook them, a blinding flash of sunlight cutting into the car, and for a moment the seven-year-old looked just like her mum, as if Billie was sitting right there in the back seat. It was such a powerful vision that Kett felt as though his mind had been cut loose from his skull, the vertigo making him grip the wheel like a drifting astronaut clutching a tether.

He turned back to the road, swallowing nothing but dust.

"Dad?" Alice said.

"Dad?" added her three-year-old sister, Evie. "I'm hungry."

"Dad?"

"Aad," went the baby, before breaking into another klaxon-like wail of fury. It was so loud that Kett had to close his eyes for a second, and in doing so he almost missed the sliproad. He indicated, pulling off, the sun mercifully falling over his shoulder. The car seemed to instantly cool by ten degrees.

"I'm hungry!" whined Evie. "I need a poo."

"Are we nearly there?" said Alice.

"We are," he said, and for the first time that day it wasn't a lie. "We are. Ten minutes, I promise."

Although it would be longer, because he couldn't quite remember where he was going. He'd spent the first twelve years of his life up here, but that was thirty years ago now and the roads had changed since then. He half thought about pulling over and firing up the satnav, but if he stopped now then the chances were the girls would pile out with or without his permission, and Moira's screams would quadruple in strength.

He scanned the forest of green signposts ahead, spotting one for the north of the city and swerving into the next lane over. Somebody leaned on their horn as he cut them up and in a moment of blind fury he almost contemplated climbing out of the Volvo, dragging them from their car and arresting them right there on the hard shoulder.

Except you're not on duty any more, he reminded himself. *Not technically, anyway. The whole point of coming up here is to get away.*

Get away from London. Get away from the job. Get away from everything that reminded him of Billie, his wife.

He slammed on his brakes just to annoy the man behind him, slowing to a crawl as he approached the traffic lights ahead. They'd just switched to red when he put his foot down, the old Volvo roaring through the lights and onto the circular. He checked his mirror, seeing the car behind him screech to a halt, a red face gurning through the windscreen.

He might not be on duty any more, but there was nothing to stop him being an arsehole.

"I can feel a poo coming out," said Evie.

"For heaven's sake," he grunted. "Just hang on, it's right up ahead."

Luckily it was halfway between lunch and pick-up and the roads were relatively clear. He raced up the circular, looking out onto a city that he had mostly forgotten—and which had entirely forgotten him. Other than flashes of the cathedral spire, etched in golden sunshine, there wasn't a single thing here that he could remember from childhood. Occasionally a police car would drive by and he waved reflexively, and the one time an ambulance blazed past in full concert mode he had to avoid the urge to chase it. He kept his head down, kept his pace steady, as they made their way up the hill.

"Evie's pooped herself," said Alice with an unkind laugh.

"I haven't! You have!" she retaliated.

"You've pooped your pants!"

"I'll poop in *your* pants!" Evie squealed.

At this, Kett almost managed a smile. He slowed, scanning the street names, finding the one he wanted and turning the car off the main road. Only when he saw the house ahead did he remember to breathe, and it felt like the first breath he'd taken all day, flooding his body with relief. The girls sensed it, all of them falling quiet.

The street was busy, cars parked up both sides, and Kett had to drive halfway up before he found a space. He pulled in, bumping up onto the kerb. Then he switched off the engine, and for a single, blissful moment there was no sound at all other than the gentle whisper of the wind in the trees outside.

"Is this it?" screeched Alice at a thousand decibels. "Are we here?"

He nodded and they broke into cheers that could have shattered every window on the street, Moira making a noise that might have been joy or might have been terror—Kett wasn't sure. He opened his door, the hinges squeaking almost as much as his joints did as he climbed out and straightened up. Alice had already unbuckled herself and was climbing into the front.

"No!" yelled Evie, wrestling with her bumper seat. "Wait for me!"

Kett closed his eyes, pushing down on a sudden wave of

anxious energy. What he wouldn't give to have Billie here right now, her soothing voice, her smile. She would have calmed the girls in a heartbeat.

But she's gone, he reminded himself. *She's gone.*

He opened his eyes, liquid sunlight searing its way into his head.

"Come on," he said, helping Alice out of the car. "Let's go start our new life."

CHAPTER TWO

As it turned out, their new life didn't want to start.

"Come on, you *fudging barstool,*" Kett said as he jiggled the key in the Yale lock. Moira squirmed in his arms, as strong as a bear cub. Her chubby hands repeatedly hit him in the face, making the job of unlocking the house even harder than it should have been. Behind him, Alice was sitting on the low wall of the front garden, Evie doing her best to climb up beside her.

The key wouldn't budge. Kett swore, hefting the baby into his other arm.

"Daddy, I really need a poo," said Evie, abandoning the wall and clutching her behind.

"I'm working on it, sweetie," he said through gritted teeth. "Give me a second. Hold it in and say *You shall not pass!*"

He cut down the side of the house. It was a three-bed semi, the walls grey pebbledash and the sash windows peeling like dandruff. Somebody, probably the letting agent, had done a half-arsed job of cutting back the shrubbery, but

Kett still could have done with a machete as he pushed through the rickety gate into the back garden. He held it open for the girls, who immediately began running in crazed circles around the yellowing grass, barking like dogs.

It seemed safe enough, so he placed Moira on the lawn, the baby waddling after her sisters. There was another door here which probably led into the kitchen and he tried the handle, knowing that he was being a little optimistic. Sure enough, the door was locked, although the whole thing shifted in its frame when he shook it.

"Daaaady!" yelled Evie, obviously in some distress.

Kett slipped his phone out of his pocket, ignoring the photograph of him and Billie on the lockscreen—Billie in blue silk, a daisy in her honey-coloured hair, grinning as she kissed him on the cheek at a friend's wedding two years ago. He opened his emails, trying to find the number of the letting agent. Behind him, Moira had started screaming again, and Evie quickly joined in. The noise spun the stress dial in Kett's head to eleven and before he was even aware of what he was doing he'd lifted his foot, stepped forward, and planted his size eleven police boot on the lock side of the door.

It didn't stand a chance, the old wood splintering as it crunched against the wall. It wobbled like a KO'd boxer as it swung back, and Kett used a hand to steady it. He glanced back, all three girls watching him with wide eyes and open mouths. A welcome bubble of laughter spilled out of him.

"That didn't happen," he said. "Come on."

He scooped up the baby, holding the door for Alice and Evie. The inside of the house was mercifully cool, the kitchen blinds pulled halfway down and the air heavy with dust. He'd been in a lot of houses over the years and he knew instinctively that this one had lain dormant for some time. The surfaces had been cleaned, the floor swept, but the handles of the cabinets looked greasy with disuse, and there were ancient cobwebs spun like silk up and down the chain of the blind. It hadn't been opened in weeks.

Still, it was dry. It was quiet.

It was home.

"Hurry daddy!" squirmed Evie.

"Come on, find the bathroom then."

He twisted the tap to get the lead out of the water, watching Alice and Evie as they barrelled from the kitchen into the hallway. Moira was making a bid for freedom again but he held onto her as he fumbled with his phone, finally finding the number for the letting agent. He walked out of the room as it rang, seeing a short corridor with a staircase leading up into sunshine. Alice and Evie were in the living room, pounding the couch into dust as they leaped up and down on it.

"Careful," he told them, his word carrying just as much authority as he suspected it would. They continued to jump, and Kett stepped out into the hall again, finding a small toilet beneath the stairs. It was a tiny house, and he cursed himself for believing the photographs he'd seen online. The tricks they worked with house brochures were magic, all low angles and good lighting. It was almost criminal.

"Evie," Kett called out. "Toilet, come on, I don't want you christening the new house."

"I don't need any more," she called back.

"Of course you don't," he grumbled. "Bloody—"

"Good afternoon, Shackley's, Dawn speaking, how may I help?"

The young voice on the phone sounded about as bored as it was possible to be. The baby heard it and shrieked a

"Hiya!" right into Kett's ear, so he gave up and put her down.

"Yeah, hi," he said. "My name's Robert Kett, I'm renting one of your properties. 8 Morgane Street."

"Do you have a postcode?" Dawn asked.

"No, but I'm pretty sure you won't have two houses at 8 Morgane Street. My key didn't work."

Dawn popped some gum.

"Right," she said. "It should have worked."

"I am well aware that it should have worked," he replied, trying to stay patient. "Keys usually do, otherwise what's the point of them? This one didn't."

"I can get a locksmith to you by the end of the day."

"We're already in," he said. "But you'll need to send somebody to fix the door."

"You can't let yourself in," Dawn said, her voice as monotone as a computer. "You have to wait—"

"Dawn," Kett interrupted. "Let me introduce myself again, properly this time. I'm Detective Chief Inspector Robert Kett, of the Metropolitan Police." Whatever Dawn was chewing, she stopped, letting Kett continue. "We need the house secure by tonight. The state of that door, you're clearly in breach of your duties as agents. If you like, I can call this in, maybe start an investigation into the security of your tenants?"

"Uh..." said Dawn. "I'll get somebody to you within the hour."

"Of course you will," he said.

He ended the call while she stuttered a response. He hated pulling rank, especially now that he technically wasn't supposed to do it, but some people deserved to have the fear of god stamped into them and Bored Dawn was certainly one of those people.

"Hey," he said, spotting Moira climbing the stairs. "Plenty of time to explore, kiddo."

He was scooping her up when his phone rang, and he answered it without looking.

"You'd better not be messing with me, Dawn," he growled.

"As if," replied a gravelly voice that made Kett stand to attention. "Not even the dawn itself would mess with DCI Kett."

"Sir," Kett said, almost dropping the squirming baby. He let her go again, watching her scoot into the living room on all fours like a wind-up toy. He heard Superintendent Barry "Bingo" Benson laugh, the booming sound of it making him feel weirdly nostalgic.

"You still driving?" Bingo asked.

"Nah, just got here," Kett replied, taking a moment to stretch out his back. "Felt like it took three weeks."

"Not surprised, Norwich is the arse end of our ancient nation, isn't it? The puckered anus on the rump of Great Britain."

"That's a little harsh," Kett said, walking to the front door and peering through the textured glass. "We've got two cathedrals here, and about three hundred pubs."

"That covers your basic food groups," Bingo said.

Kett heard the man's chair creak, could picture him leaning back and putting his feet on the desk. Superintendent Benson had got his nickname after the time he'd been called out to a triple homicide in Angel Islington one Saturday evening and he'd forgotten to take off his bowtie and bingo-caller's mic. Turned out that was what he did to relax, his baritone voice perfect for the bingo halls. Apparently, the old ladies loved him, and they weren't the only ones. As far as Supers went, he was one of the best.

"Kids okay?" Bingo asked. Kett held the phone up to the screams that were coming from the living room. Bingo laughed. "I can't tell if they're having fun or being tortured."

"They're having fun," Kett said. "*I'm* being tortured. But they're doing okay. I think the move will be good for them. It has to be."

Bingo sighed.

"It will be," he said. "For them, and for you. You're on compassionate leave, Robbie, you need this time for yourself, to heal your family. You can't do that in London."

Kett nodded.

Don't ask, he told himself. *Don't ask*. It was an order, but he heard himself say it anyway.

"Any news?"

"You know as well as I do that the moment we hear anything, you're the first person I call." Bingo cleared his throat. "If she's out there, we'll find her."

It was a telling turn of phrase, Kett thought. For the first few days it had been *We'll bring her home*. For the next few weeks it had been, *Don't worry, she'll show up*. Kett had known it was only a matter of time before the word "if" appeared, he just hadn't expected it to be so soon. Fourteen weeks was no time at all.

It was also forever.

Bingo seemed to acknowledge his mistake.

"We'll find her," he said. "Let us take care of Billie. You take care of you and yours."

Kett heard a rustle as the man stroked his thick moustache, something he always did before a big announcement. It was his tell. Bingo might have been good at Bingo, but he was one of the worst poker players on the planet.

"What?" said Kett.

"I mean it about taking this time not to work," Bingo

said. "But as you're up there, I need you to do me a bit of a favour."

He carried on talking, but his words were drowned out by a carnival of noise that marched out of the living room—all three girls doing the Conga towards the stairs and giggling manically. Kett held out a hand, redirecting them to the kitchen.

"Sorry, sir, you'll have to start over."

Bingo laughed, but there wasn't much humour to it.

"I said I need your help. As of yesterday, two girls have gone missing in Norwich."

Kett frowned. Two missing girls wasn't headline material, and nothing that the local CID couldn't handle.

"Both newspaper delivery girls," Bingo went on. "Both eleven, and both taken while on their routes."

Kett felt an unpleasant current of electricity tickle his spine, settling in his gut.

"Taken?"

"We think so," Bingo replied, sighing. "The Super in charge of the investigation is highly competent—he's an... an *interesting* guy—but this is way past anything his team has dealt with before. Norwich is a quiet place. He needs help."

"I thought I was on leave," Kett said, and he could just about hear Bingo shrug.

"Your paperwork's still on my desk," the Superintendent replied. "I haven't quite got around to filing it yet. Please, Robbie, just swing by, introduce yourself. He'd appreciate it."

Kett blew out a long breath, popping his lips. He peered past the newel post, seeing the kids parading around the kitchen, Moira using her chubby legs to try and climb onto a chair. There were a million reasons to say no, and three of them were right here. The fourth was the last missing persons case he had worked, the only one in his career that he hadn't been able to solve.

And the one that had broken him.

What do I do, Billie?

He didn't need to hear her answer. He already knew what he was going to say. There were two girls missing, after all. Two girls who needed him.

"Sure," he said. "I'll do it."

CHAPTER THREE

Thursday

"You sure it's okay?"

Kett spoke the words through a mouthful of baby dungarees as Moira tried to climb onto his head. Her hands were on his ears so he was deafened as well as blinded to the woman's response, but when he peeled the baby away he saw that she was nodding.

"She's very welcome, Mr Kett," the woman said. She gestured through the door at the nursery behind her: a small, squat, green building which sat in the playground of Alice's new primary school. Inside, twenty kids made the noise of a hundred. Evie hovered by Kett's side, one hand on his leg, peering in with a look that was half nervous excitement and half abject terror. She caught him looking.

"You'll be okay," he said. "It's just for a morning, remember? Your sister went in fine."

That was almost true. There had been a mini freak-out that morning when Alice couldn't find her new school cardigan in the suitcases they'd brought with them, but the weather was hot and Kett had let her go without one as a compromise.

"Alice would be so impressed if you were a big girl too."

Evie didn't reply, she just stood there, her little fists clenched in a way that made Kett's heart hurt. She'd been through so much, and in a way Billie's disappearance had hit her harder than it had the other two. Alice was older, but she was programmed a little differently to most of the people he met. Her last school kept mentioning things like ASD and ADHD, and they were on the waiting list for a referral, but the truth was she was just Alice, delightfully unique on some days, frustratingly awful on others. Quirky was the word most often used to describe her. Unless you were Robert Kett, of course, in which case the most common word was *annoying*.

But Evie, she took in everything, always watching, always thinking. Her big, blue eyes weren't even blinking right now, and Kett knew the storm of thoughts that would be circling her head.

"A couple of hours," he said. "I'll get you some Smarties."

Whatever doubts she'd been having, the mention of Smarties blew them clean away. With a beaming smile she offered her hand to the woman, who took it with a genuine soulful chuckle.

"Smarties," Kett said. "Crack for kids, right?"

A disapproving frown appeared on her face, but only for a second. She looked at Moira, who was once again trying to scale Kett's head like a climber on Everest.

"No Mrs Kett?" she asked, thankfully not loud enough for Evie to hear.

"I'll be back very soon," Kett said, ignoring the question. "Love you, beautiful girl."

"Love you, dad," Evie shouted back, practically dragging the nursery worker after her. Kett waited until the door closed behind them before peeling Moira off his face and holding her out in front of him.

"Two out of three ain't bad," he told her. "Let's hope the Norwich team like babies."

THE NORWICH TEAM HATED BABIES.

It hated them with a passion that made itself clear the moment Kett strolled through the station doors.

"You're kidding me," the man roared. Fortunately, he wasn't yelling at Moira, he was directing his fury at a young woman sitting in the reception area whose toddler was spread-eagled on the floor trying to punch a hole in the ceiling with the sheer power of its voice. "You do know this isn't a creche, don't you? You do know that this is a police station?"

The woman—girl, really, she couldn't have been much older than sixteen—flinched like the man had attacked her with a bat, almost in tears as she picked up the bawling kid. Kett felt himself bristle. Moira had settled a little, but she was still wriggling like a sackful of eels. He cursed himself for not bringing the buggy out of the car. Even now, after all these weeks, he still expected Billie to do it. He grabbed the baby, Billie grabbed the buggy. It was the way they'd always done it.

The angry man made an exaggerated show of stepping

around the mother and child, clutching a sheaf of papers to his chest like they had the next decade's worth of lottery results on them. He was an unpleasant guy, that was clear from the start. Some people just gave off an instantly negative vibe, like there were magnets beneath their skin that repulsed everyone they met. It was something about the tight greying curls of hair, the untrimmed eyebrows and nose foliage, the crust that had formed in the corners of his eyes—not to mention his yellow nails. He was wearing a cheap, grey suit that was two sizes too big for him, a brown belt holding everything together around his skinny middle.

There was something imposing about him too, though. He was in his late fifties and he was big, a few inches taller than Kett's five eleven. He moved in a fast, lumbering gait that reminded Kett of a rhino. An angry rhino. Kett had dealt with men like him before, on both sides of the law, and he knew they should never be underestimated.

There was a lanyard hanging from his neck, the ID card facing into his unironed shirt. That meant he was staff.

"Another one," the man growled as he approached Kett, practically snarling at Moira. "This is no place for a child, so do me a favour: if your baby doesn't have to be here, get rid of her."

Kett stood firm, blocking the man's path between the two rows of chairs. The reception of the Norwich station wasn't busy—a handful of sad-looking folk spaced evenly across the seats and a young male sergeant at the window—but the tall man had caught everyone's attention.

"How about you lighten up a little," Kett said, locking the dozen or so swear words he wanted to say behind his teeth. "They're just kids. Believe me, they want to be here as much as the rest of us."

The man snorted, then started to push past. Kett didn't

budge, standing tall and wide, and the man jabbed a finger at him.

"Believe me, son, I am in no mood to be tossed over."

"*Tossed* over?" Kett said, almost choking on the words. "I'm pretty sure that doesn't mean what you think—"

"Sit down and wait your turn, unless you want me to take you back there and let you cool off."

Kett took a deep breath, wondering if he should just turn around and leave. He didn't have to be here, he didn't have to offer his help. If this was the kind of reception the Norwich team gave him then why the hell would he even bother?

His mouth was open to say just that when he caught a glimpse of what was on the documents the man was holding: a grainy photocopy of a photograph of a young girl in her school uniform, gap-toothed and grinning. Kett recognised her instantly from the brief bit of research he'd done last night after he'd put his daughters to bed.

Maisie Malone, one of the missing newspaper girls.

"As a matter of fact," Kett said. "I wouldn't mind going in. I've got to speak with your Super."

The man frowned, the expression making his face even more unpleasant.

"About her," Kett elaborated, nodding at the paper. "My name is DCI Robert Kett, I'm with the Met. My Super, Bingo... uh, *Barry* Benson, asked me to stop by."

"He did, did he?" the man said, his mouth working like he was chewing tobacco. He wiped the white specks from his lips, looking Kett up and down then turning his attention to Moira.

"Childcare," Kett explained. "Lack of. We've only just moved up here."

"From *London*," the man said, sneering his way around the word. Kett sighed, fairly sure of what he was about to hear next: fifty quid on the words *big* and *shot* coming out of his mouth.

"Some kind of bigshot?" the man said. "Riding out to the sticks to solve the case us yokels can't get our turnip heads around."

"Something like that," Kett said, growing tired of the man's attitude. "Are you going to take me to your Superintendent, or do you have to ask one of the desk sergeants for permission?"

The man leaned in, those nose hairs almost close enough to tickle Kett's lip.

"I *am* the Super," he said. "Superintendent Colin Clare. And I'm pretty sure we don't need you, DCI Kett. Or your baby."

If Kett thought he could fit his foot inside his mouth, he might have given it a go. Instead, he took another deep breath, switching Moira to his left arm and holding out his right.

"I'm sorry," he said. "Let's start again."

For a second it looked like the man was about to push past him. Then Clare nodded, gripping Kett's hand in his own huge, dry palm. He pumped twice like he was pouring himself an ale at the pub.

"I should apologise," he said, seeming to sag. "You've caught me at a bad time. Press conference about the missing girls."

"Anything I can do?"

"Not now, but follow me there, it's being held at the Malone place. I know who you are, DCI Kett, I know the cases you're famous for. Maybe you can help."

Kett stood to one side to let the man pass.

"And my daughter?" Kett called after him. Clare didn't turn back, just shouted over his shoulder.

"You can bring her, if you promise she won't make any noise."

CHAPTER FOUR

In the entire eighteen months and four days of her life, Moira Kett had never made as much noise as she was making right now.

So much noise, in fact, that practically everyone on the street was staring at her.

"Come on," Kett coaxed. "Please, moo-moo, you're knackered."

He glanced up at his audience, almost all of whom were reporters. Maybe thirty of them spanned the width of the residential street, some leaning against their news trucks, others fiddling with their microphones, more still snapping photographs of Kett on their phones and cameras. He thought about flashing them the bird but managed to restrain himself. Besides, it was hard to stick your middle finger up when your hands were full of a stone and a half of wriggling flesh.

"No!" yelled Moira, her favourite word. "No! Shoes!"

It was what she said when she wanted to walk, and she demonstrated this by booting Kett in the face with her mini-Kickers as he tried to clip her in to the buggy.

"Goddam—" he started.

"Here, try this."

The voice came from behind him, and suddenly there was a uniformed constable by his side. She was holding an old-fashioned Peeler's police whistle and she blew a couple of quiet chirps before handing it to the baby. Moira settled instantly, her big eyes full of wonder as she investigated this strange, shiny new toy. Kett clipped her in before she could notice it was happening.

"God, thank you," he said, turning to the officer. She was in her early twenties maybe, although the coal-black pixie cut beneath her bowler hat and the sparkle in her eyes made her look even younger. She couldn't have been on the force long, nobody looked that fresh after a year of policing —not even on the quiet streets of Norwich. "I honestly thought she was about to suplex me."

The woman frowned.

"You're probably too young for WWF," he said. "Wrestling. Never mind."

"It's WWE now," she said with a smile. She held out her hand and he shook it. "I'm PC Kate Savage, happy to help."

"Savage?" Kett asked. "Nice."

"It does the job," she replied. "Especially in interviews. 'Get Savage in here!' Tends to make the bad guys open up."

"I'll bet. I'm DCI Kett. Robert."

"Local boy, then?" she asked, and it was Kett's turn to frown. "Your name. Kett. It's a Norfolk name through and through. There's a road here, Kett's Hill. It means Kite, I think, as in the bird of prey. And there's Robert Kett, obviously. The *other* one. Rebel, fought some battles against the government."

"Sounds like an awesome guy," said Kett.

"Hanged from the castle," Savage added.

"Oh," he said. "I vaguely remember it from school. Yeah, my folks were from here. My mum still lives in the county, although we haven't spoken in a long, long time. Not since my dad passed, really. I grew up across town. Mile Cross."

"The Badlands," Savage said, sucking air through her teeth.

"It's still rough?"

"Not as bad as it was, but I wouldn't want to go there alone in the middle of the night."

Moira was doing her best to blow the whistle, making little warbling farty noises with it and laughing her head off.

"They still give you whistles around here?" Kett asked, one eyebrow raised. Savage nodded.

"It's how we communicate. I mean, they tried radios but they're just too new-fangled for us country folk."

It took Kett a moment to appreciate the joke, and Savage's smile grew even broader.

"My granddad gave it to me," she said. "He was on the force back in the day, it was his whistle. It brought him good luck, or so he claimed."

"It won't bring you good luck when you try to get it back from her," Kett said.

"She can hang onto it. You've been seconded, right? To help find those girls?"

"Well, not officially," he started, but there was no time to explain as Superintendent Clare walked out of the front door of the Malone's narrow terraced house, his brogues clomping down the path. He stood to one side and ushered out a tiny, hunched woman who, at first glance, looked about a thousand years old. It was only when she lifted her head to nod at the Super that Kett saw she was only in her thirties, her eyes red with old tears and her cheeks damp with new ones. Even if he hadn't seen Maisie's face in the woman's own he would have known her as the missing girl's mother. Nothing but grief can age you like that.

They hadn't even reached the gate before the crowd of reporters surged forwards, crashing against the kerb with a thunder of voices.

"Do you have any leads?"

"Are there any suspects in custody?"

"Do you suspect that Maisie and Connie have been murdered?"

As sensitive as always, Kett thought. *Bastards.*

"Here we go," said PC Savage, wading into the melee. "I'll be back."

She joined the rank of uniformed constables, pushing the journalists back far enough so that Colin Clare and Maisie's mum could escape onto the pavement. Kett looked past them, seeing more people inside the house—Norfolk CID, he guessed.

"Thank you," said Clare, his voice loud enough to echo off the houses opposite and drown out the reporters. "Please, I understand that you are here to aid this investigation." That was a pretty generous assessment, Kett thought. "But remember that this is a difficult time for Miss Malone and her family, and I would expect you to show her nothing but respect."

To Kett's surprise, none of the reporters threw a question back. There was something authoritarian about Clare, he had the air of a headmaster who could quite easily cane you into submission.

"I am Superintendent Colin Clare of the Norfolk Constabulary, and I need not remind you that this is an ongoing case, so I will not be able to answer many questions.

Our job here today is to allow Miss Malone the opportunity to reach out to her daughter and call her home. Are we clear?"

Again, just nods and murmurs. Compared to the London press, these guys were practically saints. The Super stood to one side and put his huge hand on the woman's shoulder, guiding her forwards a couple of steps.

"Miss Malone."

Maisie's mother looked as brittle as glass, like she might shatter into fragments as soon as she opened her mouth. She stood there, hunched and bowed as if she carried the world on her shoulders, her hands clasped in front of her and her head angled up to the man beside her. He gave her a kind smile, nodding, and she turned to the reporters.

"Maisie?" she started, her voice wobbling. Once again she looked at the Super and he gently squeezed her shoulder. It seemed to give her strength.

"Maisie, I don't know if you can hear me, if you'll hear this. You never liked the news, did you?" She managed a sad little laugh that turned into a hacking cough and then a sob. "But I want you to know I love you, more than anything. I'm sorry I made you go out in the rain." The noise she made was like a woman drowning. "I shouldn't've done it. But I love you, and if... if you're angry with me, if that's why you've gone away, then please come home. I won't be mad. I'm never mad. I love you."

Kett took a deep breath that caught in his throat. He looked at Moira, thinking about her, and Alice, and Evie, and wondering how he'd cope if one of them disappeared. If one of them was *taken*. Losing a wife was one thing—an awful thing—but losing a child was a million times worse.

Miss Malone had unspun like a clockwork toy, and she

fell quiet and still. Clare kept his hand on her shoulder as he addressed the reporters again.

"I'll take some questions," he said. "Until I hear something I don't like. Then we're gone. So make them good. Alan."

He nodded at a middle-aged man in a tan suit, who lifted his iPhone.

"Do you think the missing girls have been taken by the same man?" he asked.

"We don't know they were taken, and if they were, we don't know whether it was a man, let alone the same man," said Clare. "Sarah."

"There have been complaints for years now about the reduced number of uniformed police on the city's streets," said a young woman in jeans and a yellow blouse. "Are cuts to the police force making us all less safe?"

"I'm not going to respond to that," growled Clare. "Mainly because a child could answer that question. One more. Doug."

"Me?" asked a man at the front, pointing at himself. "I'm Jim."

"Doug, Jim, I don't care, just ask your question."

"Um, okay, both girls worked for the same newsagent. Uh..." He checked a notepad. "Walker's. Is David Walker a suspect?"

"What part of *on-go-ing in-vest-i-ga-tion* is confusing for you? Last chance."

A woman at the back of the group raised her hand, almost jumping on the spot like she needed permission to go to the toilet. Clare grunted at her.

"You say this isn't necessarily an abduction," the woman said. "But you've drafted in help from the Met. That's Robert Kett."

She pointed across the street, right at Kett, and every pair of eyes swung his way.

"He found the Miller twins when they were kidnapped, two years ago. And he caught Albert Shipton after he murdered that Khan boy in 2015. If he's here, surely this is more than a missing persons case, it must be abduction or murder."

A look of disgust creased Clare's face into a mask.

"Stupid," he said, seeming to direct his anger at both the reporter and at Kett. "That's your lot. Let's try this again tomorrow."

With that, he steered Miss Malone in a tight circle and guided her back to the house. The reporters broke out in another ugly chorus of questions but they knew they'd had their lot, the ones at the back already drifting away.

Kett looked down at Moira, almost breaking into a cheer when he noticed that she'd gone to sleep during the press conference—her clammy hands holding the whistle to her lips. He jiggled the buggy a little, just to be sure.

"Told you it was good luck," said PC Savage as she walked up to him. She gently prised the whistle loose and tucked it into her pocket.

"That last question didn't feel lucky," he said. "Maybe I should have kept my distance."

"They were going to find out sooner or later," she said. "The Major Investigation Team wants to speak with you inside."

Kett sighed, wondering how he'd be able to keep the baby quiet in such a small space. Savage seemed to read his mind.

"Let me, sir," she said.

"Oh, really?" Kett grinned. "That would be great, if you don't mind?"

"It's no problem," she said. "As much as I'd love to see Clare chew you out for bringing a baby to a crime scene, I think you've had enough of a bollocking for one day. I'll keep her out of the sun."

Kett kissed Moira on the head before pulling the hood over the buggy. Then he made his way into the Malone house hoping that Savage was right, and that his bollocking was good and done with.

CHAPTER FIVE

"Do you think you could have made that a little easier for them?"

It was a bollocking, true and proper. Superintendent Colin Clare stood in the house's microscopic entrance hall—the space so small that his chest was almost touching Kett's. Any closer and they'd be kissing, not talking.

Not that Kett was doing much talking.

"It's bad enough that you even got sent up here, but you don't have to hang around outside flouncing in front of the press. Now that's all we're going to see on the bloody papers tomorrow: bigshot Londoner brought in to find missing girls."

The boss took a deep breath, shaking his head.

"I wouldn't say I was flouncing, exactly," said Kett. "I don't have the hips for it."

Clare snarled, then pushed his way inside—stopping for a moment to look back.

"It's our case, Kett," he said. "You can tag along as much as you like, but don't forget where you are. Clear?"

Kett nodded, holding up his hands in surrender.

"Use me and abuse me however you like, *sir*," he said, earning another look of disgust.

He followed the Super through another narrow door into a postage-stamp sized sitting room. Everything felt too small, as if a giant had picked up the whole row of houses and squeezed them like an accordion. It was probably more to do with the fact that three coppers stood in the room, a uniformed constable and two detectives, one male and one female. The constable and the woman gave Kett a cursory look before dismissing him.

"DS Spalding, PC Turner, and DC Raymond Figg, our FLO," Clare said. "This is DCI Kett."

The other man—a family liaison officer—nodded at Kett. His face was round and his eyes kind, and there was something almost familiar about him, in his neatly trimmed goatee and pale, receding hair. He was wearing an inoffensive chequered shirt beneath a navy blazer—despite the fact it had to be thirty degrees outside. He dressed like an older guy, but he could only have been in his mid-thirties. He offered his hand and Kett shook it.

"Kett," Figg said. "Wow. It's great to see you again."

"Again?" Kett asked.

"Sorry, yes. We've met once before. I was a second down in London, shadowed another FLO—on the Khan kidnapping. Two, no *three* years ago now."

"The Khan murder, you mean," Kett said, shaking his head like it might stop the memory from returning.

"Yes," said Figg. "But it wasn't a murder when I was there. The mother and boy were still just missing. I followed all your cases. You were the best missing persons detective I met on the job."

Not good enough to find Billie, though, Kett thought, managing a weak smile.

"I'm glad you're here," Figg said, offering his hand once more. Kett shook it again, by which time Clare looked apoplectic. He marched the five or six paces it took to get from the living room to a kitchen that was full of cigarette smoke. Another detective stood by the sink, a hulking figure who was talking quietly to Miss Malone as she smoked by the open window. Even from the back, Kett recognised him—it was impossible not to with a physique like that—and it was all he could do to stop himself breaking into a smile.

"This is DI Porter," said Clare, looking supremely awkward in the middle of the small, smoky room. The other detective turned around, smiled, turned away, then his head twisted back so hard Kett thought it might pop off.

"Robbie!" Porter said, grinning. "I heard they'd sent you up."

"Christ," Clare grunted in Kett's direction. "Is there anyone you *don't* know?"

"Pete," said Kett, shaking DI Porter's outstretched mutton chop of a hand. "Good to see you. Last I heard they'd posted you up north somewhere."

"Yeah, *Cornwall*," Porter laughed, and Kett shrugged. "I was there for a while, the wife got offered a job in Norwich last year so I transferred. How's you? How's your..."

The question died on his lips, plunging the room into silence almost as quickly as Porter's smile divebombed from his face. Kett put him out of his misery.

"Kids, they're just fine."

Porter nodded, grateful. It genuinely was good to see him. Kett had come up the ranks with Porter, right from their first beat, and they'd graduated to detectives together, both finding a home at CID. They'd only been parted after Porter had moved out of the city, something to do with his mum's health. Kett was about to ask after her when the

Superintendent cleared his throat, genuinely aggrieved that the two men had history.

"Miss Malone, this is DCI Robert Kett. He's here from London, from the Met."

His voice seemed to draw the woman out of herself, her head turning like a snail pushing out its eyestalks. She blinked at Kett, the ghost of a smile on her face.

"Is it true?" Miss Malone asked. "You found those missing twin girls?"

"A girl and a boy," Kett said, keeping his own voice as quiet as he could. "Joshua and Bethany Miller. Twins. Yes."

"Kett has found a number of missing children," Clare said. "He's one of the best detectives in the country. When we said we would leave no stone unturned, Jade, I meant it."

Clare was only singing his praises to make the department look good, Kett knew, but the words were welcome anyway.

"And you'll find my Maisie?" the woman asked. Her face had almost crumpled into itself, like it had been drawn on wet cardboard, but the expression of hope there was painfully clear.

"We'll do everything we can to bring her home, Miss Malone. You have my word."

Jade nodded, taking a drag on her cigarette before folding back into herself.

"Good," said Clare. "We have everything we need back at the station. We'll—"

"I'd like to speak with Miss Malone a little longer, if that's okay?" Kett said.

Clare looked like he was about to argue but the woman nodded. Kett rubbed his hands together, smiling at the Superintendent.

"But if you want to make yourself useful, sir, pop the kettle on."

THERE WASN'T much space in the kitchen, so Kett cleared the coppers out of the living room. Figg, the FLO, offered to stay and Kett nodded to the corner where he wouldn't be any bother. Miss Malone slumped into an armchair that looked ten sizes too big for her, and Kett took a moment to sweep the room—a sofa that didn't match the chair, a seventies faux-walnut and brass gas fireplace complete with a decorative poker, brush and shovel, woodchip wallpaper that had been painted sunflower yellow in some places and magnolia in others, jagged whorls of artex on the ceiling that had done nothing but collect cobwebs. Other than the TV and Sky box, the only thing in the room was a white Ikea Billy shelf laden with dusty DVDs and cheaply framed photographs.

"Jade, did I hear that right?" Kett asked as he crossed the room to the shelf. He'd seen one of the photographs before—the picture of Maisie in her school uniform that somebody had photocopied for the file—and he picked it up. Maisie smiled back at him, her arms outstretched and her thumbs pointing skyward.

"Yeah," said Jade, fumbling for another cigarette. It took her a few attempts to light it. "Jade."

"You and Maisie are close," said Kett, replacing the frame and picking up another, this one showing Maisie and her mum hugging in front of a giant circus tent, the kind they have at Butlin's. Jade sniffed, wiping her arm across her face.

"Yeah, she was everything to me." She seemed to hear

herself, gasping. "*Is* everything. She *is* everything to me. Her dad died when she was little, he had pancreatic cancer. Stupid bastard, only he could get pancreatic cancer at twenty-three. Since then it's just been the two of us."

"You could be twins," Kett said. "Same smile."

She showed it now, or at least something that resembled it. Kett took a seat on the sofa, scratching his fingers down the stubble he hadn't bothered to shave since leaving London.

"I'm going to be as honest with you as I can, Jade," he said. "Most cases of missing children tend to resolve themselves very quickly. Kids get angry, kids run off, kids like to make a point that they're independent. Girls especially. Trust me, I've got three."

He glanced out of the window, trying to spot PC Savage through the twists of net curtain. If she was there, he couldn't see her, and he had to push down on a sudden pulse of anxiety. *What if Kate Savage isn't a real cop? What if she's taken Moira away?* He was used to it, it was how a copper's mind worked. He wouldn't be able to do the job if he couldn't *what-if* the worst-case scenarios.

"But with Maisie, it's different," he went on. "The fact that two girls have gone missing in exactly the same circumstances suggests that there is more going on here."

Jade looked like she was about to burst into tears.

"I know," she said, looking at Figg. "He's been through it all. He's been very kind, very honest."

Figg offered the woman a compassionate smile.

"All this doesn't mean Maisie isn't safe," said Kett. "And it doesn't mean we won't find her. It just means we have to be smart, and we have to work fast. Okay?"

Jade nodded, her head slumping almost between her knees as she took a drag on her cigarette.

"Did Maisie know the other girl?" He searched his memory. "Connie Byrne? They worked similar routes."

"I already told the others," said Jade in a mumble that Kett had to lean into to make sense of. "She knew her by sight, but not to talk to. They went to different schools."

Kett fished for his notepad, remembered he didn't have one. He slid his phone from his pocket and opened up the notepad app, his clumsy thumbs writing something that even the autocorrect couldn't make sense of.

"Uh, and her employer, Mr Walker. Did she ever talk about him?"

"Yeah, of course," said Jade, blowing smoke onto the carpet. "She liked him. David's a nice man. Old. He wouldn't hurt a fly, paid the girls okay money and always made sure they were ten or over. Wouldn't let younger ones work for him."

"And Maisie always stuck to her route? Never strayed from it to visit a friend, get some chips?"

"She's a good girl. She puts her head down and just does it, always quick, always back in less than two hours. I made her fishfingers. They went... they went cold."

She sat up, rubbing at her face with her free hand like she was trying to pull it loose.

"I shouldn't've made her go, the weather was awful, it's my fault she went, my fault someone took her."

"She didn't say anything unusual before she left?" Kett asked when she'd quietened. "Wasn't talking about anything new, or any*one* new?"

Jade shook her head.

"I've said all this already. I told Raymond, and the other policeman, the big one, Peter."

"And her phone?" Kett asked.

"She had it with her," came a reply. Porter walked into

the room, two mugs of unbelievably milky tea in his hands. He set them down, tea slopping over the edge onto the coffee table. "We found it at the scene, forensics are going through it now."

Kett picked up the mug, staring into its anaemic depths before pulling a face at Porter and mouthing *This is tea?* Porter shrugged, retreating to the doorway where Superintendent Clare watched on.

"Okay," said Kett. He took a sip of what tasted like warm milk and grimaced. "I'm sorry to make you go through all this again, but it's important we know every detail. Maisie had been delivering papers for..."

"A year," said Jade. "A little less. She wanted the money, and it's not like we have a lot to go around. Three pound an hour don't sound like much but it's three hours a week, ten quid *int'it*. Ten quid's nothing to laugh at, especially for a 'leven-year-old."

"Has Maisie ever mentioned anyone ever following her, or a car she's seen more than once? Anything that made her feel nervous?"

Jade shook her head.

"Just old folk round there, bungalows full of them and most barely go outside. She knew a couple of people, but they kept themselves to themselves mainly."

Kett nodded.

"Okay, thank you," he said, finishing the disgusting tea and standing up. "I've just arrived, so let me settle in and catch up. I'll get back to you if I think of anything else."

He turned and nodded to the Super, then he frowned.

"Jade," he said. "You mentioned Maisie earned ten pounds? I thought the round took her two hours. Three quid an hour, that's six pounds a week?"

"It does," said Jade, dropping her cigarette into her

untouched tea. "But she does another route on Saturdays, up Mousehold way, by the woods. Short one."

Kett made a note of it, his phone turning Mousehold to *mouse hole*.

"Same shop?" he asked. "Walker's?"

Jade nodded, immediately fumbling for another cigarette.

"Just the two rounds?" Kett said. "No more?"

"No," she replied. She looked utterly exhausted, a bouncy castle that had been almost entirely deflated.

"Try to get some rest, Jade," Kett said "Leave it with us."

He slid his phone back into his pocket as he walked to the door, then hesitated, knowing full well he shouldn't say what he was about to say, and knowing full well he was going to say it anyway.

"We'll find her."

CHAPTER SIX

"Never gets any easier."

DI Porter spoke quietly as he closed the front door behind them. Kett rubbed his eyes, taking a deep breath of hot summer air and feeling a sudden craving for a cigarette. His headache was creeping back, probably because of the thimbleful of sleep he'd managed to grab. He'd never been good at sleeping in new beds, and last night had been worse because somehow, somewhere, he'd managed to lose the bag with all the linen in. There had been enough towels to cover the kids, but he'd spent the night lying on a sheetless double bed with nothing but moonlight to keep him warm. There hadn't been any curtains, either, so the sun had skewered him right in the eyeballs at a quarter past *piss right off* in the morning.

"Hmm?" he said, acknowledging the fact that Porter had spoken.

"This," said the other man, straightening the lapels of his jacket. His biceps looked like they were about to split the sleeves of his Tom Forde suit clean open. "Mums and dads."

Kett nodded. He'd met so many parents with missing

kids, and too many with dead ones. Jade Malone had held it together surprisingly well, but it had only been a couple of days. In missing persons cases the early days were numbed by shock and buoyed by hope. As time went on, though, you started to feel the cold and you started to sink, *fast*, like somebody was cutting the ropes that kept you afloat in a deep, dark ocean. Kett knew it from his work with other families.

And he knew it from his own experience too.

He shivered, feeling almost like he was back there in the second and third and fourth weeks of Billie's disappearance, feeling like he was standing on the edge of that precipice again, reeling.

The door opened behind them—a welcome distraction, even when it was Clare's hairy nostrils that appeared.

"That was a pointless exercise, Kett," he whispered. "We've already spoken to Miss Malone, several times. There was no need to distress her again. I don't want you anywhere near her."

Kett nodded, holding up his hands in surrender, and the Super vanished back inside.

"He's—" Kett started, and the door swung open again.

"And I don't want you talking to Connie's family either, got it?" said the boss. "We've handled that."

Clare slammed the door behind him, but only for a second. It opened again and the Super's angry face popped out for a third time.

"And while I think of it, we don't need you at the crime scenes. Forensics are already there and the last thing they need is you trampling over evidence. Got it?"

He didn't wait for a reply before vanishing again, the crunch of the closing door echoing around the street.

"He's a charmer," Kett said, wincing. "I just wanted to

get a fix on her. The mother."

"Makes sense," said Porter. "Most of the time with missing kids it's somebody in the family. You think she knows something?"

"No," Kett said. "Not unless she's the world's greatest actor. And I know she's not the world's greatest actor, because the world's greatest actor wouldn't be living in a shoebox in the arse end of Norwich."

"Good point," said Porter, walking up the path. Most of the reporters had left but a few hung around like dogs, waiting for scraps. They watched Kett and Porter with big, hungry eyes. Kett just threw a scowl their way.

"You think it's worth me checking on the crime scenes anyway?" he asked. "The houses where Maisie and Connie were snatched. Maybe I should have a word with Connie's mother too?"

"I wouldn't," said Porter. "We've done all we can do there, and it's not worth pissing off the boss any more than necessary."

"That's the only reason I want to do it," said Kett. Porter laughed, shaking his head.

"Norwich, eh. Who'd have thought it?"

"Hm?"

"Us, me and you, two of the Met's best, and here we are in Norwich. It's a weird world."

"You don't like it here?" Kett asked. Porter shrugged.

"I don't mind the city, I just don't like the fact that five minutes in any direction and you're arse deep in the countryside. All those fields and trees and cows, gives me the creeps."

"Pete Porter, terrified of cows," Kett said with a smile. "Could have fooled me, based on how much milk was in that tea."

Porter frowned.

"My tea is fine, thank you very much," he said. "Come on, let's head back to the station. I'll fill you in on the way."

Kett searched the street, spotting the bright orange iCandy buggy halfway down. PC Savage walked a few more steps, pivoted, then started back, throwing a wave and a smile Kett's way.

"Sounds good," Kett said. "But it may have to wait a while. Baby's asleep, and if I try to get her into the car now she'll bring the whole street down. She's a fudging nightmare."

Porter didn't reply, and when Kett turned to him he saw that the DI's face was warped into an expression of disgust.

"What?" Kett asked.

"You said *fudging*."

"*What*?" Kett said again.

"*A fudging nightmare*, you just said it," said Porter.

"I did not," said Kett.

"You did. You meant to say a *fucking* nightmare, and it came out as *fudging*. What the hell is wrong with you? Is this what having kids does to a man?"

Kett spluttered a laugh.

"You need to get your hearing sorted, Pete," he said. "Now fudge off."

This time it was Porter who laughed, a deep, booming roar that Kett remembered all too well from their academy days. The DI managed to cut it off after a couple of seconds, and they both turned back to the Malone house expecting Clare to appear and give them another bollocking. Fortunately, he must have been busy doing something else. By the time Kett looked back to the street Savage had almost reached them.

"Out for the count," she said. "Alright, Porter?"

"Savage," Porter replied, nodding. "Got you on babysitting duty, have they?"

"This is serious police work," she replied without missing a beat. "Working with you is babysitting duty."

"Do you two want me to step aside?" Kett asked, and when it looked like Porter was about to laugh his baby-waking guffaw again it was all he could do not to slap a hand over the big man's mouth. Porter caught himself in time.

"So we'll meet you back at HQ?" he said. "Whenever the little one decides to wake up."

"Yeah," Kett said. "But as I'm on foot, I may as well head to the newsagents. Savage, come with me, you can bring me up to speed on the way."

"Happily," she said. "I'll push."

IT WAS A SURPRISINGLY LONG JOURNEY, but there was plenty to talk about.

"Tell me about the other missing girl," Kett said as they reached the end of Maisie's street. A few of the reporters were snapping photographs and Kett didn't blame them. It wasn't often you saw a detective chief inspector, a constable, and a baby making their way into town together. Savage nudged the buggy to the left and Kett took the hint as he walked onto the main road, heading downhill.

"Connie Byrne," Savage said. "You'd think Constance, right, but it's actually short for Conifer."

"Like the tree?" said Kett. Savage nodded.

"She went missing the day before Maisie, while delivering papers. Her family didn't call it in until the next morning."

"*Why?*" Kett spluttered, loud enough to stir the baby.

Savage jiggled the buggy, making shushing noises until Moira settled.

"They're known to us," Savage said. "And to social services. A history of drugs, dad's been in and out of prison, mum's in rehab but not really. Connie did her route in the evening, she left at five-thirty. By the time she was supposed to come home dad was out and mum was off her face on Aldi's budget gin. They never thought to check on her until the next day, when she didn't show up for breakfast."

"Jesus," said Kett. The road was sloping down surprisingly steeply. For a city that had a reputation for being pancake flat, Norwich had a crazy number of hills. Cars and trucks rumbled past but the traffic was light, and compared to London it was unnervingly quiet. "Any reason she'd take off? Other than the family, that is."

"Yeah," said Savage. "And she's done it before, twice last term alone. Both times the school reported her missing, and both times they found her with friends. But this time nobody knew where she was. We checked everywhere she might have been—I was on the search team myself. Nothing. So she gets an MP alert, but it's not considered serious enough straight away."

"Because a quarter of a million people go missing every year," Kett said, nodding. "Fair enough. But when Maisie vanished delivering papers for the same shop, things changed. There was a pattern."

Savage nodded, pausing at a junction until a bus had passed, exhaust pouring from its backside. She held up a hand, parting the rest of the traffic like Moses and the Red Sea until they'd crossed.

"Connie didn't have a phone, and there was no sign of her bag or any of her belongings. No witnesses, no CCTV. She just vanished."

"But it's obvious which house she was at when she was taken, right?" said Kett. "The first one without a newspaper."

"Sure," said Savage. "I was coming to that. It was another dead house. Owner had recently passed, the house was waiting to be cleared. When we got in, we found her bag of newspapers."

The buggy hit a loose paving slab, jumping, and Savage swore beneath her breath.

"It's a bit of a beast, do you want me to take it?" Kett asked, and she shook her head.

"It's a great quads and triceps workout," she replied.

"How do you think I got a body like this," Kett replied, smiling. "Dad muscles. So, we've got an MO. The perp scopes the routes, finds a dead house, hides there and waits for his newspaper girl to arrive. Any evidence that he... that anything happened inside?"

"Forensics are still taking the place apart," Savage said. "But so far nothing. Our man's careful."

"And patient," Kett said. "People don't die that often, even old folk. He had to wait for the right person to pop their clogs, then infiltrate their home, then lie in wait for the delivery girl. This guy's a thinker, that makes him dangerous."

Despite the heat of the day, Kett felt an unpleasant chill pass through him, one that raised an army of goosebumps on his skin and tickled the nape of his neck. In the space of one conversation the case had gone from an opportunist attacker to a cold, calculating, serial kidnapper—and there was still space for it to get a whole lot worse.

"You know a lot about this," Kett said. "For a constable, I mean. I'm impressed."

"Thank you, sir. I'm going to go for detective soon."

"Something tells me you'll crush it."

She smiled a reply, then eased the buggy to a stop. They'd reached a small shopping plaza that ran up and down both sides of the main road. On this side was a chippy, a chemist, a KFC rip-off called CFK, and two charity shops, all of which clustered around a squat, half-dead pub called the Albion. On the other was not one but two off-licences, a betting shop, and sure enough a large newsagent with WALKERS written in blue italic letters above the windows —complete with racing stripes.

"The girls aren't the only thing missing here," Kett said, nodding to the sign. "What happened to that apostrophe?"

A group of five kids stood outside the newsagent looking like they were trying to audition for Norwich's own version of *The Wire*. All of them had their hoods pulled up and their trousers pulled down, and two of them had bottles in paper bags. They'd already spotted Savage's yellow jacket and they were pacing back and forth like caged tigers.

Well, caged squirrels maybe.

Kett took in the rest of the row. The whole place looked worse for wear, the paint peeling from the windows, the gutters packed with litter, at least three sad little mounds of dog shit. Two of the windows in the nearest off-licence were smashed, one covered with a board. Above the shops was a row of single-storey flats that didn't look in any better condition. The whole place stank of piss and petrol fumes.

"How do you want to play it?" Savage asked. "Shall I keep the kid?"

"No," Kett said, shaking his head. "I'll take her in, but I might need your help with the squirrels first."

Savage's confused frown was lost on him as he took the buggy and crossed the road.

CHAPTER SEVEN

Kett didn't go straight in, mainly because one of the little piles of dog shit was situated right in front of the newsagent's front door—already well-trodden in, judging by the sorry state of it—and getting the buggy around unsullied would be difficult.

Instead, he wheeled Moira towards the little door to the left of the window. It had to lead up to the flat above, and it looked as neglected as the rest of the area. Flakes of salmon-pink paint peeled like sunburn, and the quarter-circle windows were yellow with dirt and age.

In order to get closer, Kett had to walk past the teenage lads—six of them, now, as another one emerged from the weed-strewn alley beside the newsagent still pulling his grey tracksuit trousers up. He looked over with an expression of such insolence that Kett felt like slapping it out of him here and now, baby or no baby.

"Fella's got a kid to sell," said one of the lads, the rest of them laughing even though the joke wasn't the least bit funny. They were all eyeball and swagger, and they reeked of cheap booze even though not one of them could have been older than fifteen. But they were still Norwich lads, it wasn't like they'd stepped off the Willow Tree Lane Estate. Kett glanced back to see Savage right behind him.

"Got a kid to sell you're in the right place," said another of the boys, taking a few steps towards Kett—his fake limp so extreme it looked like he'd shit himself and was trying to stop it from dropping down his trouser leg. "Old paedo Walker'll give you a fiver *furrit*."

Another round of laughter, but there wasn't a shred of warmth to it.

"He's got a reputation?" Kett asked, rolling the buggy back and forth to keep Moira asleep. "Walker?"

"Fuck, he *is* here to sell a baby!" one boy roared.

"Why you wanna know?" said another. "You Five-o?"

Kett almost burst out laughing. *Five-o*. He hadn't heard that since the 80s.

"Yeah," he said. "I am. DCI Robert Kett of the Hawaii Five-o. This, in the buggy here, is DCI Kett Junior."

The boys frowned, their swagger slightly punctured. Kett had faced off against enough teenagers to know that confrontation was a sure way to light the powder keg of their aggression. But not one of the dickheads knew how to respond to a bit of humour.

"She has to take a nap between arrests or she gets cranky, but don't underestimate her, she's a supercop. So, David Walker, you've heard stuff about him?"

Savage was hanging back, and Kett couldn't help but be impressed. Most of the constables he knew, the blokes especially, would have come in all guns blazing. The boys eyed her, then Kett, and the last of their bravado seemed to drain away.

"Nah," said a kid in a red hoodie, shrugging. "Just with those girls gone missing. Walker's alright, let's us—"

That earned him a thump on the arm from one of the other boys. Kett let it go, for now.

"Shouldn't you all be in school?"

They shuffled around, feet scuffing the floor, all of them suddenly looking their age.

"Go on, now," Kett said, and they started to move away. "But not you."

Kett jabbed a finger at the boy in the red hoodie. He grumbled but stayed put, watching mournfully as his friends scattered.

"What were you about to say?" Kett asked him. The kid scratched at the blond bumfluff growing on his chin, looking at everything that wasn't the DCI. "Walker lets you..."

"*Nuffink*, man," the kid replied. "Just, you know, like fags and stuff. He lets us have them."

"He lets you buy cigarettes? From the shop?"

"Nah," the kid said, shaking his head. He pulled the red hood over his spotty forehead as if he could cover himself up completely, make himself invisible. "From the heath, you got to go over there."

"Mousehold?" asked Savage, and the kid nodded, his eyes growing moist. It might have been Kett's imagination, but he thought he could hear him whining like a baby beneath his breath.

"He gets the girls to do it, doesn't he?" Kett said. "The paper girls."

The boy nodded, those whines getting louder.

"Saturday mornings," the boy said. "You can get fags, booze, whatever."

"Drugs?" asked Kett.

"No, man, we don't do that stuff. Honest."

He looked like he was about to explode into a full-scale sobbing fit and Kett took pity on him.

"Go on," he said. "And if I catch you out here on a school day again then DCI Kett Junior here is going to book you so fast it'll make your head spin. Got it?"

The boy looked at the buggy and frowned, utterly confused.

"Go," said Kett, firmer now. The kid turned and bolted, so fast that his trainers slipped out from beneath him and he had to do a strange little jig to stay upright. Kett chuckled beneath his breath as the boy fled around the corner, then he turned to Savage.

"Did you know that? About the newspaper girls delivering the cigarettes?"

"We had a hunch. Happens all the time around here. Newsagents, ice cream vans, a fair few of them flog cigarettes and booze to minors."

Kett toed the buggy brake and walked to the door of the flat above, pushing open the letterbox and peering inside. A draft of cold, damp air hit him in the face, but the stairwell was completely clear.

"I'm not sure if Maisie or Connie were part of that, though," added Savage. "Neither of the parents seemed to know anything about it."

"Well," said Kett as he snapped off the brake and wheeled his way around the dog shit. "There's one way to find out."

THE SECOND HE walked into the shop, the sensor beneath the mat triggering a bell overhead, Kett knew why David Walker wasn't being taken seriously as a suspect.

For a start, he had to be eighty years old if he was a day. He was a small man, in height and frame, with about three strands of white hair plastered to his liver-spotted scalp. He wore a white shirt and brown tie, and a pair of gold-rimmed spectacles was perched on his button nose.

There was also the fact that he moved like a badly made and badly oiled robot in a high school science competition. Right now he was serving a couple of young men, and at the rate he was moving they'd be old men by the time he finished. He creaked and swivelled around to the till, counting out coins painfully slowly into the hands of his customers, then he bid them goodbye in a voice made up of a thousand scraps of ancient parchment.

Kett wheeled the buggy into the nearest aisle, seeing the usual collection of crisps, chocolate and overpriced, under-nutritious groceries. The shop was old, but it was well equipped. Two CCTV cameras were mounted above the tills, one in front and one behind, and a third was positioned right at the back by the staff door. CID would have everything they could get off them already, not that it would be much.

Kett glanced back to see Savage through the window. He'd asked her to stay outside, just for the first few minutes. Sometimes the bright yellow uniforms helped, sometimes they didn't, and Kett guessed that the newsagent had seen plenty of them in the last few days.

He stopped by the baby aisle to pick up an apple and banana pouch, then he made his way to the till. From this angle he could see right behind it, and he was shocked to notice that Mr Walker was actually standing on a *box*. He had to be five-foot-tall and sixty pounds soaking wet. The old man craned his head, looking every bit like Penfold from that old cartoon. His eyebrows were practically floating above his head as he nodded in greeting.

"Little one asleep then?" he croaked in a broad local

accent. "I miss 'em when they were that small, and that quiet."

"She's not always quiet," Kett replied, putting the pouch on the counter. "Trust me."

"Just this?" Walker asked, scanning it through, and then scanning it through again by mistake. "Oh, hang on. Blasted machine. Never works. Anything else?"

A packet of Marlborough reds please, is what he wanted to say. But he'd made Billie a promise, when they were first trying to conceive, that his smoking days were over—and even though she wasn't around at the moment he wasn't about to break it.

"Just the pouch, Mr Walker, thank you."

At the mention of his name, the old man looked up wearily.

"I'd ask if you were a policeman or a journalist," he said, his eyes flicking to the window and the smudge of yellow in the glass. "But I'm old, not blind."

"Sorry," Kett said, fishing a five from his wallet and handing it over. He pulled out his warrant card while he was at it. "DCI Robert Kett."

"You look like a copper," Walker said, but it was clear it was a statement, not an insult. "Just more exhausted."

"I'm more of a dad than a policeman these days," he said with a smile. "In all honesty, being a copper is *way* easier."

"Tell me about it. I had four of the buggers." He grimaced as he swallowed, opening the till using a hand that was warped with swollen knuckles. "And I was a lot younger than you when I started."

"Took me a while to get going," Kett said. "So, four kids. Is that why you're still working at, what, eighty? Eighty-five?"

"Ninety-two," he replied with a grin. "Apple a day, core'n'all. The only reason I'm still here. You should try it."

The buzzer sounded as a man in shorts walked in, wiping the sweat from his forehead. Kett leaned in.

"I'll try it," he said. "Thanks for the advice. Look, I know the Norfolk Constabulary have been in to talk to you already. I'm only helping them. I've had some experience with missing children."

And missing wives, he tried not to think.

"There are some questions that very much need answers. I'm hoping you can help."

"Anything," the old man said with genuine sincerity. "I love Maisie, and Connie too. They're good girls, bright girls. They don't deserve what's happened to them."

"They both delivered during the week, is that right?" Kett asked. Walker nodded.

"Connie on Monday and Friday, Maisie on Tuesday."

"And they did weekend routes?"

The old man swallowed again, seeming to turn a shade paler as his eyes wandered to the ceiling.

"I believe they did, yes."

"Mousehold Heath?"

He nodded, looking back at Kett.

"Selling cigarettes?" Kett asked.

It seemed impossible for a man so small to shrink any further, but shrink he did, so much that his little head only just peeked out over the counter.

"Was that your doing?" Kett asked. "A bit of extra cash?"

"I..." said the old man, shaking his head. He looked at Kett, then glanced up to the ceiling again, to the camera mounted above the DCI's head. Gradually, his shaking head turned to a nod. "Yes. It was me."

"Bit silly, don't you think?" Kett said. "How long for?"

"Not long," he said, sniffing. Kett looked to the side to see the other customer approach holding a newspaper and a can of Coke.

"Take it," Kett told him. "It's on me."

The man nodded in surprise then walked out of the shop. He paused as he reached the door, eyeing up the DVDs on a rack.

"Don't push your luck," Kett told him, sending him on his way. He turned back to Walker, who was shaking so much he looked ready to fall to pieces. "Not long as in a year? Two?"

"A year, yes," the old man said. "I'm sorry, it was stupid. I kept telling... I *knew* it was stupid."

That glance to the ceiling again, something about it was making Kett's Spidey-sense tingle. He looked up to see the little camera watching them.

"Any of the girls ever mention something about who they sold cigarettes to up there? Any parents have a problem with it? Anyone hound them?"

Walker shook his head.

"Half of those kids were buying cheap smokes for their folks," he replied, sniffing. "They never had any trouble."

Kett sighed, jiggling the buggy. Moira was still out of it, her velvet snores the loudest thing in the shop other than the hum of the ancient fridges. Chances were Walker's illicit operation had nothing at all to do with the missing girls, but he'd still have to come down to the station and give a statement.

"How much do I owe you?" he asked, but Walker waved it away.

"Don't worry," he said. "I won't be here much longer, not after this. Nobody's been in, they all think I'm... I'm a..."

He doubled over, his forehead almost on the counter. "It's a godawful way to end it all, don't you think?"

Kett didn't know how to reply, so he wheeled the buggy around in a tight circle, looking once again at the camera. What was he missing? The feeling gnawed at him, made him pause. Walker had glanced up every time there was a difficult question. It was a bad tell, almost as bad as Bingo's moustache stroking. Was it because somebody was watching him, maybe?

Or because somebody was *above* him.

"Mr Walker, are you renting here?" Kett asked, following the hunch.

"No, bought it in '73 when the whole parade was ten years old, mortgage paid off twenty years later, right on the dot."

"Just the shop? Not the flat?"

Walker swallowed again, his eyes darting skyward. *There it is.*

"All of it," he replied. "A couple of the flats upstairs are mine, but I live out in Costessey."

"Anyone up there now?"

"No," Walker said, a little too quickly. "It's sealed. Asbestos, I think. Nobody's been in for years. I should do something about it, really."

"You should," said Kett, pushing the buggy to the door. Savage was waiting for him, and she held it open as he walked through. The buzzer sounded again, and this time Moira stirred. Kett looked back, almost feeling sorry for the shrivelled ghost of a man behind the counter. "Take care, Mr Walker. We'll be in touch."

"Anything useful?" asked Savage when the door had closed.

"I'm not sure," said Kett.

He peeked into the buggy to see a pair of bright eyes and a very grumpy face looking back at him.

"Hey gorgeous girl, welcome back."

He left the grouching baby, running back to the door that led to the flat above the shop. He peeked through the letterbox again, just to confirm what he'd seen before, then he walked back. Unclipping the straps, he hoisted Moira to his chest where she proceeded to scream a needle of sound right into his ear.

"Have you ever seen an empty flat without a mountain of mail by the letterbox?" he said to PC Savage. She shook her head. "Me neither. Which means David Walker is lying to us."

CHAPTER EIGHT

Kett checked his mirrors then steered the Volvo off the dual carriageway, easing on the brakes as he neared the roundabout at the bottom of the hill. Ahead of him was the impressive bulk of the Norfolk Police headquarters, which wasn't in the Norwich city centre station but ten minutes away in a small satellite town with an unpronounceable name.

"Gen!" squealed Moira from the back seat, her feet drumming the chair. "Gen!"

"Again, I know," he replied. "I'll grab you something as soon as I can."

He'd bribed the baby into the car with the apple and banana pouch, but Moira had hoovered it up in less than a minute and had been howling for more ever since. He checked his watch as he parked the car, seeing that it was coming up for eleven. He felt bad for not picking Evie up from nursery as early as he'd promised, but technically he could leave her there until one, and the chances were she was enjoying it.

"Better get a wriggle on, eh?" he said as he clambered

out, hauling Moira out of the back door. She threw the empty pouch at him and he bent down to scoop it up, tossing it in the footwell. "They'll do you for littering, you know. Supercop or not. The law's the law, Moira."

"No!" she replied.

"Fair enough."

He walked into the reception, flashing his warrant card to the woman behind the counter. He expected her to buzz him through but she didn't, nodding instead to a row of chairs at the back of the room.

"Somebody will come for you in a minute," she said, flashing a bemused look at Moira. Kett kept his mouth sealed before he said something he might regret, waiting for considerably longer than a minute for DI Porter to emerge from the back.

Sorry! the big man mouthed as he buzzed the gate and ushered them through. They were halfway down the spartan corridor beyond before it was safe enough for him to continue.

"She's a dragon, that one. I've seen her reduce grown police to tears." He laughed, but in a way that made Kett think he wasn't actually joking. "You okay? Get much from the old man?"

"I don't think he did it, if that's what you mean," Kett said, shifting Moira to his other arm. "But I think he's hiding something. I left Savage there, told her to keep an eye on the flats above the shop."

"Yeah?" Porter said. They reached a set of double doors and he shouldered through them, guiding Kett through the bustling headquarters. "It's crazy in here. We've got a few forces helping out on the case. We're in here."

He opened a door into the incident room. A large table occupied the centre of the space, and the far wall was groaning under the weight of what had to be a hundred photographs and documents and busy whiteboards. A few people glanced up, doing some classic doubletakes when they spotted the wriggling, squealing shape of Moira.

"Yeah," Kett said, nodding to them. "He owns a couple of the flats, claims they haven't been used in years, but there's definitely been somebody in there. Recently too. What do you know about him? Have you done a friends and family check?"

"Four kids," said Porter. "All in their fifties and sixties. The youngest one's been in the nick a couple of times, robberies mainly. A few grandkids and friends, but nobody pinging the radar."

"The one with the sheet, is he local?"

"Not according to Walker. We're having trouble pinning him down. Why?"

"Let me think on it," said Kett. "I'll let you know if it's important."

Porter nodded, then clapped his giant hands together. The room fell quiet.

"Okay, everyone. Some of you met DCI Robert Kett earlier, at the Malone place. For those who didn't, here he is." Porter gestured at Kett, and at Moira, who was halfway onto his head again. Kett did his best to smile at them through the baby's legs. Porter laughed. "Robbie's the big'un, the little one's his daughter."

"Head!" Moira replied, slapping Kett on his forehead.

"I know Robbie from way back, going on twenty years now," said Porter. "He's a good man, and a great detective. He's not here officially."

"No shit," said a female detective sitting at the table. She was in her thirties, her black trouser suit looking brand new, her blonde hair tied back so tightly it made her forehead look huge. She wore a thin smile on her face. Detective Sergeant Spalding, Kett remembered from Clare's introduction earlier. "Are we even allowed kids in here?"

"We are," said Porter. "Just so long as none of the brass find out. So yeah, Kett hasn't been seconded, he's technically on compassionate leave. Uh, some of you will know why."

"Oh, shit, yeah," said another detective, one Kett hadn't met yet. He was in his fifties and so grey it looked like he'd laundered himself in the washing machine with his cheap suit one too many times. He clicked his yellow fingers. "I remember, it was all over the news. Your wife, right?"

"Do you know what compassionate means, Dunst?" Porter said. "It's the opposite of *thoughtless asshole who can't keep his mouth shut.*"

Dunst sat back, raising his arms in surrender.

"That's DI Keith Dunst," Porter said. He nodded at the woman who had spoken earlier. "DS Alison Spalding. And last but not least." Porter pointed to an older woman at the back of the room. "Head of Specialist Operations, DCI Kate Pearson."

The woman waved without looking up from whatever she was reading.

"Oh, and Figg," said Porter, nodding at the FLO across the room. "Who you already know from London."

Figg waved.

"There are others, you'll meet the whole team eventually."

"Thank you," said Kett. "It's good to meet you all. I know this isn't exactly a normal situation..."

"Head!" screeched Moira, slapping him on the ear hard enough to make it ring. Kett peeled her loose, plonking her on the floor. She immediately made a bid for the middle of the room, trying to climb onto the chair next to Dunst. He helped her up with his cigarette-stained fingers and she grinned at him like butter wouldn't melt.

"But I'm here to help in any way I can," Kett went on, massaging his ear. "I've worked a lot of missing kid cases, so if you need my advice, I'm here."

DS Spalding sneered, returning to her work.

"And if you don't need my advice," he went on, directing the words at her. "Feel free to completely ignore me."

"Good," said Porter. He clapped his hands together again and the room returned to work. "Superintendent Clare will be in soon. He's running the operation." Kett pulled a face, and Porter laughed. "Yeah, he's not everybody's cup of tea. Abrasive as hell, and he'll put the fear of god into you when he wants to. But he knows what he's doing. Spent a lot of time with the National Crime Squad before coming here, a lot of covert operations and gang stuff. Not a man to be underestimated, even with that nose hair. So that's the team. Any questions?"

"Yeah," said Kett. Moira was doing her best to fall off the chair and faceplant onto the floor, so he picked her up. He turned to Porter. "Please tell me you're not the guy who makes the tea?"

"SEE, IT'S FINE."

Porter slapped a mug of tea onto the desk, hard enough that some of it sluiced over the rim. Kett smudged a hand on it before it hit the papers in front of him, then stared into its horrifically milky depths.

"Pete," he said. "You do know what a teabag looks like, right?"

"What are you talking about?" the DI replied, looking genuinely offended.

"The little paper things with brown stuff in. Teabags."

"I used *two*," Porter replied, jabbing his finger at the tea.

"*How*?" Kett replied. "This tea's the colour of my wife's grandmother, and she's had four heart attacks. Did a cow's udder *explode* in it?"

"Don't drink it then," Porter said, crossing his arms over his broad chest.

"It's not just me, is it?" Kett said, looking up. "It can't be. Does anyone else think Porter's tea looks like, well, camel pee?"

"It's the worst," said Dunst. "It's like he makes a cup of tea then somehow sucks the soul right out of it."

"Fuck off," grumbled Porter. "Make your own bloody tea then, philistines."

"Watch your mouth," said Kett, nodding across the room. Moira was sitting in a corner with a dozen sheets of paper from the copy machine and a pack of restaurant crayons that DCI Pearson had found in her handbag. A soggy digestive was clutched in her fingers, another one already fused with the thin carpet. It wouldn't keep her occupied for long, but she seemed content for the moment. Porter pretended to zip his lips.

"*Fudge* off," he said instead. "You bunch of fudging winkers."

Laughter rippled across the room, but it was short lived. The atmosphere was heavy, oppressive. The clock above the central whiteboard said it was 11:28, which meant that Maisie Malone had been missing for going on forty-four hours. For Connie it was even longer. Every single second that clock counted out was a second more those poor girls were away from their homes, away from their families. Every single second was one they were spending in terror and pain.

If they were still alive, of course.

"Bring me up to speed," Kett said, grimacing as he took a sip of tea. "You've searched any other empty properties around both paper delivery routes? Ones that have been recently vacated."

"Yeah," said Porter. "We've had a few deaths in the last couple of weeks, old people can't handle the heat. No sign of any illegal entry in any recently vacated property other than those two houses."

"CCTV?" Kett asked.

"Maisie was caught on three cameras as she started her route, plus the ones in the shop. We've been through them, but the rain was so heavy they're practically useless. Only the shop cameras caught Connie, plus a traffic camera on the ringroad. Nothing suspicious. We've put a call out to the public for dashcam footage and witnesses, but nothing so far."

"Anyone known to both girls?" Kett asked. "Any mutual friends?"

"Other than Walker, none," said Porter. "Hey, Figg, you pick anything up from your visits with the families?"

Across the room, the FLO shook his head.

"Nothing that raised a red flag," Figg called back. "The Byrne family had some serious problems, but nothing that would lead us to believe they'd deliberately put Connie in danger."

"Okay," said Kett. "Known offenders?"

Porter looked over at DS Spalding, who must have had

one ear on the conversation. She sighed dramatically as she pored through a folder in front of her.

"I've been going through the worst offenders currently out of prison or on release," she said. "Most of the people on file are your typical, run-of-the-mill, family-member-molesting arseholes."

Kett cleared his throat, nodding across the room to the baby.

"Seriously?" Spalding said.

"Spalding," warned Pearson, and the DS rolled her eyes.

"*Arm*... holes," she corrected herself. "But the system spat out a couple of suspects who are more dangerous. Both have form for kidnapping." She slid a file over the desk and Kett found himself staring into the dark eyes of a man who looked every part the classic villain from a Charles Dickens novel. "Neil Dorey. He got eighteen years back in 1992 for the kidnap and assault of his six-year-old niece. Snatched her from school and took her to a boat house on the Broads, kept her there for three days before she managed to escape."

"Where is he now?" Kett asked, scanning the file to see a litter of smaller charges next to the big one.

"Sheltered accommodation," she replied. "Been quiet since he was released, but a monster's a monster till the day they die, right? We've already had him in for questioning, but his alibi checks out, he's been in hospital with gallstones. Hang on." She shuffled her papers, then passed the second file. A handsome man in his twenties flashed a shark-like, sociopathic smile at Kett. "This one's sneakier, and he's almost too good to be true. Christian Stillwater."

"Christian Stillwater?" said Kett. "Is he a Mid-West Gospel singer or something?"

"No. He was arrested in 2014 for abducting a child from a playpark."

"And he's *out*?" Kett asked in shock.

"Good lawyer. They argued that he thought the kid was in danger, that he'd seen the mother shoot up and that he thought he was doing the right thing by getting her the hell out of there. The girl was eight, slight learning difficulties, and technically Stillwater was right. When they spoke to the mum she was off her head on heroin. Hadn't even noticed that her kid was missing. It was the gran who called it in. Besides, the whole Lochy Percival thing had just happened."

"Lucky Percival?" Kett asked. The name rang a bell, but he couldn't quite place it. He was fairly sure he heard Spalding tut beneath her breath. She pulled her phone from her pocket and took a moment to find something, then she slid it across the table. Kett saw a press photo of a man in his thirties being led away by police, his eyes full of tears and his mouth warped by grief.

"Lochy," said Figg, who was listening in. "This guy *definitely* isn't lucky."

Spalding took her phone back as she spoke.

"Percival was a local man accused of the murder of a tourist from Liverpool, Jenny O'Rourke, in late 2013. She was fourteen. Witnesses described him perfectly, said they saw him snatch her in broad daylight from Wroxham Barns, a kind of farm attraction. By the time anyone had managed to do anything about it he'd vanished along with the girl. They found her a week later, what was left of her anyway, beneath a rotting boat on the riverside less than a mile from Percival's house. His DNA was found on the boat too."

"I remember," said Kett. "We had a briefing about it down in the Met. Because he wasn't guilty, was he?"

Spalding sighed.

"Not that we could prove."

"Not at all," said Pearson, throwing another warning look at Spalding. "He had a cast iron alibi for when the girl was taken. He was at a football match, a Norwich game. He was on CCTV for the whole thing, and he even made an appearance on Match of the Day behind the goal."

"And the DNA?" asked Kett, racking his brains. "He claimed he was a rambler, didn't he?"

"He was," said Pearson. "They found his DNA all over the woods where he'd snagged himself while exploring. He used the boat to rest on when he walked. Sat there with Jenny right underneath him, bleeding everywhere, and didn't have a clue."

"Jesus," said Kett.

"It's one of those flukes," said Dunst. "Completely unpredictable. Without that CCTV Percival would have been locked up for life for something he didn't do. They caught the actual killer a few months later, after Percival was banged up. He looked like Percival, same build, same hair, drove the same colour car—different make, though. It was a catalogue of coincidences."

"And it fuc—uh, *fonked*? It fonked him up for life." Spalding sighed. "He was fired, his house got torched."

"And he was stabbed in prison," added Figg, shaking his head. "Somebody took offence at his supposed crimes, shanked him in the thigh. I worked with him a little after his release, back when I was a therapist, he was a hollow man."

"Which is why he sued," said Pearson. "And why he won. We look in on him from time to time and he's broken. He had therapy, joined a whole heap of support groups, but you just don't recover from something like that. And it's why the CPO let Stillwater off so easily, because they couldn't risk it happening again. Without hard evidence, there was no case."

"But Stillwater *was* guilty?" Kett said. "He planned it, took his time, made sure he kidnapped the right girl. He *admitted* it. Where did he take her?"

"This is the interesting thing," Spalding replied. "Stillwater's grandfather had recently died. He owned this monster of a house over in Town Close and the place was sitting empty, falling down. Stillwater took her there. Luckily one of the neighbours saw him and got talking to him, got talking to the girl too. We think it spooked him, because about an hour later he took the girl to the police station in the city. He was arrested, of course, but the thing with the mother, and the fact that the girl—Emily, uh, Coupland, I think—hadn't said a bad word about Stillwater, I mean he'd even bought her ice cream, meant he walked right out the door."

"But he's still on file?" Kett asked. Spalding nodded.

"Nobody believed a word of his story. He was planning to take that girl and do god knows what to her. We've kept an eye on him ever since, but he's been squeaky clean. *Too* clean. And this isn't Minority Report. You can't arrest a guy for what he *might* do in the future."

"Fits our guy's MO, that's for sure," said Kett. "Smart, patient. What's he do?"

Porter smiled.

"Estate agent," he said. "Plenty of access to empty properties."

"You're bringing him in?"

"Trying to," said Porter. "He's off the grid."

Kett nodded, a shiver settling in the nape of his neck. He rubbed the hair there, studying Stillwater's photograph. The man's eyes were bright, that smile like a razor's edge.

He'd seen that look before, more often than not on the faces of the men he'd dragged in wearing handcuffs, men who left a trail of screams and tears and blood in their wake.

"Feels like our guy," Kett said. "Let's go find that bastard."

"Bar-star!" yelled Moira from across the room.

CHAPTER NINE

"I KEEP TELLING YOU, CHRISTIAN'S NO HERE."

The young, red-eyed Scottish woman—Lucy Clarke, according to the electoral register—stood in the door of the Stillwater house like she meant to barricade it, even though she was five-two and looked like she'd been carved from matchwood. She smudged her unbrushed, copper-red hair away from her face, glancing over her shoulder again at the two constables who were searching the house. Then she turned back to Kett and Porter.

"He's no been here for days now, I told the last polis, and the ones afore that. A've no seen him and I'm no wanting to either."

"You had an argument?" Kett asked, looking back to check that the Volvo was still where he'd left it. Moira peered out from the back seat, frowning. It was a pretty crappy thing to do, leave the baby in the car, but he couldn't exactly show up at the home of a potentially violent wannabe child molester with an eighteen-month-old child in his arms, could he? Besides, he'd cranked the windows down a bit.

"Aye," said Lucy. "I mean, no, not really, just one of those stupid ones that couples have."

"Mind telling us what it was about?" asked Porter. "Just between you and me."

"And all the other polis I've told?" she shot back. "Babies, we were arguing about having a baby. I wanted to, he didnae. I lost it first, told him to fuck off. And lo and behold, he did."

"Did he say why?" Kett asked.

"Why he didnae want to have a bairn?" she said, pulling a face. "What fuckin' business is that of yours. *Be careful in there!*"

She directed the last comment over her shoulder at a series of thumps and bumps from the kitchen. Then she took a deep breath.

"Just didnae like kids, although he's changed his tune from when we first started talkin'. Charmed the pants offa me with his speeches about a big house in the country, little'uns runnin' around—*literally* charmed the pants offa me. Bastard."

"How long have you been together?" Kett asked.

"Two year," she spat, rubbing her finger. The ring was gone, but the welt it had left was still there. "Proposed to me in the spring. Bastard."

"You know about his past?" Porter asked, and she glared at him.

"Aye, I do now, thank you very much. If I'd'a known it before then maybe I'd not have given him the time of day. *Bastard!*"

"I know you've already been through this," Kett said. "But anything else you know about him, any places he used to visit, anywhere he spoke about, even if it was just once. Take a moment and think. It could mean the difference between life and death for those girls. You want to see their photos again?"

Lucy shook her head, turning so pale that the freckles on her nose and cheeks looked like pen marks. She wrapped her hands around herself, sniffing. Porter had shown her Maisie and Connie's photos when they'd arrived, and it wasn't the first time they'd been thrown at her.

"Believe me," she said. "I want him caught as much as you. If he's... If he's really capable of doin' something like that, I want him sent away for good." She looked up, meeting Kett's eye. "You really think he..."

"We don't know," said Kett. "But whether he did or not, we need to speak with him. So please, think."

She chewed on it for a moment, checking over her shoulder again. The two constables were there, and one of them shook her head. Lucy sighed, kicking the door gently with her bare foot.

"He never opened up to me, not really, not truthfully," she said. "Have you ever been with somebody like that? They act like they're the most open person on the planet, and you believe it without really thinkin', and it's only after that you start to realise you didnae ken them at all."

"Classic sociopath," Kett said. "Everything is planned, their whole life is a fiction. They can make you believe just about anything."

"Aye," she said, nodding. "He didnae do much outside of being here and being at his work—he sold houses but he wasn't in every day, kept his own hours. But every now and again he'd piss off out. Always told me he was meetin' friends at the pub but he didnae have friends, not really, not that I ever saw, and his breath never smelled of alcohol. The only thing that ever smelled was him."

"In what way?" asked Kett. She shrugged her bony shoulders.

"He just smelled, just *off*, I dinnae ken. There was a sweetness to it, but an awfie sourness too. Or somethin' else. Rot, maybe? I thought he was havin' an affair at first, but it wasnae that kinda smell. I cannae describe it."

"He's gone out recently?" Porter asked.

"Last weekend, Saturday. I thought we were gonna drive out to the coast but he told me he had plans. Pissed off first thing in the mornin' in the car, came back at supper time. Six, maybe. I was furious with him, because the bastard came back and he was covered in sand. He'd been to the fuckin' beach without me. All fuckin' day."

Kett met Porter's eye. Saturday. Two days before Connie had vanished.

"You wouldn't happen to have those clothes here, would you?" Kett asked. "The ones with the sand?"

She nodded, disappearing into the darkness of the house.

"Looking more and more like our man," said Porter as the constables walked out. "Anything?"

"Nope," said the PC. "His stuff's all gone."

"All of it?" asked Kett.

"It's here," came Lucy's voice from inside the house. She emerged from the gloom carrying a black binbag, obviously struggling with the weight of it. She tossed it at Kett's feet. "All his shit's here, I was gonna take it to the tip but you've saved me the bother. He fucked off on Sunday after we argued, no seen him since."

"This is great," said Kett, picking up the bag. "You don't happen to know which beach he'd been to?"

"Aye," said Lucy, wearing the same hard stare. "A fuckin' sandy one."

She started to slam the door but Porter planted a big hand on it.

"He shows up, you call us straight away. 999 if you have to, you hear?"

"If he shows up here," Lucy said. "He's a fuckin' dead man."

BY THE TIME Kett had made it back to the car, Moira was crying. It wasn't one of her angry screams, it was a proper sob, and the sound of it caught him by surprise.

Her words, though, just about shattered his heart.

"Mamma! Mamma! Pliz."

It was the little 'please' at the end that did it, that one word jamming a lump down his throat and making his eyes wet with tears. He handed Porter the evidence bag then opened the back door of the car. He pushed his head in further than he needed to, mainly so that Porter wouldn't see the emotion on his face. But the big man would have been a poor detective if he'd missed it.

"Can't imagine what you're going through," Porter said when Moira was free of her car seat. He tied the binbag in a knot then handed it to a uniform, who carried it to the car.

Kett rested the baby on his shoulder, feeling her chubby arms wrap themselves around his neck and gently pat his skin.

"Pliz, pliz."

"Hey, beautiful," he said. "Daddy's here, it's okay."

It could go one of two ways, he knew. Sometimes the effort to sooth her would backfire and she'd have a tantrum of biblical proportions, one that would rage for hours sometimes. Billie had been the only one able to calm her, partly because she had a natural aura of peace and compassion, and partly because she had boobs. Kett had neither of those things. All he had were cuddles and kisses and kind words, and they didn't always do much to temper the storm.

Fortunately, this wasn't one of those occasions. He could feel it in the way the baby moved, those subtle motions. She didn't strain away from him, she settled against his shoulder and burbled into his neck. Kett threw an apologetic look at Porter, who waved it away.

"Robbie, we appreciate you being here, especially under these circumstances," he said. "If you need to go, just go. We'll see you when we see you, and we've got your number until then."

"It's fine," he replied, his voice low and soothing. "She just misses her mum. We all do."

"Billie's probably..." Porter started, popping his lips. "Look, you're police, you know the reality of cases like hers. But don't give up, okay? I remember seeing you on the news, with those twins. I remember you saying the same thing, that you wouldn't give up hope until they were found. You never gave up on them, not once, not even in all those weeks."

"Months," said Kett. "Seven months they were missing."

And he *had* given up hope. He'd given up hope more times than he could count.

"You're a good dad," Porter said. "Nobody would say any different. She loves you. It's clear how much she loves you, by all the dribble and snot that's dripping down your collar right now."

Kett laughed, and Moira pushed herself away, grinning at Porter.

"I mean, it's disgusting," Porter went on. "It's like a river of the stuff."

"It could be worse," Kett said, sniffing. He pulled a face. "Oh, hang on, it *is* worse."

He held the baby out to Porter.

"You want to do the honours?"

"Do I want to clean up a Chernobyl-sized radioactive turd explosion?" Porter said, shaking his head. "No, I absolutely do not."

Kett pulled Moira back, smoothing her springy blonde curls as best he could.

"Guess it's up to me again, then," he said.

"If you ever want to talk about it," Porter said. "I'm here."

"If I ever want to talk about *baby poop*?" Kett said.

"No, you idiot, if you ever want to talk about *Billie*."

Kett nodded a thank you to the man.

"I'll let you know," he said.

"DCI Kett," called one of the constables. Kett looked over to where they both stood by the squad car. The man held a phone. "Call for you, from PC Savage."

"Here," said Kett, handing the baby to Porter. He wasn't sure which of them squealed more at the change of hands. He walked to the squad car and took the phone. "Savage?"

"Yes sir," came the PC's voice, distorted by a poor signal. "I'm still at Walker's, and there's something you need to see."

CHAPTER TEN

The traffic had picked up, and getting around the city was a nightmare. Christian Stillwater lived in what was known as the Golden Triangle, an area of small but expensive middle-class houses just outside the city centre, and getting from there up to the north of the city proved to be a nightmare of buses, bikes and lorries. Kett wished the old Volvo had lights and a siren, but all it had was its croaky horn and that did bugger all to shift the people in his way.

He'd been offered sirens, of course. Porter had told the constables to escort him over, but Kett had refused. Savage hadn't exactly sounded urgent, and the uniforms would be put to better use joining the hunt for their most promising suspect. Porter had offered to come too, but Kett had told him to get the bag of clothes to forensics ASAP. If they could find out which beach Christian Stillwater had been to, they stood a better chance of finding the girls.

"Besides," said Kett as he'd hurriedly changed Moira's nappy in the passenger seat of the Volvo. "Savage seems more than capable of holding her own if there's trouble."

"And even if she isn't," said Porter with a smile. "She's

called Savage. Just yell 'Go get 'em, Savage!' and they'll be running like the devil was on their tail."

The parking bays by the shops were full, and Kett didn't want to block the road, so he drove another quarter mile and found a small Co-op store with a car park out back. It claimed it was for customers only, so he nipped in and bought a box of baby rusks as yet another bribe to get Moira into the buggy. Luckily, there was no time to feel guilty about it, because as he entered the parade and passed the dilapidated pub he heard a rap of knuckles on glass and turned to see PC Savage staring at him through the Albion's filthy windows.

He bumped and shunted the buggy through the double doors, shivering in a sudden blast of air conditioning. The pub was actually much nicer inside than out, the floor polished wood and the tables and chairs sleek and modern. Other than the sour-faced man behind the bar there wasn't a soul inside the place, and it didn't take much to work out why.

"Thanks for coming, sir," said Savage, silhouetted by the light from the window. She'd taken off her jacket and hat, but she was still every ounce the copper—and round here, coppers weren't good drinking partners. "You didn't find Stillwater, then?"

"No," Kett said, wheeling the buggy to the window. From here he had a perfect view of the newsagent's and the flat above. He could even make out the diminutive form of David Walker behind the till. "He's in the wind, which makes it even more likely that he's guilty. What about you? What caught your eye?"

Savage grinned, looking exceptionally pleased with herself.

"First, I did some research," she said, and Kett held up a hand.

"Hang on," he said, turning to the bar. "Couldn't grab a tea over here, could I?"

"I don't know," muttered the man in a tone of pure sarcasm. "Could you?" But he shuffled over to the machine and switched it on.

"And a juice," Kett asked. "For the kid."

"Oh, I'm fine, thank you sir," said Savage. Kett frowned, pointing at the buggy where Moira was chowing down on baby rusks.

"This kid," Kett said.

"I... uh... sorry," Savage said, blushing. "But anyway, I did some digging while I was sitting here. Walker has four children."

"Yeah," said Kett. "One's done time, right?"

"Burglary, two counts," she said, nodding. She picked up her phone from the table, showing Kett a photograph of a man in his fifties. He was grizzled, tanned, balding, and fat—as big as David Walker was tiny—but he was the spit of his father in his eyes and nose. "His name's Brandon Walker. Fifty-six. His last arrest was for a big job in the Midlands, he and some other guys tried to knock off a pawn shop. Turns out it was owned by the Albanian mob, and they got their arses kicked, then they got busted on top. Two years for aggravated burglary."

"That all?"

"He *aggravated* with a mallet," she said. "A *rubber* mallet. It was more for show, I think. To be honest, he's not the brightest prawn in the ocean. He was serving over in Oakwood."

"And he's still in Wolverhampton?" Kett asked.

"According to his father he is. David Walker claims he

hasn't spoken to his son since he was sent away the second time. Claims he's given him too many chances. As far as the old man knows, Brandon's still skulking around in the Midlands, and I checked. He had a job out there, farm work. Castrating sheep, if you can believe it."

Kett shuddered.

"Rented a small place, kept himself to himself. Right up until a year and a half ago, when he just didn't show up to work one day. Stopped paying his rent, officially evicted from his property."

"And?" Kett asked.

"He's been off the grid," she replied. "No job, no house, no sign of him."

"And you called me here to tell me this?" Kett said. Savage shook her head, pointing across the street.

"I called you here because the idiot just popped his head up right there."

Kett peered at the row of windows above the Walker shop. They were drenched with sun. There could have been a naked marching band in the flat and Kett wouldn't have been able to see them.

"You're sure?"

"Eighty per cent, sir," Savage replied. "About thirty minutes ago there was a cloud right in front of the sun, the whole street went dark, and I saw a face there. I'm certain it was him, he's pretty memorable."

"Makes sense," said Kett as the barman placed the drinks down on the table by the window. Despite the man's mood, he managed a smile and a wave at Moira. She blew a raspberry at him and his frown returned as he muttered his way back to the bar. "Walker was obviously lying about the flat being empty. But why was he lying about his son being there?"

"Embarrassment?" she said. "Ex con. Doesn't do much for a family newsagent's reputation."

"One way of finding out," said Kett. He took a big sip of his stale, milky tea and grimaced. "Jesus, what is it with this city and hot drinks?"

He slammed the mug down and started for the door, then his heart gave a mighty lurch as he remembered Moira. He doubled back.

"We need to get inside that flat," he said.

"You think he's got the girls in there?" Savage asked. "That's a pretty big leap, sir, I'm not sure it would stand up in court."

"He's one of only a few people who would have had some kind of access to both girls," Kett replied. "He could have found out their routes, he would have known their home addresses, and other personal information from their files that he could have used to form a friendship with them."

Savage considered this, unsure.

"It's a big leap from robbery to kidnapping," she said after a moment.

"Yeah, but Brandon knocked over the Albanians, and you know how ruthless they are. A pretty big chunk of the human traffic in the country is moved by Albanian gangs, so maybe they're twisting Brandon's arm, getting him to snatch girls as a way of paying back what they think he owes."

"That actually makes sense," said Savage. "So we get a warrant? Go talk to him?"

Kett looked over at the flats again.

"I think I can make out another person in there," he said, knowing how obvious the lie was, and well aware that Savage knew it too. "Maybe two other people. They could be girls."

"You're really going there?" Savage asked, her face deadly serious.

"Yeah," he replied. "And one day I'll tell you why. Don't worry, I'll do it, you don't have to get your hands dirty. I need you in here to make sure he doesn't bolt. And, you know, to make sure *she* doesn't drink a whole bottle of rum."

The baby seemed to find this hilarious, her chest heaving with cartoonish chuckles.

"I'll call it in," Savage said. "We can wait. We can have half a dozen PCs here in ten minutes."

Ten minutes. It was how long he'd waited on his first ever case.

Those ten minutes had cost a young boy his life.

"Walker Senior is sharp, he probably knows we're here, and if he knows then there's a chance that Brandon does too. If—and I know it's a big if—those girls are in there, he could be doing anything to them."

Savage nodded, her young face etched with concern.

"Call it in," Kett said. "Just let them know I'm in there."

He started for the door, but Savage called him back. She popped a stud on her belt and pulled out her telescopic baton.

"Take this," she said.

Kett nodded a thank you, then strode out of the pub.

CHAPTER ELEVEN

A FRESH BANK OF CLOUDS WAS MOVING ACROSS THE sun, and the temperature plummeted as Kett closed the door of the pub behind him. The road was thick with traffic but there weren't many pedestrians, the parade of shops almost entirely deserted.

He tucked the heavy baton into the inside pocket of his jacket, glancing up at the flats across the road—but only for a moment, because he didn't want to give himself away. He ignored the crossing, cutting between the stationary cars and walking to the off-licence next to Walker's. Down here he'd be practically invisible to anyone in the flat above, and he kept close to the giant windows as he passed the newsagent's. David Walker was still there, but he was facing the shelves behind him, restocking cigarettes.

He reached the door of the flat and peeked through the letterbox again, then he put his ear to it. There was a definite current of air in there, which was weird because none of the windows were open. Kett knew when a house was empty, and this one didn't feel that way at all. The way the air moved, the quiet noises it carried, made him think that someone was up there.

Someone holding his breath.

He let the letterbox close slowly, then he cut down the alleyway beside the shop. It was thick with weeds, strewn with empty bottles, and it stank of piss. It led around to the rear of the parade, which was made up of a small paved area and a handful of bike racks—three lonely, severed wheels locked to the metal bars. Across from them was a collection of rickety, graffitied fences and barbed wire that shielded the row of houses beyond.

There were two more doors back here, both of which led to more flats above the shops, and both of which were sealed tight with metal panels. Kett was surprised to see that Walker had been telling the truth: signs on both of the doors mentioned hazardous materials. Shielding his eyes from the reappearance of the sun, Kett saw the windows of both flats were boarded up on this side too. Only the one above Walker's looked in any way fit for habitation.

He made his way back to the door at the front. There was no handle, just a Yale lock, but Kett had faced off against doors like this a million times. He popped the letterbox again and slid his hand through, grunting as the metal rubbed against his flesh.

"Come on," he said, straining, his fingertips brushing against something metallic. "Get over here, you bastard."

He found it, twisting the latch and shoving with his shoulder at the same time. The door popped open, the hinges as fresh as a daisy. Quietly, Kett crept inside and closed it behind him. Then he pulled the baton from his pocket and flicked it to its full length. He hadn't used one in years, not since his uniform days, but it felt good. It took some of the edge off breaking into the home of a convicted thug.

He took the steps as slowly as he dared, every creak deafening in the small, quiet space. His heart revved hard behind his ribs and all the tea he'd drunk that morning boiled inside his empty stomach. This wasn't strictly legal, of course, but he'd been doing the job long enough to know that it was better to trust your instincts and smooth out the wrinkles later, otherwise—

Thump.

Kett's breath caught in his throat. The noise was close, from right at the top of the stairs. He hesitated, holding the baton by his shoulder, ready to bring it down hard.

Thumpthump.

That definitely wasn't the sound of an empty flat.

Taking a deep breath, Kett charged up the last few steps and burst through the door at the top.

"Police!" he roared.

No reply.

The dark, narrow hallway was empty, but it hadn't been for long. He sniffed, making out the distinctly unpleasant aroma of an unwashed male.

"Brandon?" he said. "Brandon Walker? If you're in here, make yourself known. I've got a baton here that really doesn't want to play hide and seek."

Nothing.

Kett walked through the nearest door, finding a living room that was empty apart from a mattress covered in a bundle of filthy sheets and a full ashtray. If there had been any doubts about the flat being occupied they were immediately shot down by the wisps of smoke that still rose from the butts there.

"Brandon," Kett said. "I've seen your photograph, man, I know there aren't many places you can hide."

He left the room, crossing the corridor and seeing a kitchen that was almost too small for him to fit inside. There was nothing at all in the cupboards, and only half a pint of milk in the fridge.

"You're running out of room, Brandon," Kett said, adjusting his sweaty grip on the baton. "And I'm running out of patience."

There was nobody in the lime green bathroom, or the airing cupboard, which left the flat's only bedroom. Kett peeked through the crack in the door, frowning, then he walked inside. It was empty, just a small chest of drawers against the far wall, and a broken mirror facing the window. He shivered in a sudden breeze.

"What the..." Kett muttered. He walked to the window and tested the handle, but it was locked tight. Cupping a hand to the glass he made out the pub opposite, seeing Savage sitting in the window, Moira bouncing on her lap. The PC looked relieved to see him, then confused as Kett lifted his shoulders in an exaggerated shrug.

He walked away, doing another quick search of the flat and finding sweet FA. But there had definitely been somebody here. How the hell had they managed to get out? It had to have been just before he arrived, maybe even as he was speaking with Savage in the pub. Kett swore. Not only had he broken the rules of a search, he'd managed to lose the suspect—and there wasn't even any sign that the paper girls had ever been here.

He folded the baton, sticking it back in his pocket and wondering if he could make it out before backup arrived. That way he could let the uniforms in, and they could *officially* discover that the flat was empty. He made his way back down the corridor, stopping only when he heard that noise again.

Thump.

There was no sign of an attic hatch—and no room for one either, given how low the roof was. The floors, too, were fake wood laminate and positioned right over the shop beneath. It could have been birds scratching overhead, he guessed. Maybe a delivery van dumping stuff on the street. But it sounded too close for that.

It sounded like it was coming from next door.

Kett walked back into the bedroom, his eyes falling on the chest of drawers. It was too small to fit a person, especially a fat bastard like Brandon, and when Kett pulled out a drawer he saw that it was empty.

There was that breeze again, though, kissing its way up his sleeves and making his skin break out in goosebumps.

He suddenly understood. Grabbing the corners of the chest of drawers, he yanked it across the floor.

"Fuck me."

There was a hole in the wall, maybe two feet across and lined with jagged teeth of brick and concrete. It was empty apart from an unfathomable darkness and that same ghostly current of cold air.

Kett took a deep breath, rubbing his face. Under normal circumstances there was no way in hell he'd stick any part of his anatomy through a hole like that, but these weren't exactly normal circumstances, and for all he knew there were two eleven-year-old girls bound and gagged on the other side of this wall. Two girls who Brandon Walker might be leaning over right now, who might be gasping for their last breaths as he strangled them...

"Fuck me," he growled again, flicking the baton to its full length and using his other hand to fire up the flashlight on his phone. He leant down and shone the light through the hole, revealing a bedroom identical to this one —only crawling with shadows. "Brandon Walker, if you are in there I'm giving you to a count of three. If I get to three, I swear to god you're leaving this place on a stretcher. One."

Trying not to scream, he pushed an arm into the hole, then his head, kicking his way through. Bricks dug into his skin, snagging his belt, and for a horrible second he thought he was going to be stuck there. Panicking, he swung the phone back and forth, waiting for a shape to come bounding out of the dark. He wriggled, grunted, his foot finally catching on the chest of drawers in the other room and giving him enough leverage to push himself through. He plopped to the floor with a groan, scrabbling to his feet and wiping the sweat from his brow.

"Two," he said, clutching the baton and itching to swing it. This guy was *seriously* pissing him off.

The bedroom was empty, and Kett made his way into the hallway that mirrored the one next door. It was so dark in here, not even a crack of light able to break through the boards on the windows. The little flashlight did its best to compensate, but it was almost powerless against the vast weight of gloom.

Nothing in the bathroom. Nothing in the airing cupboard. Nothing in the kitchen.

That left only one place for Walker to hide.

"Three," said Kett as he positioned himself by the closed living room door. "A stretcher it is."

He raised his boot and gave the door a mighty kick. It didn't stand a chance, almost disintegrating under the attack. Three steps was all it took to reach the centre of the room, the baton raised and the torch sweeping from side to side—a huge wooden table piled with stuff, a desk chair, and there, in the corner...

No.

Two binbags, wrapped tight with tape, each the size and shape of a small, thin, broken body.

"No," Kett spoke aloud, running to them. He dropped to his knees, putting down the phone and the baton so that he could work at the plastic with his fingers. "Come on, don't be—"

He heard the footsteps too late, twisting his head in time to see a man running out from behind the table. He was big, *huge*, but he moved fast, the edges of the torchlight just catching the lump hammer in his hand.

Kett ducked as the man swung, adrenaline taking over. He wasn't quick enough, the hammer's heavy head skimming the top of his scalp. The room burned flashbulb bright for a second, Kett's ears ringing like he was standing inside a cathedral bell. He dived—at least he thought he dived, he couldn't even be sure which direction was down any more—scrabbling over the binbags.

The man roared, pain flaring in Kett's shoulder as the hammer hit again.

Get up! he screamed at himself. If he didn't, he was going to be pummelled to death right here. He thought of Moira, of Evie, of Alice, knowing that if he died then they would be orphans. It was like a burst of nitrous oxide in the engine of his rage.

"No!" he found the wall, pushed himself up, turning just in time to see the hammer drop towards his face. He sidestepped to his left, the hammer crunching into the wall hard enough to put a hole in the plaster.

Kett bunched a fist and threw it up into the man's solar plexus. Brandon was a big guy, plenty of padding, but the shot was true and he made a noise like he was vomiting. He lumbered back, trying to pull the hammer out of the wall, and Kett threw a second punch right into the flabby pouch of his throat.

Brandon attempted to breathe as he staggered away but the double whammy of a strike to the gut and to the windpipe was making it impossible. His foot landed on Kett's phone, cracking the flashlight, and suddenly the room went dark.

"On your knees!" roared Kett, his boot scuffing the ground to try to find the baton. "Now!"

There was a soft thump, and for a moment Kett thought the man had obeyed. Then a deeper shadow barrelled out of the dark and suddenly Brandon was on him, his immense arms pulling Kett's face into his chest. A fist hit him in the ribs but it was a badly thrown blow that didn't do much damage. Another followed, this one harder. Kett tried to breathe but his mouth was full of the stench of BO. He threw a punch of his own into Brandon's stomach but the man didn't seem to feel it.

A third punch, this time to his back, and Kett reacted before he even knew what he was doing—his teeth clamping down on what could only be the man's nipple. He chewed, hearing Brandon unleash a glass-shattering screech. But it worked. He was free. He fumbled for the wall, found the hammer, swung it blindly in the dark. Something cracked, and this time the sound of falling flesh was unmistakable.

"Fuck," Kett said, his voice just a whisper. His head was pounding like somebody was taking another hammer to his brain. With every heartbeat the room flashed white, and he felt like he was out at sea, like the whole building was swaying. He put a hand to the crown of his head, his fingers coming away warm with blood.

But Brandon Walker had it worse. He was rolling on the floor making wet, sobbing noises. Kett reached down and found him.

"Stay there," he said, fighting to form the words. "Don't give me an excuse to put this hammer through your face."

Crunch.

The sound of a door being knocked down, then the thunder of feet and voices from the flat next door.

"In here!" Kett shouted, the effort making the pain in his head sing. "Through the hole in the wall."

He got onto his knees, feeling his way back to the corner of the room. The binbags were tough and he couldn't break them with his fingers. He kept trying, though, kept working at them, because there was a chance the girls inside were still alive. There was always a chance.

Lights, the room suddenly swimming with them.

"Kett? Sir?"

Five constables burst into the room, three of them piling on the squirming shape of Brandon Walker. Savage was there too, and she dropped down beside him.

"Sir, you're hurt."

"The bags," Kett croaked. "The girls."

Savage pulled a pocket knife from her belt and slid it carefully through the closest binbag, ripping at the plastic until she'd formed a hole. It took every last ounce of energy Kett possessed to lean in and see what was inside.

Pills. Hundreds of bags of little white pills.

And he wasn't sure if it was the effort of the fight, the crack with the hammer, or the sheer relief of not seeing two dead bodies in those binbags that tipped him over the edge into unconsciousness.

CHAPTER TWELVE

"Robbie?"

The voice was muted, distant, as if he was lying inside a coffin deep beneath the earth. Kett groaned, trying to open his eyes. Nothing seemed to work, and he was filled with a sudden terror that he'd gone blind—or worse, that he was dying. He reached into his memories but there was nothing there.

Nothing but Billie.

He suddenly saw his wife, her generous smile, those big, blue eyes that had been passed on to all of their children. She leaned in and wrapped her arms around him, pulling him to her chest. Something exploded inside Kett's heart, a rush of warmth and happiness that was almost overwhelming.

You've come home, he thought but couldn't say. *You've come back to us.*

"You're going to be okay," Billie said, holding him tight. "Just don't move, it's going to be okay, sir."

Sir?

Kett attempted to make his eyes work again, and this

time one of them peeled open. He shut it immediately as a blade of light twisted its way into his aching head. Then he tried again.

A room filled with coppers, torchlight, and PC Kate Savage on her knees beside him.

Not Billie, then.

The disappointment was almost too much, and it was only slightly tempered by the relief that he was still alive.

He started to sit up, the room cartwheeling over his head.

"Easy," said Savage. "Walker brained you good and proper. Ambulance is on its way."

He tried to form a word.

"Moira?"

"She's fine," Savage said. "Safe. There are two constables with her right now, teaching her how to use a taser."

Kett almost managed a laugh. He lifted a hand to his head, feeling a sticky crust in his hair. The bleeding seemed to have stopped, but it hurt like a bastard.

"How long was I out?" he said.

"Uh," Savage checked her watch. "Ninety seconds, give or take. How does it feel?"

"Like an angry fat man hit me in the head with a lump hammer," he replied.

"You're lucky he didn't put it clean through your skull," Savage replied. "He was trying to kill you."

"Where is he?" Kett asked. He tried to sit up again and this time Savage helped him, her skinny arms surprisingly strong. Kett screwed his eyes shut against the phantom wave of bright lights and nausea, his mouth full of battery acid.

"On his way downstairs," said Savage. "Then to the hospital. You caught him right in the jaw, he's not making a lot of sense. And..." She leaned in. "Did you, uh, bite off his nipple?"

"I bit it," said Kett, grimacing at the memory—and at the taste. "I don't know if it came off."

"Well, either way. Looks like he was running his own little pharmaceutical factory up here."

"The girls?" Kett asked, squinting at her. She shook her head.

"But it was a good bust. Those bags were full of ecstasy and MDMA, thousands of pills. Nasty stuff, too, cut with all kinds of poison. Brandon Walker was a piece of shit, and he's going to go away for a very long time."

"His dad?" Kett asked.

"They've taken him in too, as an accessory," said Savage. "Brandon was behind the drugs, and he was the one making the girls sell cigarettes too, but David Walker knew about it. There's no way he didn't. I think he was scared of his own kid."

Kett started to nod, then thought better of it. He grabbed Savage's shoulder and pulled himself to his knees, then somehow managed to make it to his feet. For a second he thought he was going to vomit but he swallowed hard until the feeling went away.

"Sir, please," said Savage, standing up beside him. "You need to get checked out."

"I'll be fine," he said. "It only glanced off me. What time is it?"

"Just gone one," she replied. Kett swore.

"Look, I've got to go. Evie's going to be wondering where I am."

"You can't go," Savage replied. "The boss is on his way over. Bust or no bust, he sounded pissed."

"Yeah, all the more reason I need to get out of here."

He started to walk and Savage blocked his path, her fingertips touching his chest like she was a nightclub bouncer.

"Sir, I have orders," she said.

"Yeah, and I've got kids," he replied. "Sorry. Blame it on the concussion. Tell Clare I was a crazy man and you couldn't stop me."

He walked around her, pushing through the constables into the hallway, then clattering down the stairs. Somebody had pried the metal frame from the door and the blast of fresh air was beautifully welcome. The heat and sunshine were less so, but he pushed through it, and by the time he reached the little party of police vehicles blocking the entrance to the parade he was starting to feel okay.

Still in a horrific amount of pain, of course, but okay.

"Addy!"

Moira spotted him before he spotted her. She was in the back seat of a cruiser chewing on a little silver whistle that Kett instantly recognised. She tossed it into the footwell, both of her hands straining in his direction. Two constables standing beside the car followed the direction of her fingers and smiled at Kett.

"She's adorable," said the woman, an older PC with greying hair but a bright smile. "I wish they let us bring kids to work more often."

Her smile faltered when she saw Kett's injuries.

"You probably want somebody to take a look at that," she said. He waved her away.

"Hey beautiful girl," he said to Moira. "You ready to get out of here?"

He scooped the baby out of the seat.

"Can one of you do me a favour and make sure PC

Savage gets her whistle back?" he said. "I'd do it myself, but I've got to run. Late for pickup."

"*School* pickup?" said the constable, raising an eyebrow as she studied his head. "Please tell me you're going to get that cleaned up first."

"It's just a scratch," he said, wincing at her. "Nobody's even going to notice."

"DEAR GOD! WHAT ON EARTH HAPPENED?"

The nursery worker looked like she was about to pass out right there on the floor of the cloakroom. Both her hands were on her cheeks, and her eyes resembled a couple of pickled eggs. She looked DCI Kett up and down, then turned her attention to the baby in his arms.

"Is *she* okay?" she asked.

Moira yawned, then waved at the woman. Kett squinted through his headache to read the badge that hung from her Hufflepuff lanyard.

"Betty, everything is fine," he said.

"Debbie," she replied, frowning. Kett leaned in, his double vision clearing for a moment.

"Debbie," he said. "Sorry. It's been a long morning, but I'm fine, I promise you. I've just come to collect Evie."

"She was expecting you some time ago," said Debbie, the lines on her forehead deepening. "She was quite upset."

He nodded, and started to walk past her, but she stood her ground.

"I am not going to let you through this door until you clean yourself up," she said, surprisingly firmly. "There's a disabled toilet in the main school building across the playground."

"Sorry," he said. "I'm a policeman, there was—"

"I don't care," said Debbie. "Here, you're a father, and I'm not going to let you put the fear of god into these children."

She opened her arms for Moira, and although Kett hesitated the baby threw herself towards the woman without hesitation. He let her go, muttering an apology as he stepped back out into the day. The school reception staff were just as surprised to see him, and they guided him to the disabled bathroom as surreptitiously as they could.

As soon as he caught sight of himself in the mirror, he knew why they had been so cautious. He looked dreadful, like he'd just crawled out of a grave. The injury on his head was worse than he'd thought, trails of blood winding down his cheeks and pooling around his collar. His eyes were red and rimmed with shadows, his suit jacket was torn beneath the right armpit and streaked with dirt and blood and god knows what else from Brandon Walker's floor. He was coated with a fine, white powder, too. If he tried to walk through an airport terminal now, he knew, the drug dogs would chew him to pieces.

His reflection made him understand, as well, how close he'd come to not making it out of there.

"Stupid," he said. He couldn't help but imagine it: a copper arriving at the school—maybe Porter, or Savage, or god forbid Colin Clare—and asking to speak to Evie and Alice Kett. A quiet room, a terrible, aching silence, then those words.

"Girls, I'm so sorry, your father's been in an accident. He's not coming home."

And then what? What would happen to them after the tears, the screams? Billie's family were all in the States, and other than his mum—who had practically disowned him nearly two decades ago—he didn't have anyone worth mentioning. Care, then, foster homes, adoption, separation. Just like that, the family was gone. After a while, Evie and Moira wouldn't even remember him.

"Stupid stupid *stupid*," he said again, gripping the sink.

Going into the Walker flat alone had been reckless, and selfish. He couldn't afford to make that mistake again.

He ran the tap, easing off his jacket then his shirt. His shoulder was a marbled mess of yellow and black where Walker had caught him with the second hammerblow, and he couldn't lift his arm past ninety degrees. He didn't think anything was broken, though. Bending down, he splashed water over his head, locking a growl behind his teeth as the pain burned out of his scalp. It wasn't bleeding any more, and once he'd worked his fingers through his hair a few times the water ran clear. He scrubbed the worst of it from his face and neck, and from his hands, then he dried himself as best he could under the whiny little hand drier.

The result wasn't perfect, but it was passable. He looked a little less like a policeman, and a little more like a dad.

A half-naked dad.

He slung the shirt on again, reaching the middle button when somebody knocked on the door.

"Hang on," he said. "Nearly done."

"It's Carol, from reception," came a voice. "I told the principal what had happened, he has some clothes here if you'd like them."

When Kett opened the door she was standing there with a T-shirt in her hand.

"It's just a PE shirt," she said. "But it's better than..."

She nodded at the bloody mess he was currently wearing.

"He knows you're a policeman. He said anything you need, just ask."

"That's very kind," said Kett, pulling the shirt off then the T-shirt on. It was a little tight around the chest, but it looked fine. The school logo sat there proudly and Kett patted it. "Thank you."

"Any time," she said.

It was just a wash and a change of clothes, but it worked miracles—even his headache seemed to be ebbing. At least it was, until the woman cleared her throat and spoke again.

"Look, as you're here, perhaps you could have a word with Miss Gardner?"

It took Kett a moment to remember.

"Alice's teacher, right?" he said. "Is everything okay?"

"Alice is fine. She just got into a bit of bother at lunch. Frances will explain everything."

"Can I grab my other kids first?" he said, wondering why he felt the need to ask permission. "Evie's waiting for me, and the little one too."

"It will only take a minute," said Carol, holding the door open for him. Kett sighed, shoving the shirt in the bin. There was no washing powder on earth that was going to get the stench of Brandon Walker out of it. He followed Carol down the same corridor, past reception, and to the door of a classroom. A picture of a turtle floated on the glass, and past it he saw thirty kids all sitting on their tiny chairs doodling on scrap paper. It took him a moment to find Alice, and seeing her there, so big and yet so small, was like a fist around his heart.

Carol knocked twice then pushed the door open.

"Frances? Mr Kett."

"Dad!" yelled Alice, beaming. She was out of her chair in a heartbeat, knocking past the other kids to get to him.

The hug she gave him made him wince, but it was worth the pain.

"Hey, kiddo, how's it going?" Kett asked, smoothing back her hair.

"She's doing great," answered Frances as she crossed the room. She gestured into the corridor and they all shuffled out, Frances closing the door behind them. "A smashing kid, I can see that already."

Alice's smile had become one of her legendary scowls, and she pushed her face into Kett's side.

"But?" asked Kett.

"But there was an episode at break. Alice pushed a boy over."

"He was being an idiot," barked Alice. "I hate him."

"Hey, easy," said Kett. "Was there a reason for it?"

Alice didn't say anything, and Frances sighed.

"We're not sure, she won't say, but it's not the kind of behaviour we expect here. I asked her to apologise and she refused."

"Sorry," Kett said, the same way he'd done a million times before in her old school. "She has trouble picking up on social cues sometimes, trouble processing her emotions. Don't you, Alice?"

Alice grunted something.

"It's just been a very difficult time for her, for all of them," he went on. "It will take her a little while to settle, but she will. Right, kiddo?"

Alice grunted something else, but the strop was passing.

"It's my fault," Kett said. "I shouldn't have brought her in so soon. The plan was to take a bit of time to get to know the new house, the new city, before starting the new school. But something... something came up."

As if trying to prove his point, Kett's phone began to

ring. It was loud, and it was a horrendous version of the Mexican Hat Dance which Alice had installed and which he couldn't work out how to change.

"Uh..." he said. "Excuse me a moment."

He fished it out of his pocket, seeing a Norwich number. It was probably Clare, or somebody else from the Major Investigation Team. Jabbing a finger on the screen to end the call, he slid it back into his pocket.

"We'll talk about it tonight," he said to his daughter, stroking her hair. "But maybe it's best for now if you come home with me?"

Alice nodded, clutching his hand.

"We can try again tomorrow," he added, and Frances smiled.

"It was lovely to meet you, Alice," she said, bending down to the girl's level. "We'll see you in the morning. Go home, chill, take some time to be normal with your mum and dad. Everything will be just fine."

CHAPTER THIRTEEN

Everything wasn't fine.

For the entire journey home the back row of seats in the Volvo was a sea of hard stares, all of them directed at Kett. Evie had been furious with him for being late, even though she didn't even know how to read a clock. Apparently, nursery had been awful, everybody had been a "fart head" and they'd tried to make her eat crumpets for lunch. With *butter*. Judging by her expression, which looked like a pug that had eaten a hornet's nest, the world had pretty much come to an end.

Alice, on the other hand, was mad at him because of what her teacher had said. *Take some time to be normal with your mum and dad* was about the worst thing that could have come out of Frances Gardner's mouth. Alice hadn't said anything about it as they'd walked to the car, but he could read her mind well enough, and he knew the thoughts that ran through it.

Why can't I see mum?

Where is she?

Is she dead?

Why didn't you save her?

He knew those thoughts because they were exactly the same as his own.

Moira was the only one who wasn't glaring at him, and only because she was still in a rear-facing car seat. She directed her shrieks at the window, her legs drumming the seat and her hands pinching Alice's arm, making her yell too. By the time he'd found a parking space along their new street all three of them were screaming a soundtrack that would have been more at home in Guantanamo.

"Alright, enough!" he said, popping his door and clambering out. He took a moment to catch his breath, checking his watch and wondering how on earth he was going to get through another six hours of this before bedtime.

Give me a fight with Brandon Walker any day of the week, he thought. *It's got to be easier than three young girls.*

He opened Evie's door, unclipping her booster seat. Then he walked to the other side and released the Kraken. They all tumbled into the house together, the cool, dark interior seeming to take the edge off their anger.

"Go find your iPad," he told Alice. "Put something nice on for everyone, you can crash on the sofa for a bit, okay?"

She ran upstairs, and Kett put Moira down on the living room carpet. The baby continued to scream, rolling onto her back and kicking the floor. Evie dropped onto the sofa and folded her hands across her chest, still glaring at him. Her disgruntled expression was so comically exaggerated that it brought a smile to Kett's lips.

"Yeah, I love you too, Evie," he said.

He walked into the kitchen and ran the tap. A proper cup of tea, maybe a biscuit, and everything might be okay. Just so long as there were no more surprises.

He was just grabbing a mug from the drainer when the

doorbell rang. He sighed, wondering whether it was worth even answering it. But Alice took the decision out of his hands.

"Someone's at the door!" she yelled, thundering down the stairs. He heard her fiddling with the lock. "Dad! Someone's at the door!"

There was a tall, curly-haired silhouette in the frosted glass that could only belong to one person.

Great.

"Out of the way," he said to Alice as he twisted the brand-new Yale and opened the door. Superintendent Colin Clare stood there with an expression that almost perfectly matched Evie's. He was holding a manila folder in one hand and a large carrier bag in the other.

"Sir," said Kett. "You didn't have to come all the way out here."

"I did," he replied. "Because you weren't answering your phone."

"Who are you?" Alice asked, indignant.

"Alice, be nice," Kett said. "This is Colin, he's my boss."

Clare grunted at Alice, and Alice grunted back.

"Why is your nose so hairy?" Alice asked, craning up on her tiptoes to get a better look. Kett didn't know whether to laugh or cry, so he just stood there, waiting for Clare to react. To his immense surprise, the boss just smiled.

"It's for when I go undercover," he said. "All this nose hair pulls out into a moustache and beard so nobody knows who I am."

Alice pulled a suspicious expression, looking at her dad.

"It's true," said Kett. "The hair in his ears pulls out into a wig as well."

Clare gave him a look: *don't push it.*

"Come in," Kett said. "I was just making tea."

"Do you make it better than Porter?" the boss asked as he stooped beneath the lintel.

"God yes. That man wouldn't know tea if he had to identify it in a line-up."

Clare hissed a small laugh through his nose, hovering in the doorway to the living room. Moira was still bawling on the floor, but she stopped when she spotted the giant above her.

"Ook!" the baby said, pointing. "Ee-ee, ook!"

Evie did as she was told, staring. She picked up a cushion and held it over her face, her standard response to any stranger.

"Boss, this is Moira, and Evie on the sofa. And Alice, of course."

"Good to meet you all," he said. "I hope you don't mind. Porter told me you didn't have a chance to get bed linen, and that the movers aren't coming until the weekend. I took the liberty."

He unloaded the carrier bag over the easy chair, releasing bundles of brightly coloured sheets, pillowcases and duvet covers. Alice and Evie dived in like it was Christmas, Moira doing her damnedest to clamber into the middle of the melee.

"They've all been washed. My lot don't exactly need them any more."

Kett nodded a thank you, steering Clare through to the kitchen. He grabbed another mug from the drainer and rinsed it, then filled the kettle.

"That was kind of you, thank you," he said as Clare took a seat at the little table. "You've got kids?"

"Six," he replied, smiling at Kett's shocked expression. "We were going for four. The last batch were triplets, they run in Fiona's family. We should have been more careful."

"How old?"

"Youngest three are fourteen, the oldest is twenty-one." Clare gave Kett a sympathetic look. "It was nightmarishly hard, and that was with two of us and a whole village of support. This... How are you coping?"

This wasn't the conversation Kett had expected at all.

"Fine," he said as he popped the teabags in. "As well as can be expected, anyway." He paused, listening to the kids in the living room. "It's hard, to be honest. Every day I wake up and think I can't do this."

"And every day you do," Clare said. "Trust me, I've been there. There is nothing in this universe harder than being a parent. Except maybe being a single parent. Except maybe being a single parent of three girls."

"It's only... it's only until Billie comes back."

He'd called Bingo last night, of course, even though he'd tried not to. Just a quick call, with an even quicker answer: *no news, sorry Robbie.*

"She was taken, wasn't she?" Clare asked. "I remember seeing the security footage on the news."

Kett nodded. He knew the CCTV off by heart, a grainy video of Billie heading to Gospel Oak after meeting a friend. Moira in the buggy. Then a white van with no tags, two men wearing children's animal masks, smoking tyres as they burnt down the road—three seconds and it's over, no more Billie, just Moira's ghostly face in the buggy screaming and screaming and screaming.

And that was three and a half months ago.

"We searched everywhere, we checked out every lead. I was convinced it was the Otley crew, you know them?" Kett glanced at Clare and Clare nodded. "The ones who kidnapped that politician's son. I worked that case too, put three of them behind bars, including Jonus and Philip

Otley, the brothers. Saved the kid. They put a price on my head, tried and failed to kill me. I thought they went after Billie instead."

"And?"

Kett poured water into the mugs, letting it steep.

"We tore them apart, every den, every brothel, every safe house. By the time we'd finished with them there wasn't a stone left they could hide under. But Billie wasn't there. Lead after lead we followed, but nobody connected to me or to any of my cases knew anything. It just felt like a... like a random attack."

He heard footsteps, turned to see Evie charging down the hall. She glanced warily at Clare, then held up a Spider-Man duvet cover.

"I want this one. Can I have it?"

Moira was right behind her, trying to carry a Trolls pillowcase even though it kept getting stuck beneath her feet.

"You can have it," Kett said. "But only if you go back through. Watch the iPad with your sisters."

She bolted, and Kett fished out the teabags and added a dash of milk to both mugs.

"Sugar?"

Clare shook his head, moving the folder so that Kett could put the mugs down.

"Anyway," Kett said, picking up Moira and putting her on his lap. "It's still an active case, and some of the Met's best coppers are on it. We'll find her."

"I don't doubt it," Clare said, looking at the wound on Kett's head. "Benson told me you were thorough, that you gave everything to a case. I see now that he wasn't just trying to sell me a story."

Kett started to reply, but Clare held up a hand.

"You've done this job long enough to know what I'm about to say, but let me say it anyway, just so it's on the record. Your decision to enter the Walker property was based on extremely tenuous evidence. Luckily, you have PC Savage backing you up. She claims to have seen Brandon Walker inside, and she told me your reasoning for an immediate search. It's not what I'd call solid, but it will hold up."

He leaned forward, pointing a cracked nail at Kett.

"What doesn't hold up is you going all Errol Flynn on me, bursting in there without a plan, and without backup. You may not be one of mine, Kett, but I still have a duty of care to everyone who works under me, whether it's you, or even *her*."

He nodded to Moira, who was using the pillowcase to play peekaboo.

"You cannot use my officers as a babysitting service, is that clear?"

Kett nodded, and Clare sat back.

"Brandon Walker is going away for a long time," he said. "And that's on you. It was good work. More importantly, it gives us access to everything in the Walker shop. We swept the place after you'd gone, found a whole bunch of documents detailing what they were up to in Mousehold. The paper girls were distributing the pills inside the cigarette boxes."

"Maisie and Connie too?" Kett asked.

"Maisie, yes, although I doubt she knew she was doing it. We're still trying to find out about Connie. Mousehold was their turf, if you like. David Walker knew his son was up to something, but I believe him when he said he didn't know about the drugs. I don't think he dared even ask Brandon about it."

"Could this be a gang thing?" Kett asked. "Could the

girls have been taken as part of some territorial dispute? A warning? Brandon Walker had ties to the Albanians."

"It's something we're looking into," said Clare. "It would be unlikely, but there has been an increased level of organised violence in the city in recent years, and this would certainly follow that trend. Trafficking too, although this doesn't have any of the hallmarks of a trafficking case. More and more gangs are coming up the A11 from your part of the world, DCI Kett, and it's causing me any number of headaches."

He gave Kett a look that implied this was all his fault, but it was short lived. He sighed, opening the manila folder.

"Our main line of enquiry remains the same," he said. "That this isn't related to organised crime, and that the girls were taken by a single, dangerous individual. Of course, when they've finished wiring Brandon Walker's jaw, and he remembers how to hold a pen, we may know differently."

He gave Kett another accusing look.

"But the focus has to remain on finding Christian Stillwater. Porter filled me in on your talk with Lucy Clarke, the girlfriend, and forensics came back an hour ago with a report on the sand found on his clothing."

"Daaaaady!"

Evie's shout from the living room coincided with Alice charging down the corridor holding the iPad.

"Evie wants to watch *Peppa Pig*," she said, stamping her foot. "But it's my iPad."

"Put something on that's suitable for everyone," Kett said.

"No, that's not fa—"

"Alice," Kett snapped, making her jump. "Until we've got our TV, you have to learn to share. Find something, or I'll decide."

She growled like a werewolf, then stormed back. Moira slid off Kett's knee and ran after her.

"Sorry," Kett said. "The sand. Lucy said she thought he'd been to a beach."

"He hadn't been to a beach," Clare said. "There were deposits of clay and iron in it. It's sharp sand."

"From a building site?" Kett asked, and Clare nodded. "Okay, so this fits his MO, right? Our guy likes abandoned places, or at least places where there aren't many people. Stillwater got the sand on his clothes on Saturday, according to his girlfriend. Commercial building sites don't generally run at the weekend, but they'd be back to work on Monday, when Connie went missing, so it doesn't make any sense that he'd be preparing something on site. Somebody would see him, and he made that mistake last time, right? With the other girl, um..."

"Emily Coupland," said Clare, taking a sip of his tea.

"Right, Emily. So he wouldn't pick anywhere where there's a chance of being spotted. Unless he was on a building site that's in limbo. We should check to see if there are any stalled construction works in the city, any sites that aren't currently in use."

"Spalding's already on it," said Clare. "We're working on the theory that Stillwater snatched both girls and took them somewhere pre-planned, someplace that was set up to contain them."

"A location he'd already prepared," said Kett, nodding. He gulped down a mouthful of hot tea, wincing as it burned its way into his empty stomach. Then he shook his head.

"What's wrong?" Clare asked.

"I don't know," he replied. "I'm not feeling the whole building site thing. Stillwater's all about control, he's a planner. There are too many variables in a large, open construction zone. If I was him, I think I'd be looking for somewhere smaller, more private. I think we need to be looking for a renovation project, a house that's getting an extension, maybe a new build."

"I bloody hope not," muttered Clare. "This city's on a boom. There are five or six extensions being built on my street alone, and at least a hundred new build estates across the county."

"So cross reference as many as you can with people who've recently died," Kett said. "I think we're looking for a vacated property that was undergoing significant renovation."

Clare nodded.

"Have there been any letters? Any communication at all?" Kett asked.

"None. Why?"

"It's just with a case like this, there's usually something. People like Stillwater want the world to know how clever they are. They thrive on being smarter than the people who are chasing them. Stillwater's a clever guy, he's chosen to disappear, he knows that we're going to suspect him. It feels odd that he hasn't reached out."

"Maybe he's waiting until it's too late for us to do anything about it."

"Maybe," said Kett, taking another sip of tea. "Just be on the lookout for it, it might be subtle. Psychopaths are bastards."

"There's a lot riding on your theory that Stillwater is a psychopath," said Clare.

"There's a lot riding on your theory that it's him at all," replied Kett.

Clare nodded, polishing off his tea in three huge gulps. He stood up, leaving the folder on the table.

"Everything's in there, take a look when you get a chance," he said. "And Kett, I know I can sound cranky."

"Really, sir, I hadn't noticed," said Kett, getting to his feet.

"But we do appreciate you being here. I just want to bring those girls home, okay? We'll be working through the afternoon, and the night, so anything you think of, call us."

"Sir," said Kett with a nod that set the ache rolling around his head again. "If you want, I can find a sitter, I can come in."

Clare stopped at the front door and looked back.

"You've done enough for today," he said. "Spend some time with your girls, let us do the hard work."

He let himself out. Kett stared into the living room to see all three girls smacking the hell out of each other with the sofa cushions, half-laughing and half-screaming.

Sure, he thought, almost longing for the quiet and the calm of the incident room. *Because this isn't hard work at all.*

CHAPTER FOURTEEN

To give them their due, the kids calmed down after Clare had left. Alice found *Moana* on Amazon Prime and the three of them snuggled side by side on the sofa, enraptured, their eyes full of blues and greens and oranges reflected from the screen. Kett bundled them up in a couple of the duvet covers, opened a family sized packet of crisps, and left them to it.

He took a photo first, to show Billie when she turned up. His phone was full of them.

He wasn't sure what was creakier as he made his way to the first floor: the stairs, or his joints. He washed out the bath, chasing away the spiders from the corner of the room, then ran the water. He'd forgotten a tonne of stuff when he packed up their old house, but he'd remembered their toiletries, and after a quick search he squirted some bubble bath into the water.

While it ran, he made his way back downstairs, boiling the kettle again and grabbing a bag of crisps for himself. He sat at the table with his brew, flicking through the folder that Clare had given him. Most of it was information about the two girls, copies of their Instagrams, messages from their phones, their paper routes, the CCTV footage, even school reports. Kett noticed a couple of posts from Maisie that hinted at the extra money she was earning dealing cigarettes —and, unknowingly, class A narcotics—out of her newspaper bag, but other than that they were just your typical pre-teen girls. It was hard not to imagine that they were his own children, especially Connie, who with her big blue eyes and chubby cheeks bore a passing resemblance to an older Evie.

The forensic report for the sand was there, and Kett glanced over it before putting it to one side. Beneath it was everything they had so far on Christian Stillwater. On the surface the guy was as clean as a whistle—apart from the incident that had got him arrested in 2014—but still waters ran deep, Kett knew, and his were probably as polluted as they came. They hadn't found his computer, he'd probably taken it with him to wherever he was hiding, but if Kett's experience with men like this was right, it would be full to the brim with *bad things*.

The last documents in the folder were the files for other suspects, including the Neanderthal-like Niel Dorey and, to Kett's surprise, Lochy Percival, the man wrongly accused of the murder of a tourist back in 2013. Kett read his file, seeing absolutely nothing there that would make him a person of interest. And Dorey's gallstones and hospital stay ruled him out entirely.

That was it. That was everything they had.

Clare had scribbled the MIT's phone number in the top corner of the folder, plus his and Porter's mobile numbers. Kett fished his phone out of his pocket and dialled Porter, heading upstairs as he waited for it to ring through.

"DI Porter," came the reply.

"Pete."

"Hey, Robbie, how you holding up? Savage tells me you got your arse kicked."

"Yeah, pretty much. Anything new?"

He heard Porter scoff.

"Nope. Wait, yeah. Sand was from a building site."

"Heard that already," said Kett. "Clare came over."

"Yikes, he give you a bollocking?"

"Actually, no." Kett put a hand in the water then pulled it straight out again. It had to be close to a hundred degrees. He made a mental note to check that the boiler wasn't on fire.

"Robbie," said Pete. "Please reassure me about something."

"What?" said Kett.

"It's just, I really don't want this image in my head, but the echo in your voice, the gentle lapping of water... you're not in the bath, are you?"

Kett laughed as he turned on the cold tap.

"You bet, stark naked, washing my arse crack as we speak."

Porter made a vomiting noise.

"That's it. I quit."

They shared a laugh, and it felt good.

"We've got every spare officer out scouring the city," Porter said after a moment. "Clare made the decision to go public with Stillwater, the media have been briefed that he's a POI, not a suspect."

"Risky," said Kett, wondering why the boss hadn't mentioned it. "It might make him panic, which might make him ditch the girls."

"Agreed," said Porter.

"But if Stillwater's a genuine psychopath then it might

draw him out," Kett went on. "And if it's not Stillwater, it will buy us some time. Our guy will think he's in the clear."

"Fingers crossed," said Porter.

"Hey, why was Lochy Percival's file in the incident report?" Kett asked, sitting on the edge of the bath.

"Oh, yeah, it's an algorithm thing," said Porter. "He wasn't guilty, but the system spits out his name as a possible suspect in every related case. Poor bastard."

"You don't think he's worth checking on, even just to rule him out?"

"No!" yelled Porter. "Do *not* go there."

Kett heard a voice in the background, maybe Kate Pearson's.

"Kett wants to go after Percival," Porter said.

"No!" Pearson yelled.

"See, that's a bad move. I'm pretty sure Stillwater's our guy, we just have to find him."

"I'm working on it," said Kett.

He almost hung up, then hesitated.

"Hey Pete, you remember Lucy was talking about Stillwater, about how he used to go out with friends. Only he didn't have any friends."

"Sure," said Porter. "She said he always used to come home smelling weird. Sweet and sour, wasn't that how she described it?"

"Off," said Kett. "I don't know. It was a weird thing to mention. If Stillwater's been planning this for a while, it might be relevant. You know anywhere in the city that smells sweet, sour, off?"

"I'm guessing your bath," Porter said. "But sure, I'll put some thought into it. Go on now, lather up. I'll catch you tomorrow."

The call went dead. Kett turned off the cold tap then

closed the bathroom door behind him, walking downstairs to find out if anything different was happening to Moana in her 500th viewing.

KETT LAY IN BED, the brand-new duvet already rucked and loose inside its *Paw Patrol* cover. He was conscious of every sound, every passing car outside, every shout from the city, every creak from the settling house, and every breath and muffled groan from the rooms next to his. It always took a while to get used to a new house, but it was harder this time because he knew this place would never feel like home, not really. Not until Billie was here beside him.

God, he missed her. He missed everything about her, even the things that had driven him crazy—the way she'd always cleaned up right after dinner, even when he and the kids were still eating, the way she'd always clipped her toenails in front of the TV, even the way she'd hogged the bed in her sleep, sometimes so violently that her flailing knees and elbows had sent him running to the couch for the rest of the night.

He just missed *her*, he missed having somebody to orbit around. Without her gravity, he felt as if he and the kids were comets, floating out into the freezing silence of space.

Of course, he missed her functionally as well. After he'd bathed the kids he'd dressed them in fresh clothes, bundled them into the car and driven them across town to a retail park. A quick dash around Dunelm had got them all the duvets and pillows they needed, then they'd stuffed themselves silly in Pizza Hut. But the trip had been exhausting because the kids were like magnets packed positive to positive, they pushed each other away, so that when one of them ran the other two were guaranteed to head in the opposite direction, leaving him spinning in circles. When it had been the two of them, he and Billie had been able to manage them without any trouble. But three against one were hopeless odds.

He rolled over and checked his phone. 11:43. He'd been lying here for two hours, with Moira finally settling in the little camp bed in Evie's room just before half nine. She was the hardest to get to sleep because she still wanted boob every night. And she'd be awake again by midnight.

But Kett couldn't sleep. It wasn't unusual, he hadn't slept a full night through since Billie had gone. His brain wouldn't let him. As soon as he put his head down, as soon as there was any kind of silence, his mind just fired up Billie's case and bombarded him with theories.

They were always the worst-case scenarios, of course. Billie inside a coffin, gasping for her last breath. Billie in a sealed room, tied to a bed. Billie being dismembered by a shadow with a grinning face. They were so unbearable that sometimes, on the bad nights, he would happily find out she had died just for the relief of closure.

No. That wasn't true. However bad his imagination got, there was always hope. Until he saw her body for himself, until he felt for a pulse that wasn't there, there was *always* hope.

Across the hall, Evie moaned in her sleep, muttering something about flapjacks. Kett turned again, kicking the duvet off his feet. His shoulder roared despite a chemist's worth of paracetamol, but the good news was that he hadn't experienced any of the symptoms of concussion since returning home, so he was pretty sure the wound on his head wasn't too bad. He'd live.

He'd just have to suffer a little more *while* he was living.

He screwed his eyes shut, praying to find sleep in the darkness. But all he saw was Billie and, in the shadows behind his wife, two young girls. Connie and Maisie called to him, their voices like the whisper of the wind.

Find us, please.

Their faces tortured him, pleading, desperate. He wondered if they, too, were inside a coffin, or tied to a bed, or being dismembered. It could be happening right now, and he wasn't there, he couldn't help—

Enough! he roared at himself. Then, quieter: *Enough, Robbie.*

He was on the case. He was doing everything he could. He'd get up tomorrow—at some ungodly hour, of course, thanks to Moira—and he'd find those girls.

He just had to pray that they were still alive.

CHAPTER FIFTEEN

SHE WAS STILL ALIVE.

She had to keep reminding herself of that fact, because in the crushing darkness, in the deafening silence, it was so easy to believe that she was dead.

A fly landed on Maisie's cheek, tickling her, and she instinctively tried to move her hand to wipe it away. But her arms were still bound tight, and the pain sliced through her wrist, burning all the way up her shoulder and burrowing into her neck. She screamed, the sound muffled by the gag but still impossibly loud.

Don't come, *she begged.* Please don't hear me.

Because the monster didn't like noise. He hated noise. It was the first thing he'd told her in the darkness of that awful bungalow where he'd caught her.

"Horrid girls who spoil the fun do not get to keep their tongues."

He'd said it again when he'd balled up a newspaper and stuffed it in her mouth, and again when he'd bound her hands behind her back with wire, and again when he'd pulled a bag over her head and led her out of the back of the house, into the rain, then into the boot of a car.

"Horrid girls who spoil the fun do not get to keep their tongues."

There was no thump of footsteps, no creaking of old stairs, no sudden wash of stench from outside as the door swung open.

Maisie tried to sit as still as she could, but it felt like there was somebody drilling into the small of her back. Her legs had gone numb a long time ago, and she'd lost count of the number of times she'd wet herself—and worse. It wasn't fair that she wasn't even allowed to use the bathroom. It wasn't fair that she was here. It wasn't fair! She just wanted her mum, she just wanted to feel her arms around her, to smell her, even with the cigarettes. Where was she? Why wasn't she trying to save her? Why—

"No!"

Pain lanced through Maisie's neck as she twisted her head around. She was so disoriented, so dehydrated, that at first she thought she'd made the noise herself. Then it came again, a low, mournful cry.

"No!"

Shut up! *Maisie called out inside her head.* The monster will hear you!

"No! I want to go home!"

The cries were louder, full of grief and fury. There was no way the monster wouldn't hear—

Thump. Thump. Thumpthumpthump.

Oh god, no.

He was running up the stairs.

Thumpthumpthump.

Running down the corridor.

THUMPTHUMPTHUMP.

Click.

The door opened, and the sun might as well have been burning right outside because a shaft of light burned its way into Maisie's eyes. She screwed them shut, partly because of the pain, partly from the terror. But she couldn't keep them closed for long.

"Who said that?" the monster asked.

Maisie kept her mouth closed, clenching her jaw so forcefully that her teeth felt ready to shatter out of their gums.

Notmenotmenotme.

"I just want to go home," came a voice from the other side of the room. "Please."

Maisie peeked, her eyes adjusting to the glare of the bulb that swung in the corridor beyond. The monster stood there, just a silhouette against the light. He wore the same mask as before, a hessian sack with two crosses in black ink where the eyes should be.

In his hand was a scalpel.

"Oh Connie," said the monster, taking a step towards the other girl. She'd somehow managed to work the gag from her mouth, and her jaw was trembling so hard that her teeth sounded like castanets. "My dear Connie, don't you remember the rules?"

How could she have forgotten them, Maisie thought. They were so simple.

Horrid girls who spoil the fun do not get to keep their tongues.

"Please no!" the girl called Connie screamed. But the monster wasn't listening. He towered over her, the scalpel glinting in the light, and Maisie forced herself to look away, forced herself to look across to the other side of the room.

To the third young girl who sat there, tied to her chair, her eyes overflowing with fear.

CHAPTER SIXTEEN

Friday

On any normal day, Kett was woken up at the crack of dawn by one of the children. If it was Evie doing the waking, it usually involved being yelled at from a distance of about three inches. If it was Alice, it would be her sitting next to him in bed with the iPad blaring. Moira went for a more effective method, usually climbing onto his neck and slapping him hard across the cheek.

Which is why it was a surprise that he stirred from his dreams to the sound of the Mexican Hat Dance.

"Hmmm?" he said, wondering if it was Billie turning on the radio the way she always did in the morning.

Of course it isn't, he told himself as his thoughts clicked into place. *Billie's gone.*

It took him a moment to remember his phone, and a moment more to remember how to speak. "Kett."

"Sir?"

"Kate?" he said, sitting up. His entire body ached from the fight with Brandon Walker, like he'd spent the whole of yesterday at the gym. "Sorry, *Savage*. Is everything okay?"

He took the phone from his ear to see that it was coming up for seven. The shock of sleeping in so late meant that he completely missed what she was saying.

"Hang on, sorry," he said, clambering out of bed. He tripped on the duvet that he'd kicked off in the night, stumbling out onto the landing and peering into Evie and Moira's room. It was pitch black in there, the curtains proper blackout ones, but he could just about see the outline of Evie in the bed.

The cot was empty.

"Shit," he said, his heart giving a mighty kick, and he was on the verge of telling Savage to put out an alert when he spotted the extra head on Evie's pillow. The baby must have crawled into her sister's bed in the night.

Thank Christ, he thought, his heart still turning over like an old engine. He put his spare hand to it.

"You okay?" Savage asked.

"Yeah," he said, leaving the room and pulling the door to. He checked on Alice, then made his way downstairs as quietly as he could. "Just in shock. Kids are still asleep."

"Did I wake you?" she said. "Sorry, the boss asked me to call to check your status."

"My status?" he said, stifling a yawn. He filled the kettle and clicked it on. "Dog tired and in need of tea."

"He meant, are you coming in this morning?" she asked.

"Yeah, but I need to get the girls to school."

Her voice was muffled as she spoke to somebody else.

"Can school start at seven?" she asked after a moment. "His words, not mine."

"I'll see what I can do. Why the urgency?"

"We might have a lead," said Savage. "Stillwater just surfaced."

"MORNING, ROBBIE," said Porter as he opened the door of the incident room. The big DI looked like he'd been there all night, his shirt crumpled and untucked, his face unshaven. "It's great to see you without your entourage. Did you manage to find a sitter?"

Kett shook his head, waiting for Moira to catch up to him. She waddled down the corridor like somebody brought in for the drunk tank, earning as many 'awwws' as she did scowls from the coppers who passed her by.

"Oh," said Porter. "That's a no then."

"I've got one," Kett said as Moira pushed her way past Porter's legs. "One of the women at Evie's nursery has a daughter who works as a childminder. She called her as a favour, but she isn't free until ten."

He'd managed to get Alice into breakfast club at school, and Evie stayed with her—even though it wasn't strictly school policy.

"Until then, the baby's in charge," Kett said with a sigh. Moira was already barking unintelligible orders at the police inside the room. "Hope it's not a problem."

"With me, no," said Porter. "With the Super..."

As if on cue, Superintendent Clare's voice boomed out, ringing Kett's name like a church bell. Moira retreated at a pace, thumping into his legs and holding her hands up for an emergency rescue. Kett picked her up, pain flaring in his injured shoulder, and she burrowed her head into his neck.

"Ni-Ni-Saw," she said.

"Dinosaur," Kett translated, and Porter let loose a cannon shot of laughter.

"You're not wrong, kiddo," the DI said. "You're not wrong. Come on."

Porter stood aside to let Kett through. The incident room was packed, everyone from yesterday and a platoon of new detectives who gave him nods of welcome—plus one who was looking at Moira like she was Jack the Ripper. DC Figg, the FLO, gave Kett a wave with his pen. Kett saw Savage across the room and nodded at her, and she smiled back.

Clare was standing at the head of the table, in front of the whiteboards and pinned photographs. On the monitor behind him was a photograph of Christian Stillwater sitting at his desk, dressed in a pinstripe suit and wide tie, and flashing that same shit-eating grin.

"Thank you, everyone," said Clare, giving Kett a warning look. Kett shifted Moira to his other arm and mouthed: *sorry boss*. Clare replied with a grade A glare. "As you know, Stillwater pinged onto the radar an hour ago when his debit card was used in a petrol station in Drayton. He bought a can of Coke and a sandwich. We have officers on scene and witnesses and CCTV confirm that Stillwater was definitely present—dressed in overalls. His face has been all over the news, so it's only a matter of time before he's spotted again."

Kett frowned. Something didn't feel right.

"For now, Stillwater is our chief suspect for the abduction of both girls," Clare went on. "Not only does he have form for this kind of crime—remember, he snatched a young girl from the park a few years ago—but he also went off the grid at the same time as the newspaper girls, and he hasn't responded to our calls for contact even though he must be well aware that we are treating him as a person of interest."

"Maybe he's scared, sir," said Spalding from where she sat. "It wouldn't be the first time a wrongful arrest has ruined somebody's life."

"Lochy Percival." Dunst coughed the words into his hand.

"Agreed," said Clare. "Which is why we have to do this very carefully. Our number one priority is bringing Stillwater in as peacefully as possible. Is that clear?"

Kett put his hand up, and so did Moira. Clare nodded at him.

"Stillwater is smart," Kett said. "We already know this. Smart enough to be aware that using his debit card will draw us to him immediately. He didn't use the card for essentials, or for petrol, or for a plane ticket. He used it for a drink and a sandwich. That has to mean—"

"Ni-Ni-Saw," Moira squealed, pointing at Clare.

"That has to mean," Kett said a little louder, "that he wants us to find him."

"You think he's trying to be caught?" Raymond Figg asked from the other side of the table, his pen in his mouth. "What kind of criminal wants to be caught?"

"Maybe you're right, and he's scared," Kett said, speaking to Clare. "Maybe he wants us to go to him and this is his way of connecting with us. But he doesn't seem like the kind of guy who'd be scared."

"What are you saying?" Clare asked.

"I think he's got something else in mind," Kett went on. "I think he's been planning this abduction for a long time, maybe even as far back as 2014, when he took Emily Coupland from the park. Whatever he's doing, he's expecting us to respond in a particular way. He's in control of this situation, and I don't like that."

"Like I said," Clare said, resting his knuckles on the table. "We do this very carefully. I want all teams working on finding Stillwater, *today*."

Something told Kett that wouldn't be a problem.

"I'll come with you," Kett said to Porter as the coppers began to organise themselves. "I've chased guys like this before, they—"

"Kett," Clare bellowed. "Come here."

Kett sighed, but did as he was told. Hoiking Moira up, he crossed the room to the boss.

"Look, I know—"

"Not happening," Clare interrupted. "I told you yesterday, we can't offer babysitting services, especially not to a detective who isn't even on the payroll. You're grounded, Kett. Until the kid goes someplace safe, I don't want you out of this room."

It was pointless arguing, so Kett shut his mouth. Moira spoke for him, firing a heartfelt raspberry in Clare's direction.

"Ni-Ni-Saw," she said again.

Clare ignored her, gathering his papers and leaving the room along with everybody else. Well, *almost* everybody. Raymond Figg remained, and PC Savage stood on the other side of the table with a folder in her hand.

"You too?" Kett asked her.

"The boss is a little annoyed with me for letting you go into the Walker flat yesterday," she said. "He hasn't, like, said it, but it's pretty easy to read his mind."

"Sorry," said Kett, but she waved it away.

"I'm just lucky to be in here at all," she said, putting the folder on the table. "I feel like I'm pretending to be a detective."

"Join the club," said Figg as he carted a bunch of files to the photocopier. "I'm actually a detective and I still feel like a complete imposter here."

"Nothing pretend about it," Kett said, putting the squirming baby on the floor. "You're first class police, Savage. What's he got you working on?"

"Phone duty," she said. "We're calling the other paper girls who worked for David Walker, seeing if they know anything. To be honest, we've spoken to most of them already and none of them have a clue. A few have 'fessed up to selling cigarettes on the heath, and a couple even knew that there were drugs inside. They're all scared shitless, and none of them are delivering any more. But he wants me to go through them again, push them for anything they might be hiding, maybe try some of the other newsagents too. Figg's helping out, aren't you, Raymond?"

"Anything to get these bastards," he replied as he hammered buttons on the copier.

"Sounds like fun," Kett said, pulling out a chair and groaning as he eased his aching body into it. "Well, there are three of us now, so what do you want me to do?"

Savage smiled, pushing the folder across the table.

"You any good on the phone?"

"YEAH, yeah. Okay, thank you. And if she thinks of anything else make sure she gets in touch immediately."

Kett muttered a goodbye and replaced the handset on its cradle, rubbing his eyes.

"I can't believe you got me out of bed for this," he said.

It was only just gone half nine, but he felt like he'd been awake for days. The buzzing strip lights in the windowless room had kickstarted his headache again, the pain not helped by the fact he'd just had exactly the same conversation with twelve different mums and dads.

"Why aren't you doing anything?"

"Why haven't you found them?"

"It could have been my girl, do you realise that? She's extremely upset."

"Are they going to be compensated for the hours they miss?"

People really were dicks.

Savage held up a hand to silence him, the other holding her own phone to her ear.

"We will keep you posted, Miss Swain. Thank you."

She ended the call and looked at him.

"Huh?"

"I said I can't believe you got me out of bed for this," he repeated, checking on Moira. Savage had given the baby her mobile phone, and as much as Kett hated the idea of beating his child into silence with an endless run of *Peppa Pigs* he was grateful for the break. She hadn't moved or spoken for about forty minutes. It was a miracle. Figg had made a few calls too but had left after a while, heading for the cafeteria, his stomach rumbling.

"Who's left in your pile?" Savage asked. "Mine's done."

Kett leafed through the four remaining files.

"Do you want Delia or Abi?" He laughed. "Delia. Only in Norfolk, right?"

"I couldn't get through to either of those two yesterday," Savage said, taking Abi's file. "Better luck today, eh?"

Kett dialled the number on Delia's file, staring at her information as he waited for somebody to pick up. *Cordelia*

Patrice Crossan, eleven, 14 Drayton Close Road, Date of Employment: 23.03.18, routes: Drayton North, Fakenham Road, Friday / Saturday / Sunday.

On the other side of the table, Savage was speaking to Abi's family, but his line kept on ringing, eventually clicking into silence. He put the handset down.

"Thank you," said Savage, ending her own call. "Anything?"

Kett shook his head.

"No answer. You say you couldn't reach her yesterday?"

"No, although I don't know if somebody else did."

"You brought in Walker's files from the shop, didn't you?" Kett asked. Savage pointed over her shoulder to a mountain of evidence boxes in the corner of the room.

"He was about as good at keeping records as Porter is at making tea," she said as she scooped the last two files from Kett's side of the table and started to call. "We haven't had time to go through it yet, but it's all— Oh, hi, this is Police Constable Kate Savage calling from the Norfolk Constabulary."

Kett left her to it, crossing the room to the boxes and opening the lid of the top one. Savage hadn't been lying, they were stuffed with seemingly random pieces of paper, receipts, payslips and notebooks full of route logs. He picked up a book and opened it, seeing entries from last August. He tried another, then another, eventually finding one from this month. Each page had a list of customers, papers, and which route they were on. Stapled to every corner was a timesheet for each delivery girl. The goose-bumps stood to attention on his arms when he saw Maisie's name on Tuesday. Flicking back a couple of pages he found Connie too. He carried the book back to the table and found Delia's file again.

"Friday, Saturday," he muttered to himself, running his finger down the entries for both days. There was a note next to Delia's name on the space for Sunday afternoon.

No show, Eleanor to cover.

"Hey," he said when Savage had hung up the phone. "Delia Crossan, the girl you couldn't get hold of. She didn't show up for work on Sunday."

Savage looked at him, a frown creasing her forehead.

"That's odd," she said. "Worth a visit?"

Kett checked his watch. It was nearly ten.

"Definitely," he said. "I've just got to make a quick stop first."

CHAPTER SEVENTEEN

The stop wasn't as quick as he'd hoped. By the time he'd found the address the nursery worker had given him—a cute semi-detached house south of the city, 'Welcome to Bumblebees!' written on a sign above the door—it was way past ten, and even though he'd insisted he was in a hurry, the girl who met him at the door had a ream of paperwork for him to fill in.

The good news was that Moira had been all too happy to stay there, waddling into the large, airy living room to join the two little kids that were already inside. She hadn't even noticed Kett saying goodbye. It had been hard to leave her, of course, his 'what ifs' going into overdrive as he walked out of the front door. He had to resist every urge to pin the childminder to the wall and grill her about whether she was a serial killer or a child trafficker. In the end, Savage had practically pulled him out of the house and thrown him into the Volvo.

"She'll be fine," she said as Kett started the engine. "I promise. I Googled them when you were signing the paperwork, four-point-eight on Trust Pilot. Moira's in safe hands."

"She'd better be," he grumbled as they headed to the circular again. His anxiety chewed away at him while they ground their way through traffic, easing only when they pulled into a quiet residential close on the other side of town twenty-five minutes later. He cruised past the houses, counting numbers, before stopping at a detached, two-storey chalet bungalow with a floral 14 painted on the gate post.

"By the book, this time, okay?" Savage said as she popped her door and clambered out.

"Hey, I basically wrote the book," he replied, stretching until his spine popped. He'd automatically walked to Moira's door before he remembered he was child free. It was such a strange feeling that he wasn't sure whether to laugh or cry.

"Curtains are drawn," said Savage. "All of them, upstairs too. Must have a loft conversion."

"Maybe they're just late risers," Kett replied. "Or on holiday."

"If they were on holiday, they would have let Walker know," Savage said as she opened the gate and stepped onto the uneven flagstone path. The garden was overgrown, but what was growing there was beautiful: great piles of lavender and rosemary and even a rosebush against one of the windows. The smell of it was intoxicating. "Walker wrote 'no show'. She just didn't turn up. And their car is here."

She nodded to the driveway on the other side of the garden, an ancient blue Renault 4 parked there."

"You should be a detective," he said with a smile.

"I'm working on it, sir. Do you want to do the honours?"

"Nope, this is all yours."

He stood back as Savage rapped on the door, the sound of it making his ears ring.

"That's some knock you've got," he said.

"My granddad taught me," she replied. "You want them to know you're here, and that you're in charge."

The street was incredibly quiet, the only sounds the pigeons warbling in the trees and the faint buzz of somebody's lawnmower. It was hot again, too, the air seeming to swim. If there was somebody in the house, they weren't answering. Savage knocked again, so loud that Kett half expected the glass to shatter.

"Mrs. Crossan? Delia? It's the police."

Nothing. Kett was getting that feeling again, an instinct gnawing at his intestines. There was nobody inside the house. There was something in the stillness of the place, its immense silence, that made him sure of it. He pushed through the garden, brambles snagging on his trousers and the smell of herbs exploding. There was an integral garage, and past that a small, weed-littered gravel passage that led to the back garden. He crunched his way down it until he reached the kitchen door. A cat sat there, scrawny and ginger, and as soon as it saw him it came over and started rubbing itself against his leg.

"Hey," he said, reaching down to tickle its head. It purred like a generator. "You live here?"

The cat meowed a reply, but it wasn't really necessary. There was a cat flap in the white PVC door, a food dish beside it that was empty of anything except flies. The noise they were making made his skin crawl, because what he was hearing wasn't the buzz of a few bluebottles, it was the sound of *hundreds*.

"Savage," he called out. "Better get back here."

Gently nudging the cat out of the way, he crouched down beside the cat flap. He didn't even have to open it to know what he was going to find in there, the smell hit him like a fist, right in the back of the throat. He put one hand to his mouth then used his knuckles to push open the flap. The smell roared out like it was trying to escape, a few flies batting against his hand. It was too dark inside to see much, but despite the shadows and the stench-induced tears in his eyes he was pretty sure he could make out the outline of a body lying in the middle of the kitchen floor.

"Sir?" Savage said as she emerged from the passageway. She sniffed the air. "Oh fudge."

"It's okay, Savage," he said. "I think this is one of those occasions where the word 'fuck' is perfectly acceptable. Call it in."

She put a hand to her radio and started talking. Kett stood up, tried the handle, then grabbed a large piece of flint from the shrubbery.

"Stand back," he said, turning away as he lobbed the stone at the glass panel in the door. It punched through with surprisingly little mess, and Kett kicked the rest of the glass from the frame before reaching in and finding a key in the lock. Twisting it, he opened the door and stepped into a thunderous vortex of flies. "Police!" he yelled. "If anyone is here, make yourself known immediately."

It took him a moment to find the light switch, the fluorescents blinking on reluctantly, as if they didn't want anybody to see what lay there on the cracked linoleum.

"Fuck," said Kett, taking a deep breath through his mouth.

It was the body of a woman, or maybe a girl, dressed in denim dungarees and a cream blouse, her bare toes pointing to the sink. It was impossible to tell how old she was because she was face down beneath a shroud of blood-matted hair. It was as if somebody had covered her in a blanket of flies.

They crawled everywhere, the angry noise of them making Kett's skin itch.

"Oh shit," said Savage as she walked in behind him, waving a hand to chase away the insects. "Ambulance on the way, backup too."

"It's a little late for an ambulance," Kett said. "But Delia might be here."

"I'm on it," said Savage, stepping carefully around the woman and vanishing into the darkness of the hallway. It was impossible not to have flashbacks from yesterday, a shape bouldering out of the shadows, a hammer gripped in its meaty fist.

"Just be careful," he shouted after her, and in response he heard the sound of her flicking out the telescopic baton.

He turned his attention back to the woman, fishing a pen from his breast pocket and using it to pull the hair from her face. An eye stared up at him, bloodshot and broken like a cracked egg. Her skin was mottled and black where the blood had pooled post mortem, and the flies had laid eggs there, hundreds of them. He couldn't make out much, but he could see enough to know that this wasn't a young girl.

He didn't want to disturb the crime scene, so he let the woman's hair drop and followed Savage out of the room. She'd found the light switch in the hall, the bulb doing nothing to fight the oppressive shadows that had gathered there like ravens. All Kett wanted to do was rip the curtains open and crack the windows, but there would be forensic evidence everywhere.

There could be girls too, he knew. Maybe three of them.

"Dining room is clear," said Savage, appearing beside him. "I'll check upstairs."

She creaked her way up the narrow wooden steps, and Kett peeked into the small toilet before heading through to the living room. He switched the lights on with his knuckle, seeing a cosy space full of photographs, a sagging couch covered in homemade cushions, a small TV perched precariously on a bookshelf.

"Nothing up here," Savage called down. "Two bedrooms and a bathroom."

She walked down the steps, her face ghostly.

"Living room is clear as well," Kett said. "You okay?"

"Yeah," Savage said. "I will be. I've never actually, you know, *seen* one before."

She didn't have to say what, it was written all over her expression. He'd been exactly the same the first time he'd witnessed a dead body—a road traffic accident in his second week of duty as a PC. He hadn't been able to stop seeing the young man's face for months, the way his jaw had been cleaved off by the windshield of his motorcycle. That face had been everywhere, in every thought, in every nightmare, enough that he'd almost handed his notice in three months later. It had been a grizzled sergeant who had talked him through it in the end, who had taught him how to push the memory from his skull and keep it out of his dreams.

Don't think about them dead, picture them living, laughing. Picture them the way they were before the end.

"I'll deal with the rest," Kett said. "Head out and wait for the ambulance. Does the boss know?"

"I couldn't get through to him, but dispatch will. I spoke to Porter." She took a deep breath, a soft groan spilling out of her. But she stood tall. "I'm okay, sir. If that's Delia's mother then we've got to assume the worst about Delia, right?"

Kett nodded.

"Find out if she was staying with any relatives," he said. "I don't see any sign of a dad here, no photos on the wall.

Maybe she's with him. Grans, aunties and uncles, friends, anyone she might be with."

It would be a futile search, he knew. Delia hadn't shown up for work on Sunday, and it was clear her mother had been dead for days.

"But I'm pretty sure this was an abduction," he said, walking into the living room again.

"You think it's our guy?" Savage said.

"Same age as the other victims, same employer. Yeah, it's our guy. I think it went wrong because this was his first. The suspect got to her here, killed the mother, then took Delia. That would have been Saturday night or Sunday, because she was supposed to be working on Sunday but didn't show. Might be why he snatched the others from dead houses on their routes, when he knew they'd be alone. He didn't want to murder any more parents."

"Jesus," said Savage.

Kett walked to the fireplace, studying the grid of photographs that had been hung there. Most showed a grinning young girl and her mother—in Paris, at the seaside, bundled up in duvets together on the bed—and Kett had that same awful feeling of disconnection he always felt in these situations, the knowledge that the woman in those photographs was now a cold, stiff piece of meat in the other room. Had she ever suspected that this was how her life would end? That her last sight would be of her killer dragging her daughter out of the house?

You never see it coming, he thought. *You never think it's going to be that way*. Billie hadn't. Billie had never suspected that one day a van would screech to a halt beside her and that two men in animal masks would tear her kicking and screaming from the world.

Kett screwed his eyes shut against the wave of vertigo

that swept through him. Only when the dizziness had passed did he dare open them again, and when he did he found himself staring at another photograph. This one wasn't in a frame, it had been blu-tacked just above the mantelpiece along with a handful of others, one corner peeling away from the wallpaper. He grabbed it by the loose side and pulled it free.

Delia was there, but maybe five or six, and her mother, the two of them standing in what might have been a caravan park. There were pine trees behind them, the corner of a picnic table, a litter bin. Standing hand in hand to Delia's left were two elderly people, a man who looked too much like the dead woman not to be related to her, and a short, stooped woman that had to be his wife.

It was the guy on the other side of the group that had caught Kett's attention, though. He was in his late twenties, maybe early thirties, his mousy hair already showing signs of extensive thinning. He wasn't tall, maybe five-six, and his black shirt was tucked into the front of his jeans, showing off a fair-sized paunch. The beaming smile on his pale, rounded face seemed genuine, his eyes open and welcome. There was something about him that was familiar. Kett had seen him before, and recently.

He flicked the photo over, seeing small, neat handwriting in pencil. *Delia, me, mum and dad and Uncle L, 2013.*

"Savage," he said. No reply. He looked around to see her on her haunches stroking the cat, who had followed them in. "Hey, Savage."

"Sorry," she said as she walked over. "Poor thing. What's up?"

He turned the photograph to her.

"Who's that guy?"

"The younger man?" she replied, squinting at it. She puffed air between her lips. "I don't know, I don't think I... Wait, *do* I?"

Kett heard the growl of a large engine outside in the street, the squeal of brakes and the creak of a door opening. It would be the ambulance. He stared at the photo again, straining for something that was frustratingly just out of reach.

"Holy shit," Savage said, straightening up. "I know who it is. Picture him thinner, gaunt, in tears."

Kett looked, shaking his head.

"I can't see—"

And then he did, just like that.

"Holy shit," he echoed. "That's Lucky Percival, the guy who was falsely arrested back in 2013."

"*Lochy*," said the PC, frowning. "Lochy Percival. But what's he doing here?"

"Uncle Lochy," said Kett, reading the text on the back of the photograph again. "Delia Crossan is Lochy's niece."

He popped his lips, watching the cat as it jumped onto the sofa and began kneading, its purr even louder than the engine outside.

"Maybe your innocent guy isn't so innocent after all."

CHAPTER EIGHTEEN

"Fucking fuckety fuck on a fucking bike!"

It was safe to say that Superintendent Colin Clare wasn't happy. He paced restlessly in the back garden of the Crossan's bungalow, the photograph of Delia's family and a younger Lochy Percival clenched in his latex-gloved hand.

"I refuse to accept this, Kett," he said, marching over and doing his best to loom. It wasn't hard. Kett was tall, but Clare was a giant, and when he was angry he seemed to grow an extra six inches. Kett did his best not to stare up the man's nose, turning to look through the back door instead where a forensic team was collecting evidence. The flash of their cameras lit up the house like there was a lightning storm inside, revealing glimpses of the dead woman who still lay there.

It was impossible not to imagine Billie lying there instead, butchered in a kitchen somewhere, left to rot.

"You do realise that Lochy Percival is off limits," Clare went on. "After what happened to him last time, the false arrest, the law suit, he's untouchable."

"I didn't exactly plan this," said Kett, pushing Billie out of his head. "We just found the photo."

And at least eight others scattered around the house, all of which showed Percival with the family. The early ones were your typical extended family group shots, all smiles or silly faces on holiday or at Christmas. But after 2013 Percival looked like a different man entirely, like he'd aged and withered overnight. No more smiles—at least none that reached his eyes—no more cheerful Uncle L.

Kett could see where he'd been stabbed as well, his body listing to one side like a sinking ship, and more often than not a walking cane gripped in his hand.

"We've checked," Savage added. "Lochy is Evelyn Crossan's younger brother, Delia's uncle by blood. He lives across town, a nice place."

"Yeah, *we* bought it for him," said Clare. "With the payout he got when we falsely accused him last time. I will *not* let it happen again."

"Even if he's guilty?" Kett asked. Clare shot him a look that looked like he wanted to actually shoot him.

"Let's get this straight," the boss said. "You think Lochy Percival murdered his own sister in order to abduct his niece?"

"She's the same age as the girl he was accused of murdering in 2013," said Savage. "Approximately. Even if he didn't commit that crime, there's nothing to say he didn't do this one. That case really screwed him up."

"The house is secure," added Kett. "All the windows were sealed from the inside, both doors were locked. There's no sign of a break-in, other than the rock I used to gain entry. It makes sense that the family would open the door to somebody they knew, somebody they trusted."

"But why?" Clare said. "It doesn't make any sense that a

man like Percival would go after his own niece. Christ, I sat in on some of the interviews with him back when he was arrested, he didn't give off the slightest whiff of a serial arsehole. Part of me wasn't surprised when they found out he was innocent."

"So we interview him again," said Kett. "Hear his side of the story."

Clare shook his head.

"I'm not going anywhere near him," he said. "Not until you find a handwritten note with his signature and fingerprint and goddamned DNA saying, 'I just killed my sister and kidnapped my niece.' Okay?"

Kett looked past the boss to the swing set at the bottom of the garden, the little chalk mural on the fence, two figures whose bright eyes and smiles had survived the rain. It didn't need to be said, because everyone was thinking it, but Kett said it anyway.

"What if he has the other girls?"

"Ah fuck you," said Clare, stomping down the garden and resting his head against the fence like a schoolkid sent to the naughty corner.

"That's some mess," said DI Porter as he stepped out of the kitchen, a napkin pressed to his mouth. For a big man, he looked awfully squeamish. He caught sight of Clare, keeping his voice low as he approached Kett. "So, he took the news well then?"

"Oh, sure," said Kett.

"No, *seriously*," Porter said. "He actually is taking it well. I once saw him throw a chair through a window when he had a warrant denied. You think this is Percival?"

Kett shrugged. Clare was already on his way back.

"I wouldn't bet on it, not yet," Kett said to Porter. "Any indication of what killed her?"

"My guess is the knife in her heart," the DI said. "One wound, driven upwards beneath the ribs, the blade was still in there."

"That's not the move of an amateur," said Kett. "There would be smaller wounds, hesitation. A crime of passion would have multiple injuries. This feels more like an assassination. Whoever killed her wanted her out of the way, and fast. Doesn't exactly sound like Percival, but we need to speak with him anyway."

"Fine," muttered Clare. "Christ, bring him in. But do *not* make an arrest. We just need to speak with him. Is that clear?" He looked back. "Do *not* arrest him, even if he's coming at you with a samurai sword in one hand and a chainsaw in the other. Porter, take Spalding."

"And me, sir?" Kett asked. Clare looked him up and down, glaring.

"I think you've done enough for one morning, don't you?" he spat. "I need you and Savage back at the station on paperwork duty. If, and it's a *big* if, Percival has anything to do with this then we need to make certain this case is watertight. Is that clear?"

Kett nodded, and so did Savage—although her expression made it clear what she thought of the idea. Clare looked at them both, then at the photograph in his hand. Finally, he tilted his head back and bellowed at the big, blue sky overhead.

"Fuck!"

"THIS IS EXACTLY what I dreamed it would be," said Savage as Kett pulled them out of Drayton Close Road.

"Riding around in a Volvo, heading back to the station to do paperwork. It's not exactly Bad Boys, is it?"

He glanced at the young constable as he pulled up to a set of lights. She was doing her best to smile, but her mouth was set in a grim line and her eyes were full of something dark and painful.

"They'll offer you counselling," he said. "If you're like me you'll say no, then regret it. Don't be like me. It can be a lifesaver."

She looked away from him, staring at the street outside as they started moving again.

"I'm okay," she said. "Honestly. I kind of psyched myself up for it, I did for years. It wasn't exactly what I thought it would be, but I wasn't completely unprepared. My mum was a doctor, she never sugar-coated death. We grew up hearing about it."

"Was?" asked Kett.

"Was as in retired, not passed," said Savage, finally turning to him. "Well, she still works, but over at the university hospital. She is the most mechanically minded person I've ever met. To her the body is an engine with a billion moving parts. Anything can go wrong, almost anything can be fixed. But she's religious too, church every week, had me and my brother baptised. I could never get my head around that."

"People will do anything to make it through the day," said Kett, hitting a line of traffic.

"How do *you* get through the day?" she asked, looking like she immediately regretted the question. "Sorry. Is that too personal? I just... I looked you up, read about your wife. I can't even imagine what that must have been like. How do you go on?"

Kett exhaled through pursed lips, easing the Volvo forwards.

"Sorry," Savage said again. "Forget I said anything. It's the detective in me, I'm just nosy."

"It's fine," said Kett. He snorted a humourless laugh. "Okay, it's not fine. None of it is fine. I just feel guilty, you know? Like I should still be down there, still looking for her. But it wasn't fair on the kids. Every single day Billie was missing I was missing too, I just wasn't there for them. I vanished."

He drummed the wheel with the heel of his hand—seeing Billie, hearing Billie, smelling Billie, then forcing her face from his head. And it suddenly struck him, what he was doing—chasing her away the same way he chased away the visions of dead people so that they wouldn't keep haunting him. Something exploded inside him, a wave of phosphorous-bright panic that almost made him steer the car onto the pavement.

Breathe, he ordered himself. *In. Out.*

That's how he got through the day. One breath at a time.

"I do it for them," he said. "Alice, Evie, Moira. Everything I do is for them. When you have kids, they become the very centre of your universe."

"I'm pretty sure the centre of the universe is a black hole," said Savage with a gentle smile. Kett managed one too.

"Yep, that fits my analogy perfectly. A black hole that pulls you in and swallows everything you ever were or ever could be. A force so strong that nothing can escape."

He thought of them now, and all of those 'what ifs' began charging through his head like a strip of old movie. Alice being sent out of her classroom for fighting, Evie bawling because he wasn't there to take her into nursery, Moira screaming and screaming and screaming because she was surrounded by strangers.

What the hell am I doing? he asked himself as they approached a junction. *I came up here to be with them, and here I am losing myself to a case again—and this one isn't even personal.*

What a *bastard.*

"Look," he said as he pounced on a break in traffic and turned left. "I'm honestly not sure how much more help I can be. I should probably just drop—"

PC Savage's radio squawked, loud enough to make Kett jump. The voice that came through was rough with static.

"All units, we have a confirmed sighting of Christian Stillwater in Hellesdon, on the Low Road. Spotted walking south past the junction with Hospital Lane. Repeat, all available units head to Low Road."

Savage didn't hesitate.

"Dispatch this is PC Savage, I'm currently just three minutes from Hellesdon."

She broke the call, looking at Kett. The question was written in her expression.

Yes or no?

And even though his head was full of Billie and the girls, the answer in his smile was silent, immediate, and unmistakable.

Fudge yes.

CHAPTER NINETEEN

THE VOLVO DIDN'T HAVE SIRENS, BUT IT HAD A HORN.

Kett rammed it as he overtook the cars in front, earning glares and worse from drivers in the opposite lane who had to swerve to avoid him. Savage slapped a hand on the hazards then wound down her window, leaning out as far as she dared so that her uniform could be seen. Most people got the hint, pulling in to let Kett past as the old car roared down the main road.

"Next right," Savage yelled, and Kett jabbed his hand on the horn again before twisting the wheel. The car swept in a wide arc, almost glancing off the front of a bus. Then they were on a quieter road with trees on both sides. The sun burst through the branches, splattering across the windshield like paint, but Kett kept his foot on the accelerator, hitting fifty as they passed the entrance to a hospital. An old lady was pulling out and Kett slammed the horn again, blasting past fast enough for the shockwave to rock her little Fiat.

"Easy, sir," Savage said, one hand on the dashboard and the other gripping her chair. "Sharp left up ahead."

There was, and he almost didn't slow down in time. The car shuddered as it decelerated, crayons and teddy bears rolling off the back seat into the footwell. A kid in a Golf was coming the other way, taking the racing line around the bend, and the two cars passed close enough for their wing mirrors to clip.

"You've done this before," Savage said.

"Not for a long time," he replied, and the truth of that was in the way his heart seemed to pound against his tonsils.

"This is Low Road," Savage said after the turn. "Some big houses down here."

She wasn't lying. On the right-hand side of the road was a row of mock Tudor mansions with wide fronts and black beams. Opposite them was dense woodland.

"They said right after the junction, didn't they?" Kett asked.

"Round here somewhere, yeah," Savage said, scouring the trees.

"Where are you, you bastard?" Kett said, slowing the car to a crawl. Somebody in a Corsa honked as they overtook, but he ignored them, watching as the Tudor houses gave way to some art deco brick ones. "He could be in any of these."

"Or none of them," said Savage.

A patrol car appeared ahead, its lights blazing. Kett flashed his headlights at them, winding down the window as they neared.

"Anything?" he asked. The two PCs frowned at him, then one of them caught sight of Savage in the passenger seat.

"No sign," he said.

"Close off the road at the north end," Kett ordered, nodding over his shoulder. "If he's on foot he can't have gone far. Radio for somebody to shut it down at the other end too. Then we go door to door. You guys start with that great big mansion back there. Anything suspicious, call it in."

"Sir," said the driver, gunning the engine and driving off.

Kett started moving again, scanning each house.

"Any reason he'd be down here?" he asked.

"Not that we found. His address is across the city, and his family live down by the Suffolk border. He doesn't have any immediate links to this side of town."

"Did Walker have a route on this street?"

Savage shook her head.

"Too far out, but somebody would deliver papers here."

"Can we check to see if there have been any recent deaths? Looks like there would be plenty of old people round here, some empty houses."

"I'm on it," said Savage, pulling out her phone. Kett kept driving, kept searching, nothing but pristine houses on the right, so grand that he almost missed it.

A break in the woods to the left. A metal gate.

A For Sale sign.

He pulled the wheel, bumping the car up onto a dirt track.

"You see something?" Savage asked.

He didn't answer, he just put the Volvo in park with its nose to the gate, then popped his door. The heat of the day flooded in, almost suffocating. He hobbled over the ridges of dry mud, seeing that the track stretched up a little way before curving into the trees.

"You know if there's a house up here?" he asked.

"No idea, but there's got to be something, right?" Savage replied. "It's for sale, so it could be empty. I'll do a Land

Registry check, and search Right Move, but that sign looks like it's been here for donkey's years."

"It's quiet, out of the way," Kett said. "Good place to keep a few girls."

"Sir..." said Savage, and he could tell by her tone what she was about to say.

"It's your call," he said, turning to her. "I don't want you to get in any more trouble."

She puffed out her cheeks, popping her lips, deep in thought.

"It's just trouble, right?" she said. "How bad can it get? But I'm calling for backup, and I'm coming with you this time."

She vaulted the gate with impressive ease, dropping down the other side while speaking into her radio. Kett was glad her back was turned as he slipped on the first bar, almost chinning himself. He grunted over the top and eased himself slowly back onto the track. They walked side by side, keeping close to the trees. They weren't far from the city here but it felt like the middle of nowhere. After a couple of minutes Kett couldn't see the road any more, just a wide, open, grassy space with a distant fence to the south-east.

"A farm?" he asked.

"Horses, probably," she replied. "Lots of the land round here is used for them because the river's just over there. There's a golf course in the other direction."

They kept walking, every scuffed stone and broken stick like a gunshot going off. A minute or so more and the path curved to the left, leading into a row of ancient-looking lime trees.

Beyond them, nestled in the dark, was a house.

"Jackpot," said Kett, hunkering down behind a felled

tree that was drowning in ivy. The house was old and it looked like it had seen some fire damage—or maybe a falling tree. One side of the roof had a hole punched through it, the chimneystack in pieces on the ground below. All of the windows were boarded up.

But the front door was wide open.

"Backup knows we're here?" Kett asked. Savage nodded.

"They'll be with us in seconds. You want to wait?"

No, he thought. But yesterday was all too fresh in his aching head. Brandon Walker had been a thug, armed with a hammer and defending nothing but drugs. There was a good chance Stillwater was a psychopath, armed with god only knew what, and guarding three terrified young girls.

"Yeah, we should wait," he said.

They wouldn't have to wait long. He could already make out the shimmer of blue lights between the trees. Sure enough, a series of pounding footsteps grew in volume until two more uniformed officers appeared. Kett waved them over, motioning for them to keep their voices down.

"If our man's here then he could be dangerous," Kett said. "On a perfect day we'd hold up and wait for a negotiator and a firearms team, but we can't risk those girls turning into hostages. You two, take the back, wait there in case he breaks for it. Savage, with me."

He stood, then hesitated. Something was nagging at him.

"What's up, sir?" Savage said.

"It's that sandwich and Coke," he said, looking at the house again. "Why would he use his debit card? Feels so unnecessary. So *deliberate.*"

"Maybe he was just hungry?" she said. "Shop's a fair bit from here, he might not have expected us to track him back.

Like you said, guys like Stillwater are clever, and sometimes that makes them cocky. I've read enough true crime to know that's how a lot of them are caught."

"And he might not even be here at all," Kett said, nodding. "Okay, come on, let's do this."

He set off at a jog, trying to be as quiet as possible. Savage ran noiselessly beside him, her baton extended. The two PCs were already out of sight as they cut behind a small, brick workshop. Kett slowed to a walk as he neared the open door, resting against it for a second before peering inside.

It was dark, of course. If there had ever been electricity here it had been switched off a long time ago, and the windows were all blinded by plywood sheets. The place stank of piss, but Kett was pretty sure it wasn't human. He'd been in London long enough to know the stench of rats when it clawed into his sinuses.

He pulled his phone from his pocket before remembering the flashlight still didn't work. Savage was way ahead of him, aiming her torch ahead of her as she crossed the threshold. Kett followed, trying to work out if the house felt empty or not before realising that he didn't need his instincts for this one.

Somebody inside was whistling.

Savage had reached the first internal door, the baton held above her right shoulder. She nudged it open with her foot and Kett looked past her to see a small, bare room—nothing here but a fireplace. There was only one other door in the hall, and Kett nodded towards it. He couldn't be sure, but it sounded like the whistling was coming from right behind it.

He held up three fingers, Savage nodding at him to show that she understood.

Two fingers.

One finger.

Kett stretched himself to his full height, lifted his size eleven boot, and kicked the door as hard as he could. It didn't so much open as come clean off its hinges, dropping in a cloud of dust.

"Police!" Kett roared as he charged into the room. "Down on your knees!"

"Police!" Savage echoed.

There was just enough time to make out a small kitchen illuminated by the hole in the ceiling, a table, a man in overalls, before the back door crashed open and the two PCs barrelled inside yelling their heads off. If they were going for shock and awe, it worked. The man—even in the swirling dust and half-dark Kett could tell that it was Stillwater—fell back against the sink, something clattering from his hands.

"Stay where you are!" Kett shouted, crossing the kitchen in three strides and grabbing Stillwater by the shoulder. He was covered in something wet, and sticky, and warm, and there was a vicious little knife at his feet. Kett kicked it away, spinning Stillwater around and yanking both of his hands behind his back.

"Hey!" Stillwater yelled. "Get off me!"

"Cuffs," Kett yelled, but Savage was already there. She snapped them onto Stillwater's wrists then drove her foot into the back of his leg, sending him crashing to his knees so forcefully that his chin rang off the cast iron sink.

"What the hell do you think you're doing?" Stillwater cried out, his voice muffled and broken. "Let me go!"

"Keep struggling," Kett growled. "I'll be happy to knock the fight right out of you, son."

Stillwater groaned, but his movements slowed. He sat

back on his haunches, craning his head around to try to see behind him. He'd hit his face pretty hard, but that didn't explain the mess he was in.

The bastard was soaked from head to toe in blood.

"Where are they?" Kett said, grabbing Stillwater's hair and wrenching his head back. He turned to the other PCs. "Check the house, the outbuildings, the woods, they're here somewhere."

"Who?" whined Stillwater.

"Don't fuck with me," Kett said. "Where are the girls? What have you done to them? Is this their blood?"

"No!" Stillwater cried. "I don't have any girls."

He was interrupted by the sound of more coppers arriving, the kitchen suddenly flooded with them. Dunst was there, his grey face turning greyer at the sight of Stillwater's overalls.

"They here?" Dunst asked.

"They have to be," said Kett. He dropped his head so it was just inches from Stillwater's. "And they'd better be alive."

Stillwater wriggled away, twisting so that he was sitting on his backside. He'd split his lip on the sink and he sucked at the blood there, snot pouring from his nose.

"I don't know what you're talking about," he said. "There's nobody here but me. It's rabbit blood."

"Rabbit?" Kett said. Stillwater nodded to the table, and Kett saw the animals there—skinned, and in the process of being gutted. The little nest of organs glistening on a plate made his stomach churn. The rabbits, three of them, stared at Kett with their dark, dead eyes.

"Just rabbits," Stillwater said.

One of the constables leaned through the hallway door, shaking his head.

"You have got to be kidding me," said Kett. He looked down at Stillwater, resisting every urge he had to stomp on his head. "You're here slaughtering rabbits?"

"Pest control," he said. "The place is overrun with them. Rats too. I'm helping a friend, making a little money on the side selling rabbit meat." He held up his cuffed hands in a display of innocence. "I swear, that's all I'm doing."

Kett met Savage's eye, reading her thoughts.

Fuck.

"Get him up," Kett said to her. "Take him to the nick. Make sure all this goes to forensics immediately."

"You're arresting me?" Stillwater said. "I don't understand."

"Yes, you do," Kett said. "And yes, I am. Christian Stillwater, you are under arrest for the abduction of Delia Crossan, Connie Byrne, and Maisie Malone. You do not have to say anything but it may harm your defence if you do not mention, when questioned, something which you later rely on in court. Anything you do say may be given in evidence. Got it?"

Stillwater shook his head in denial. PC Savage grabbed his elbow and helped him up, leading him to the back door.

"Stillwater," Kett said, and the man turned back. "If they're here, we will find them."

"No," Stillwater replied. "You won't."

And even though it was dark, even though the room was still choked with dust, Kett could swear that the fucker was smiling.

CHAPTER TWENTY

Kett drove back to the station alone. A few coppers had stayed on site, a search team of detectives and constables working a line from the farmhouse out into the woods and over the neighbouring golf course—much to the fury of a bunch of badly dressed old farts. Kett had spent half an hour scouring the house and its outbuildings for any piece of evidence that might implicate Christian Stillwater, but there was no indication at all that the missing girls had been there.

He thumped the wheel, accidentally sounding the horn just as a woman pushing a buggy walked onto the zebra crossing in front of him. She almost jumped out of her skin, yelling obscenities at him as she scuttled across. He waved an apology that probably came across as sarcastic before accelerating into the city centre. Stillwater had been brought to the nick in town, where he'd be stewing inside a cell. If he was smart, he'd already have called his lawyer.

And Stillwater was smart. Kett had no doubt about it.

There was nowhere to park, so Kett pulled the Volvo into the underground car park of the huge library opposite, tucking the ticket into his wallet as he jogged back to the surface. He checked his phone for messages, clocking the time—half eleven—and reminding himself that being late to collect Evie two days in a row would result in a strop of Biblical proportions. He wasn't even sure what time he was supposed to pick Moira up. In his rush to get to Delia Crossan's house he had completely forgotten to ask the childminder.

"Hey," he said to the sergeant on duty as he walked through the door. It had only been a day since he'd last been here, but it felt like a century or two. "Stillwater?"

"He's out back," said the man without looking up.

Kett walked through the double doors into the bustling heart of the police station. It was much smaller than the Wymondham headquarters, and older too, but it was currently buzzing like a hive. Kett crossed the bullpen, spotting Porter standing by a window. Colin Clare was on the other side of the room with a face like a gorilla's arse.

"Pete," Kett said. "Any word on Percival?"

"Hey Robbie," Pete said. He looked exhausted. "Spalding's bringing him in, but she's doing it as gently as possible. I didn't go in the end, we thought I might terrify him too much. Apparently when he opened the door he broke down in tears before Spalding could even say why she was there."

"Did he know about his sister? His niece?" Kett asked, and Porter shrugged.

"Kett," yelled Clare from across the room. "Get over here. You too, Porter."

They did as they were ordered, standing in front of the boss like two kids in front of the headmaster. He finished reading the document in his hand then looked at Kett.

"What is it with you and beating up suspects?" he

asked. "That might be how things work in London, but it's not how we do it here."

Kett opened his mouth to argue, then decided to save his energy. It was a good move, because Clare's expression softened—only slightly.

"But we've got our main suspect in custody," he said. "That's a good thing. The bad thing is there's absolutely no evidence connecting him with the missing girls. Unless you want to charge him with cruelty to rabbits, we can't touch him."

"So we press him," said Porter. "Put the pressure on, find a chink in his armour."

"It's going to be tough," said Kett. "I've interviewed guys like him before, too many of them. They're clever, they can tell a lie, and they've rehearsed their story so many times they probably believe it."

"That's why I want you in there," said Clare. "You're as annoying as all hell, but you've done this before. I'm coming in with you."

"Oh, sure," said Kett. "Now? It's just I have to pick—"

"Now," said Clare. "We've got Percival coming in at some point too and god only knows how we're going to handle that one." He looked at Kett with a strange expression. "Wait, were you about to say you're picking your kids up?"

"Yeah," he said. "Evie at one, Alice at three, and Moira at some point between now and midnight. Why?"

Clare chewed on it, then shook his head.

"Nothing," he said. "Come on. I want you to be the bad cop."

"Yeah?" said Kett. "And you're the good cop?"

"I'm the *devil* cop," said Clare with a grim smile.

THEY'D STRIPPED STILLWATER of his bloody overalls, dressing him in a jumpsuit that might once have been orange, but they hadn't let him wash the blood from his face and hair. It was a deliberate move. The room was hot, the air close, and the smell of him was cloying. His bottom lip was black, his hands filthy and his wrists swollen where the handcuffs had been clamped then removed. His eyes were bright, though, regarding Kett with an arrogant curiosity as the DCI sat down on a chair on the opposite side of the desk. Clare pressed the record button on the deck but remained standing, a caged bear, his mouth-breathing the loudest sound in the small space. Kett waited for the boss to make the first move. Then, when he didn't, he sat back and looked Stillwater up and down.

"You waived your right to counsel?" Kett asked.

"I've got nothing to hide," the man replied. "You're making a big mistake. *Another* one."

"Ian Brady, you know him?" Kett asked, his voice quiet, calm. Stillwater sniffed, his blue eyes watching Kett with a frightening clarity.

"The Moors Murderer," he said after a moment. "Sure."

"Killed five children," Kett went on. "But he didn't start there. His first kill was a cat. He was ten. He burned another cat alive, and he stoned a dog to death. Do you know what else he did?"

Stillwater didn't reply, his eyes not wavering, barely even blinking. It was an intimidating stare, and every cell in Kett's body was sending signals to look away—the same way he'd look away from an aggressive dog—but he held his ground. He'd faced off against far worse people in the interview room.

"He cut the heads off rabbits," Kett said. "Is that what you were doing, Christian? Rehearsing?"

"You have to cut their heads off," the man replied, breaking eye contact to look up at Clare. "It's too hard to peel the skin otherwise. And nobody wants to cook a rabbit with its head on."

"But look at you," Kett said. "You're drenched in blood. You look like you've been bathing in it."

Stillwater ran a hand through his sticky hair, shrugging.

"Must have happened when you tackled me," he said, a blatant lie.

"You're selling the rabbits," said Kett, moving on. "Who to?"

"Anyone that will have them," he replied. "I get a fiver a rabbit, and the farm is overrun with the furry little bastards. Eat some myself, too."

"Whose farm is it?" Kett asked.

"It belongs to a man called Peter Dalton," Stillwater said. Kett didn't react, because Stillwater was telling the truth. The Land Registry had returned the same information. Dalton was an ex-pat living in Spain, and they hadn't been able to reach him yet. Stillwater's mouth twitched, almost a smile. "He's away at the moment. He's had that place on the market for about three years and nobody wants to touch it—not for the price he's asking anyway. Not just rats, half the ceiling is gone and there's rot everywhere. I keep the site as free of rodents as I can."

"You don't need the money," Kett said. "You're working a good job. Estate agent, right?"

"Yeah, but it's boring," Stillwater said. "You must get that? I don't see you sitting behind a desk—well, apart from this one. You're bursting into houses smashing people's heads into sinks." He gingerly prodded his lip. "I want the same thing, to be outside, to live a little, to be human."

"To get your kicks," Kett said, nodding. "Killing rabbits. Kidnapping girls."

"Where are they?" Clare dropped both hands onto the desk, the sound of it like a bomb going off. Kett wasn't sure who jumped harder, himself or Stillwater. The boss was *loud*. "You've still got a chance here, a chance to avoid spending the rest of your life in jail. Hell, maybe you can use the same lawyer you did last time and you might walk free again. Just tell us where they are, and you can make your life a hell of a lot easier."

It was the wrong tactic, Kett knew that immediately. Stillwater's smile grew, his forehead furrowing.

"You're talking about those paper girls, aren't you?" he said, turning back to Kett.

"You know exactly who we mean," Clare said. He opened the folder he'd brought in with him, pulling out three large photos. Kett had seen the two of Maisie and Connie already. The one of Delia Crossan was new—a blown up picture of the young girl in her Brownies outfit, caught mid-laugh. Clare fumbled and the photograph fell to the floor with a slap. Stillwater smiled as he watched the Superintendent pick it up and slam it down. "Maisie Malone. Connie Byrne. And Delia Crossan. Those girls don't deserve the hell you're putting them through."

Stillwater reached out, brushing his fingers down Delia's cheek in a way that made Kett's skin crawl. He had to resist the urge to rip the photograph away before it was contaminated.

"Sweet girls," he said. "I saw them on the news. She's new, isn't she? I wasn't aware there were three of them."

"Bullshit," said Clare. "Anything happens to them and I swear to god I'll make your prison life hell."

"Let's talk about Emily Coupland," Kett said, trying to get back some control. "The last girl you abducted."

Stillwater's smile sat motionless on his lips.

"I was cleared of any wrongdoing," he said eventually. "It was all a terrible misunderstanding. I was worried about her, and I did what I thought was right. As it turns out, Emily was removed from her parents after that whole incident because they were putting her welfare in danger. I was right."

"You were," said Kett. "You chose your victim well. You just weren't quite smart enough to make it work."

For the briefest of moments, too small for Kett to be sure he'd even seen it, Stillwater's expression changed.

"I—"

"No, don't get me wrong," Kett said, riding over him. "I can see what you were planning, but you fucked it up. There were too many moving pieces."

Stillwater chewed on something that he wasn't quite willing to say, his jaw bulging.

"Killing rabbits, anyone can do that," said Kett. "Hell, I've done that, a long time ago. It's amateur stuff. But taking children, that's not easy. That's not an amateur job at all. It's tough, and most people aren't smart enough to figure out how to do it without being caught."

"You think you're going to bait me," said Stillwater. "Is that all you've got? What, you think I'll buckle and cry and confess my sins?"

"Something like that," said Kett. "Floor's all yours."

Stillwater regarded his bloodstained fingertips, then bit off a loose piece of thumbnail. He chewed it for a moment, then spat it onto the desk—never looking away from Kett.

"Okay, so why these girls?" Kett asked. "All eleven. Skinny as rakes. Freckles. Is that your thing? Because don't forget, we've met your girlfriend."

That look again, his mask slipping.

"Oh yeah," Kett said. "She's, what? Twenty-four? But if you squint she could pass for a lot younger. You ever make her dress up in a school uniform? Maybe watch her cycling around on a bike with a newspaper bag over her shoulder?"

"No," said Stillwater, but Kett had obviously touched a nerve. "That's disgusting."

"Is that what we're going to find on your laptop, *when* we find your laptop? Young girls?"

Stillwater was still smiling, but his eyes looked sharp enough to cut glass.

"I'm not one of *them*," he said.

"A paedo?" said Kett, working at those frayed edges. "Why are you telling me that? What are you hiding? Why are you making such a big deal about it?"

"I'm not telling you anything," Stillwater said, an edge of panic to his voice.

"You know what they do to men like you in prison, don't you?" Clare said, leaning on the table again so that he could spit the words into Stillwater's disintegrating smile. "You must know. There's only one way of making sure that doesn't happen. Tell us where they are."

"You should be careful," said Stillwater, regaining his composure. "Both of you."

"Yeah?" said Kett. "Why's that?"

"You're both family men."

Kett's hand went automatically to his wedding ring.

"You both have children," Stillwater went on. "How old are your triplets, Superintendent. Fourteen? And Robbie, you've got three little girls, haven't you? Where are they now?"

The rush of fury that boiled up from Kett's stomach was almost too powerful to resist. He clenched his fists, breathing steadily, trying to ignore the desire to rip Stillwater's shit-eating grin from his face. He could almost feel the interview seesaw, the balance of power shifting to the other side of the desk. Clare's eyes looked ready to pop out of his head, flecks of white foam on his lips. He was going to explode, and that was exactly what this arsehole wanted.

"Where were you on Monday afternoon?" Kett said, keeping his tone as civil as he was able. He felt Clare stand down, the boss's breaths returning to normal. "Between five-thirty and, say, midnight?"

Stillwater looked miffed that nobody had taken the bait. He made an exaggerated show of deep thought.

"Monday, let me see."

Kett knew from the man's grin that they were about to get some shitty news.

"Oh yeah, that's right, I was out of town. On a train, in fact."

"Yeah?" Kett said.

"I left Norwich at three-thirty, heading to London."

"Business or pleasure?" Kett said.

"Bit of both," he replied. "But you'll have me on camera, both here and at Liverpool Street Station. I had a meeting in Whitechapel."

"Jack the Ripper territory," muttered Clare, which struck Kett as a weak move. Stillwater just sneered.

"Dinner, a couple of drinks. I got the last train back, arrived in the city past 1am."

It wasn't impossible that he could have taken Connie, Kett thought. The girl's home life hadn't exactly been much fun. If she'd stayed with a friend after her round, then walked home later that night, Stillwater could have snatched her after he'd arrived back in Norwich. It was unlikely, though.

"We'll check the CCTV," Kett said, and Stillwater shrugged, chewing his bloody nails again. "And Tuesday afternoon, where were you around three?"

Another smile, and Kett sighed.

"You should know," he replied. "I was right here."

"What?" said Clare.

"In the station," Stillwater said. "I had an appointment. Tuesday, a quarter to three, I think. I'll check. Or you can. You kept me waiting for hours."

"You were *here*?" Clare said.

"I came in as a witness. There was a fight outside my work, a week or so ago. A kid ended up in the hospital. I saw the whole thing, offered to come in and give a statement. To be honest, I thought it would be a five-minute job. So much for being a good Samaritan, eh? This world just doesn't seem to like good people."

Kett drummed his fingers on the table, trying to think of a way around his story. Clare had obviously given up. The boss cursed beneath his breath then stormed to the door, banging his hand on it twice. The lock snapped open and he left the room, and even though it closed again straight away Kett could hear him cursing as he walked down the hallway.

"Interview terminated at, uh, twelve-oh-three," Kett said, ending the recording. He didn't get up immediately, and the two men sat there in silence, staring each other out.

"Charge me if you like," Stillwater said. "I'll get my lawyer in here and I'll be out in a heartbeat. No forensic evidence, plenty of witnesses, CCTV footage from a police station, and no reason on earth why I'd want three young girls. Any jury would see this for exactly what it is, a personal vendetta. And it is. You guys really messed me up last time, I had to have a tonne of therapy just to get my head straight after you accused me of kidnapping Emily. You're out to get me, to try to make yourselves look better, to cover up your past mistakes, and anyone in their right mind would see that."

He was right, Kett knew. Stillwater was a cold, calculating arsehole. He was a bad man. It didn't take a lifetime of detective skills to work that out. But unless he was a magician, he didn't take the girls.

"You mind yourself now," Kett said as he stood. "And make yourself comfortable, we've got twenty-three hours left to get to the truth."

"Oh I'm just fine," Stillwater said, lacing his fingers behind his head and leaning back on his chair, his feet thumping onto the desk. "You're the one who's in the shit, detective."

There was that arrogant grin again, and this time Kett couldn't stop himself. He leant across the desk, planted a hand on Stillwater's chest, and gave him a hefty shove. For all his attempted composure, the man made a noise like a squawking chicken as his chair toppled.

"Whoops," Kett said, knocking on the door. "Like I said. Mind yourself."

CHAPTER TWENTY-ONE

"I don't believe it," said Porter, leaning closer to the screen. "There he is. That's him."

Even in the grainy feed Stillwater could be seen as clear as day, sitting on the row of chairs by the wall of the city centre police station waiting room. He had a book in his hand, and every now and again he'd walk over to the desk and speak to the duty sergeant. The timestamp said that he walked in at 2:43, went in to give his statement at 5:38, then left the station four minutes after six.

"Wasn't even him that made the appointment," Porter went on. "We asked him to come in."

"Maisie left her house just after quarter past three," said Dunst. "The alert went out less than an hour later when she dialled 999 from her phone, and when she didn't pick up emergency dispatch's return calls. Cops tracked her down and arrived on scene at five, give or take, and her bag was found long before Stillwater left the nick."

"He's not our man," said Clare, who was standing over the group. "Fucking hell, what a mess. You really tossed this one all over yourself."

"I *what?*" Kett said. "Look, we should keep him anyway, because he's an arsehole."

"So you can pull another stunt like the one back there?" Clare growled. "Get us involved in a brutality lawsuit?"

"He just fell off his chair," Kett said, lifting his hands in a display of innocence. "Shouldn't have rocked it back on two legs, it can be dangerous. I was reaching out to try and help him."

He paused, suddenly serious.

"He knew about my kids, sir. Yours too. Don't you think that's weird."

Weird was one word. Terrifying was another.

"So he did some research," Clare said. "It's not exactly a secret. My NC profile online says I have six children, including triplets, and you were all over the TV after your wife went missing. I saw the press conferences with you and the girls. You're right, he's bad news, but it's not him."

"Sir," Kett said, but Clare growled in his direction.

"Let him go. Forensics are still working on it, but they haven't pulled anything from his body or from the house that isn't animal blood. There's not even trace DNA that could link him to the girls. For now, our attention remains on the other suspect, Lochy Percival." He grimaced as he said it. "He is to be treated with the utmost care, is that clear? If he's our man, we need to prove it beyond a doubt. If he's not, then the slightest hint of a cockup on our part will land us so deep in the shit we'll need a submarine. Is he here yet?"

"*En route,*" said Porter. "Spalding's bringing him in."

"Don't put him in an interview room," Clare said.

"Sir?" Porter frowned.

"I don't want him freaking out. He's not under arrest,

and we want to keep him calm. Dunst, do me a favour and clear the canteen."

"At lunchtime?" he replied. "You're asking for a riot."

"Just do it," said the boss. "And Kett, I need to ask you for a favour. A big one. An *unusual* one."

Kett lifted an eyebrow, waiting.

"Go fetch your kid and bring her back here."

KETT RANG MOIRA'S childminder as he drove across town to the nursery. It was only a five-minute trip so fortunately the call didn't go on for long.

"Oh gosh, she's adorable," she said on the line. "She hasn't grumbled at all. She ate some toast and honey, and a digestive—sorry, I didn't ask if she could have biscuits but I figured it was okay. She practically ripped my fingers off trying to get it out of my hand."

"They're fine," Kett said, trying to remember the woman's name. "I just couldn't recall if we'd fixed a pick-up time."

"Anything up to three," she replied. "Longer is fine, but after-school rates are different and I have some bigger kids arriving."

"I'll collect her before three," he said. "She's definitely okay?"

"Mr Kett, she hasn't asked for mummy or daddy once."

In one way that was a relief, Kett thought as he hung up. In another, it was a disappointment. All it took was a morning and Moira had made herself a new home, a new family. It was heartbreaking, too, because that's how babies worked, their memories didn't etch deep. The awful truth of it was that Moira was already beginning to forget her mother.

He parked on the zigzags outside nursery, leaving the engine running. As soon as the staff let him through the door Evie launched herself onto his leg, gripping it like he was a lifebuoy during a storm.

"Hey, gorgeous girl," he said, ruffling her hair. "Good morning?"

"She was great," said Debbie, handing Kett Evie's water bottle. "Quiet as a mouse, but she was playing with some of the other kids today."

"You're late," Evie mumbled into his leg.

"I'm not!" he protested. "I'm actually early."

"Am not," she said. He tried to prise her loose but she refused to come, and he was forced to do a Monty Python silly walk out of the room with her still attached to his leg. By the time he'd reached the car she was howling with laughter, grappling him so hard in her effort to stay on that his trousers were in danger of coming loose.

"Hey, Evie, that's enough," he said, grabbing her beneath the arms and hauling her loose. He held her for a moment until she'd stopped wiggling. "I need your help with something. Official police work. You think you can handle it?"

"Will I be catching bad guys?" she asked.

"You will," he replied, and it wasn't exactly a lie.

He buckled her in to her booster, checking it twice before closing the door and clambering into the car. He'd known immediately what Clare was going to ask him, and he had been impressed—partly because it was a good idea, and partly because he didn't think the boss would be so happy flaunting the rules. He looked over his shoulder and smiled at his daughter.

"I need your help talking to a man."

THE CONTRAST COULDN'T BE starker.

Stillwater had been composed, intelligent, ready for anything. Surrounded by the scarred walls of the interview room, drenched in blood, he'd looked every part the villain.

Lochy Percival, on the other hand, looked like a wreck.

He was practically curled into himself on a chair in the far corner of the canteen, his legs drawn up to his chest and his hands wrapped around his knees. He peered over his kneecaps like an injured rabbit, and his dark eyes flitted back and forth beneath a scuffed and filthy yellow Norwich City cap, waiting for somebody to come and put him out of his misery.

And that somebody was DCI Kett.

"Remember," said Clare, his lips practically touching Kett's ear as they both stared through the greasy little window in the canteen door. "Go easy on him. The wrongful arrest suit gives him a weapon of mass destruction and plenty of ammunition."

"Pow pow!" Evie said in her deafeningly squeaky voice.

"You sure about this?" Kett asked. "Evie doesn't really go easy on anyone."

"I want him to feel relaxed," Clare said. "I want this to be as far from a police interview as it's possible to be."

"Your call," muttered Kett as he pushed open the canteen door. Evie was in like a shot, bolting to the fridges like it was Christmas morning. Percival looked ready to scream at the sight of her, then he calmed down, his expression softening as he watched the child picking things up then dropping them again.

The room had been emptied, then partially filled again. Spalding and Dunst were sitting together at a table pretending to have an intimate conversation, and Porter nibbled a protein bar beside the door, studying his mobile phone with an Oscar-worthy expression of concentration. All of them had removed their jackets and loosened their ties.

"Can I have this?" Evie asked, holding an orange jelly pot over her head.

Kett walked in after her, a smile on his face. He nodded at Percival, still smiling, then walked to Evie's side.

"Jelly for lunch?" he said. "How about a sausage roll? They do sandwiches here as well."

"Jelly," said Evie, with a face that told him not to bother arguing.

"Go get a spoon," he said, watching her run past the tills. He turned to the woman behind the counter, surprised to see DCI Pearson there. "Can I pay for this later?" She nodded, and he turned to Percival again. "Hi, sorry about this."

Percival didn't reply, but his legs dropped to the floor. He rested his elbows on the table, playing nervously with the frayed brim of his cap. He looked nothing like the photographs they'd found in Delia Crossan's house—the early photos, that was. He looked *broken*. Beneath the cap his thinning hair was greasy and unwashed, his face pocked with spots. His clothes looked like they hadn't been laundered in weeks, and even from here Kett caught a whiff of him—strong enough to put him off the idea of grabbing a sandwich from the shelf. The man's hands rubbed at his left thigh, massaging it. It was where he had been stabbed, Kett remembered.

"I really am sorry," he went on, taking a few steps

towards his table. "I know how difficult this must be for you. I want to assure you that—"

"I don't like it," Evie said. She was standing behind Kett, leaning on a canteen table. The jelly was open, juice running to the floor.

"Come on, Evie, you're making a mess."

He took the jelly from her and put it on the closest table while she ran back to the counter to look for something else.

"You want anything?" Kett asked Percival, and the man shook his head. From the look of his complexion he hadn't eaten anything other than garlic bread in years. Kett took another step in his direction. "Mind if I sit down?"

Percival still didn't respond, like he'd lost the ability to communicate. Kett took a chair from a neighbouring table and positioned it far enough from Percival not to appear threatening, but close enough for them to talk quietly.

"My name is Robbie," he said. "I'm a detective, but not here. I'm not officially on duty, as you can see."

Evie was doing her best to open a Kitkat, firing wary glances back in case Kett asked her to stop.

"That's my daughter, Evie," he said. "She's been at nursery, haven't you sweetie?"

Her mouth was far too full of chocolate for the question to even register.

"I didn't do it," Percival said. "I swear. She was my... my sister."

"Nobody is saying you hurt Evelyn," Kett said, keeping his voice low so Evie wouldn't overhear. "We just want to make sure we know all the facts. Have you seen them recently? Delia and her mum?"

Percival shook his head, his eyes scouring the surface of the table like there were answers written there. The smell coming off him was unbearable, making Kett's breath catch in his throat.

"I haven't seen them for ages," Percival said, sniffing. "Or those other girls. I mean I haven't seen *them* at all."

"Do you know anything about them?" Kett asked. "Maisie and Connie?"

Percival retreated into himself like he'd suffered a physical blow, shaking his head so hard that spittle fanned out from his lips.

"I swear it, I swear it, I don't know where they are."

"Do you know anyone who would have wanted to hurt your sister?" he asked. "Any enemies, old boyfriends?"

"No," Percival told the table. "Everyone loved her. She was so gentle."

He looked up, his expression full of alarm.

"Who's going to look after Franklin?"

"Franklin?" Kett asked.

"The cat," Percival said. "Who's going to feed him?"

"We will," Kett lied. "Until we bring Delia home. Okay? Franklin's going to be just fine."

"I like cats," said Evie from the other side of the canteen. She was working on her second Kitkat and Kett fired a warning look at her. She turned away, defiant as always as she wrestled with the plastic wrapper.

"Yeah," said Kett. "She likes *Kit*kats."

At this, Percival almost managed a smile. It was like somebody had left a Halloween pumpkin out for too long, his face weirdly mushy, *loose*. Kett wondered if he'd taken to drugs since the wrongful arrest, meth maybe. He had the teeth for it. But he seemed sober enough now.

"It's an unusual name, Lochy," Kett said. "Do you know what it means?"

Percival scoffed, his eyes darting from Kett to the table

to Evie, never staying in one place for more than a second or two.

"Mum always told me it meant God's gift," he said. "I don't know. Evelyn means bird. I always liked that more."

"Well, Lochy, do you mind if I ask you a couple of questions? I want you to remember that nobody is accusing you of anything. This is just a chat, okay? So we can find out who did this."

He glanced back to see Evie guzzling a four-arm Kitkat practically in one go, like a sword swallower.

"Evie, that's enough," he said. "No more chocolate."

Any more and she'd be climbing the walls for the rest of the day.

"Sugar is her weakness," Kett said, turning back to Percival. "Mine is tea, I drink way too much of the stuff. What's yours?"

Go on, just say it and save us all some time: snatching young girls.

"Weakness?" Percival said, straining his way towards an answer. "I don't... I don't know. I drink. Drink too much. Wine, mainly. Is that what you wanted to hear?"

"I want to hear whatever you want to tell me," Kett said, stifling a yawn. The arrest and interrogation of Stillwater had worn him out, his mind padded with cotton wool like somebody was packing it up for a house move. "No pressure. Were you drinking last weekend?"

Percival shook his head the same way he had before. It reminded Kett of his kids when they refused to do what he asked, so exaggerated it was almost comical. The man rubbed his eyes.

"You're going to say I did it," he moaned. "You and *him.*"

Lochy looked at the canteen door, and so did Kett—just

in time to see Clare's head drop out of sight through the window.

Idiot.

"He was there last time, back in 2013, he asked me the same question again and again and again, about that girl who died, the one they found beneath the boat. He was so angry and he wouldn't stop, he never stopped. It's him who wants to do this, he wants me to suffer."

"Forget about him," said Kett, leaning forward and keeping his voice low. "I'm in charge right now, and if I say you didn't do anything then he has to believe me. Okay?"

Percival nodded, calming down, but the guy felt like a powder keg, ready to blow at any moment.

"You weren't drinking, then? On Sunday?"

"I was," Percival said, his hand trembling as he wiped away a tear. "Just a little. Just to keep the... keep all the bad stuff away. The pain."

He rubbed his leg again.

"It hurts all the time."

"How much are we talking, Lochy?" Kett went on. "A glass? Two? A bottle?"

"A bottle," he replied with a shrug. "Enough to know what I'm doing. I didn't hurt my sister."

"Nobody's saying you did," Kett said. "I like a drink too."

"To take away the pain of your dead wife?" Percival asked.

The question felt like a kick to the bollocks, and for a second Kett couldn't get a breath in. He looked back, Evie thankfully out of earshot as she tried to open a bottle of Coke.

"How did you know about my wife?" he managed after

a moment. Percival squirmed in his chair, refusing to make eye contact. "Lochy, how did you know?"

"I don't know," he whined, his words almost insufferably desperate. "I didn't do anything. I can show you I didn't."

It was like somebody had flicked a switch in the man's head, a desperate smile appearing there.

"Yeah, I can prove it," he said. "I can prove I was in all weekend. I can prove I'm in all the time, I never go anywhere."

One big hand dived into the pocket of his stinking sweatpants and he pulled out an iPhone—a brand new one, by the look of it. Unlocking it with his thumb, he swiped through a few apps then opened one up. He passed the phone to Kett, who found himself looking at a large living room, two sofas, shit everywhere, and a couple of cops obviously in the middle of a search.

"That's my house," Percival said, leaning close enough to jab a finger on the screen. "That's live. I said they could look around as much as they liked, I don't have anything to hide."

Kett squinted, realising that one of the uniformed officers on the screen was PC Savage.

"Live?" he asked.

"Sure. You can talk to them if you want. Press that microphone thing."

Kett pressed the icon and the phone chimed. On screen, both cops looked up.

"Savage?" said Kett.

Savage frowned, walking closer. The camera was obviously hidden because her eyes roved left and right, up and down.

"It's behind a frame," Percival said. "A silver one. It's empty."

Savage must have heard him, because she suddenly locked eyes with Kett. She said something but the sound wasn't working.

"Take your finger off," Percival said. "It's like a walkie talkie."

"...there?" Savage asked. "Porter?"

"It's Kett," he said as he pressed the mic again. "I'm looking at you through Percival's phone."

"Nest cam, by the look of it," Savage said, and the world spun as she picked it up from the shelf.

"There's one in every room," Percival explained, sitting back in his chair. "Except the bathroom."

"You film yourself?" Kett asked. He heard a hiss and a whoop of success, looking back to see Evie with the Coke bottle to her lips. "Oh Jesus, hang on. Evie, no!"

He ran to her and grabbed the bottle.

"Coke? Are you insane? You're *three*! Give me that."

"No!" she screamed. "It's mine! I opened it myself!"

"Just sit there," Kett said, pointing to a table. "No more sugar."

For a second he thought she was about to erupt, but she huffed into the chair and folded her hands over her chest, eyeballing him until he turned away.

"Fart head," she muttered.

"Yeah," Kett said, returning to his chair. "Sorry. These cameras, you film yourself on them?"

Percival nodded, pressing the heels of his hands into his eyes for a second and making them even more bloodshot than they were before.

"It wasn't my idea, somebody suggested it in group," he said.

"Group? Like a support group?"

"For trauma. I went for a little while after I was, you know, arrested. Put in prison. It didn't really help, but somebody there gave me the idea to film myself all the time. If the cameras hadn't caught me at that Norwich match, I'd be in prison now. I'd be dead. I'm never going to let it happen again, not ever."

Kett couldn't help but feel a rush of sympathy for the man. Uncle L, he'd been, good old Lochy Percival. Then a series of almost unbelievable coincidences had turned him into *this*. Paranoid, depressed, filthy. It had eaten him up from the inside out.

Kett was starting to feel something else, too. Panic was gnawing at his guts, the fear of what he was about to find out.

"You keep it all?" Kett asked. "The footage from your house?"

"Daddy, I feel sick," said Evie.

"One minute," he replied, still looking at Percival, waiting for an answer. The man nodded.

"It's stored online for a week, but I keep it all. Hard drives."

"You keep it all?" Kett asked. "Going back..."

"Going back five years," he said. "Nearly."

"Daddy I'm bored," Evie went on. "And sick. And I need a poo."

Kett turned his attention to the app, navigating the interface to see a bunch of little folders labelled with the days of the week. He clicked on Sunday, then scrubbed through the footage. The living room cam picked up Percival throughout the day, and even though he came and went it was pretty clear he couldn't have made it out of the house and across town in time to kill his sister and snatch Delia.

"Fudge," he said beneath his breath.

"Daddy I really feel sick."

"Am I okay to keep this for a few days?" Kett asked. Percival looked unsure. "It's totally voluntary, of course. The whole point of the cameras was to do exactly this, wasn't it? We'll take a look, then we can be absolutely sure you had nothing to do with those girls going missing."

After a moment, Percival nodded.

"Thank you, Lochy," Kett said, standing up and offering the man his hand. Percival stared at it like he couldn't remember what to do, eventually stretching out his arm and gripping Kett with fingers as damp and limp as salad leaves. The smell pulsed from him, enough to make Kett's eyes water, but he fought through it. "We really appreciate you coming to talk to us. And remember, if you need anything at all, you only have to ask. Things are different now. We're on your side."

Percival swallowed, his eyes bulging. He was sweating, even though the canteen was air conditioned.

"Can I go?" he asked.

"Yeah," said Kett, standing back to let the other man up. Percival limped towards the door, glancing at Evie as he went.

"Bye," Evie said, waving at him with her chocolate fingers. He had a hand on the door when Kett called to him.

"Lochy," he said. "Can I just ask you one more thing?"

The man didn't turn around, he just stood there panting, his eyes dark beneath the brim of his cap. His grip on the door was so tight his knuckles had blanched.

"You seemed concerned about your sister, and rightly

so. It was terrible, what happened to her. But you didn't ask about Delia. Why not?"

Percival licked his lips.

"Have you found her?" the man asked after a moment.

"No," Kett said. Another pause.

"I was too frightened to hear the answer," Percival said. "That's why I didn't ask. I didn't want to hear that she'd died too."

He stood there, motionless apart from the rise and fall of his shoulders.

"Can I go?"

"Yeah," said Kett. "You can go."

CHAPTER TWENTY-TWO

The bullpen in the city centre nick was less like a hive now, and more like a funeral parlour. Two dozen coppers sat on chairs or perched on desks, their hands folded in respectful silence, their eyes downcast. Superintendent Clare was in charge of the ceremonies, marching left and right across the full width of the room, his expression as black as a priest's robes. Nobody dared talk. Nobody dared make the slightest sound.

"Daddy? What's happening? When can we go home? This is boring."

Nobody apart from Evie, that was, who sat on Kett's knee and played with his shirt buttons. Clare pretended not to notice the girl, his nostrils flared like a bull ready to charge. DI Keith Dunst, who leaned against the desk next to Kett's chair, squinted at Evie like he couldn't figure her out.

"She was smaller yesterday, wasn't she?" he said quietly. "Like, a *lot* smaller."

"It's a different girl," said Kett, one eyebrow raised.

"Oh," said Dunst, still unsure.

"Aren't you a police detective?" Kett asked with a smile.

"You think this is *funny*?" Clare said, coming to a halt and practically stamping his shit-coloured brogue on the floor. He glared at Kett. "You know what I think? I think we've separately accused two men of abducting our missing girls, both of whom have a known relationship with this constabulary—one of whom successfully sued us for the better part of a million pounds—and both of whom have rock solid alibis for the crimes. There is *no* forensic evidence, there is *no* solid motive other than rampant speculation, and both men are now free. You, DCI Kett, are largely responsible for this, and to be brutally honest with you, you have tossed up all over yourself, me, and this entire department."

"Sir," said Kett. "I really don't think *tossed* means what you think it—"

"I'll toss over you!" he roared back. He started pacing again. "This is a disaster, we have no suspects, no leads, and right now three young girls are out there, scared out of their minds—that's if they're even still alive."

Kett did his best to cover Evie's ears, but she squirmed out of his grip, listening intently.

"Does anyone have any good news?" Clare asked, his voice cracking with desperation.

"Percival is in the clear," said Porter from two desks away. "His cameras check out. I spoke to Nest and they say it's impossible to change the timestamp without hacking the whole system, and they'd know if it had been done. He was at home during all three abductions."

"That's *good* news?" said Clare.

"It's, uh, good for Percival," muttered Porter with a shrug.

"And Stillwater," said Raymond Figg, the FLO spinning his pen between his fingers like he was twirling a baton. "All his alibis check out. No video footage for Sunday, but he's clear on the other two. It's not him."

"Any other leads?" Clare asked. "Anything at all?"

"We're still looking into the idea that it was a gang-related crime," said DS Spalding as she tied her hair back. "We've rounded up a couple of minor players who've been caught squabbling over control of the heath. Pressed them pretty hard, but there's no indication things were serious enough for multiple abductions. It's too risky, the gangs would never want heat like this."

Clare swore at the ceiling.

"So you're telling me you think the Walker father and son are in the clear for this as well?" he asked.

Nobody replied, but the answer was obvious.

"They can't have just vanished," the boss said. "They're out there somewhere. Somebody has taken them. From now on, I don't want anybody going to sleep, I don't want anyone sitting down to eat, I don't even want any of you taking the time to sh—"

"Boss?" came a voice from the back of the room. Kett looked over to see the desk sergeant there. He looked nervous.

"This better be something positive," Clare said.

"Uh..." the man went on, wringing his hands together. "It's just that the press has arrived."

"Which one?" Clare asked.

"All of them," the sergeant said. "They want to know why you've arrested Lochy Percival again."

"Fuck!" Clare yelled, spittle soaring across the room. He kicked a chair, everyone watching it squeak across the floor on its rollers before crunching into a desk. "Don't let them in, and don't talk to them, any of you—on pain of death. Everyone, I want a new lead by the end of the day, something to take everybody's focus off this tossing disaster, or I'll bust you all down to constables. Okay? And Kett."

Kett looked at Clare. Everyone else looked at Kett, the room ringing with the echo of Clare's voice.

"You've done all you need to do here. If you'd been less rash, if you'd taken your time before arresting Stillwater, then maybe this wouldn't be such an immense clusterfuck. Take your daughters and go home. We'll call you if we need you."

"Sir," said Porter. "That isn't really fa—"

"Porter, unless you want to sit this out with *him*," Clare interrupted, jabbing a finger at Kett, "then shut up, and get out."

Kett sighed. He stood up, holding Evie. He could have argued, of course, but Clare was right. He'd arrested Stillwater before he knew all the facts. He'd arrested him on instinct—on *bad* instinct.

"Sorry, sir," he said, turning to leave. Evie glared at the Superintendent over Kett's shoulder, getting the final word in just as they were walking through the door.

"Fart head!"

THE SERGEANT HADN'T BEEN LYING, it seemed like the whole of the city's press corps was trying to get inside the building. They'd amassed on the street outside, maybe thirty reporters all jostling for position while the sergeant did his best to hold the pass like a balding, overweight Gerard Butler minus his 300 Spartans. Even through the closed door Kett could hear their questions.

"Are you any closer to finding the paper girls?"

"Why were two men arrested and then released?"

"Is Lochy Percival guilty? Do you now suspect his involvement in the death of Jenny O'Rourke in 2013?"

The poor bastard, Kett thought as he came to a halt in the middle of the waiting room. Percival was never going to be clear of that cloud.

"I'd take the side entrance, sir," said the sergeant. "They'll eat you alive out there."

"Thanks," Kett said, heading back the way he'd come. He bumped into Porter and Figg on the way. His old friend looked about twenty years older than he had yesterday.

"Don't listen to the boss," Figg said with a shrug, smoothing down his goatee. "He's just looking for somebody to take it out on. He'll call you back in time. It's this case, whoever did this is smart, and Clare feels outfoxed and outwitted. He feels stupid, and a man like him can't handle that. Give it time, everything will become clear. It will be just like it was on the Khan case back in London."

Kett squinted at the FLO.

"I hope not," he said. "That little boy died."

"Oh, god," Figg said, a hand flying to his mouth. "Sorry. He did. Well, you know what I mean, just don't be too hard on yourself. Sorry."

Kett waited for Figg to scuttle away, then he turned to Porter.

"Sorry about that," the big DI said. "He bollocked me pretty good too, after you'd left."

"It's my fault, Pete," Kett replied. "He's right. Ever since Billie... I don't know. I went for the jugular before I took the time to work out exactly what I was trying to kill."

"Don't kill anyone, daddy," said Evie, genuinely

concerned. She put her little hand to his cheek, her eyes full of worry, and it took some of the pain from the day.

"I won't," he said. "In fact, I'm not going to do anything else today except take you guys home and chill."

He felt guilty for saying it, because there were three girls out there who needed all the help they could get. But he hadn't been lying to Porter, Billie's disappearance had changed him. It had made him desperate, and that made him dangerous. The Norfolk team were good, they were clever, they knew exactly what they were doing. It would be better for everyone if he got out of their way.

"Well we're right here," said Porter. "If anything pops into your head, let me know. And thank you, Robbie. Whatever the boss says, it was good police work."

Kett shook the man's offered hand as they parted, then navigated his way through the warren of corridors until he found the side exit. There was nobody around in this part of the building and he lifted Evie onto his shoulders before heading down the side of the nick and making his way into town. It was baking, the heat sapping his strength, but the longer walk was worth it because by the time he'd fought his way through the tourists and the shoppers and circled back to the library he was well out of the reach of the reporters. He could see them, though, further down the street. Clare was out there already, presumably giving a statement that involved much kissing of Lochy Percival's arse.

"Come on," Kett said to Evie. "Let's forget about all this and go get your sisters."

FORGETTING about it proved more difficult than Kett would have liked. The instant he pulled the Volvo out of the concrete tomb of the library car park the news fizzled onto the radio, the three missing girls in Norwich now the headline on national radio. The man speaking wasn't Clare, it was the top brass, the Chief Constable, and he was doing his best to plaster over a lot of mistakes. Kett prayed he wouldn't hear Percival's name, but there it was, bright and clear and just about perfectly pitched for a second lawsuit.

"Fudging artholes," he muttered as he drove through the narrow streets. It was only just gone two, a little too early to pick up Alice—although he was pretty much driving past her school. Instead, he made his way out of town and headed for the childminder. Most of the traffic was coming the other way, and it didn't take long to reach the house. He was almost disappointed when Moira didn't want to come home with him.

"It happens all the time," said the woman, whose name Kett still couldn't remember. "It lets me know I'm doing something right."

Or that I'm doing something wrong, Kett thought, picking up the screaming, wriggling blob that was his youngest daughter.

"Email me an invoice," he said. "And thank you."

Moira settled on the way back into the city, so tired that for a while he thought she'd actually fallen asleep with her eyes open. It was a little late for a danger nap, but fortunately Evie was there prodding and shouting and generally doing all she could to piss off the baby. He couldn't be bothered to tell her to stop.

He parked the Volvo on the road behind Alice's school, taking the girls to the little park there to pass the time. Evie was happy to explore, and Moira just wanted to fall asleep on the swing, so he pushed the baby for a while and did his best not to think about his failings. But how could he not? Arresting Stillwater had been an amateur move. He'd just been so sure that it was him, everything had been lined up—almost too good to be true. Here was a man who'd kidnapped a girl before, who displayed all the traits of a genuine psychopath, who was standing in an abandoned house with a knife in his hands and blood all over him. If he'd wanted to bait the police, he couldn't have done it any better.

But the cameras never lied. Stillwater was innocent.

"Daddy, I need a poo," said Evie after what felt like five minutes but which, when he checked his watch, turned out to have been nearly half an hour.

"Is there ever a moment in the day when you *don't* need a poo?" he asked Evie as he pulled Moira out of the swing. They walked down the street together, using the school's toilet. Both girls went wild in the playground as they waited for Alice's class to finish, but Kett did his best to avoid meeting the eye of any other parent. He wasn't in the mood to talk.

Alice wasn't in the mood to talk either. She stomped out of her classroom, almost elbowing her teacher as she went. Mrs. Gardner flashed Kett a look that said, *don't worry, we'll deal with this tomorrow*, and he nodded back in gratitude.

"You and me both, kiddo," he said to Alice as they walked through the gate. "It's been a bad day all round."

AS IT TURNED OUT, the bad day wasn't done yet.

Kett saw them before he'd even pulled up, two men and a woman sitting on the low wall of his house. They were on their feet and running towards him as he parked, the woman rapping on the window with her knuckles.

"Daddy who are they?" Alice asked, her eyes almost wild with fear. "I don't like it."

It didn't take much to make Alice hysterical, and Kett popped the door of the car, clambering out with murder on his mind.

"There are kids in here," he hissed. "Why don't you piss off and bother somebody else?"

"There are kids out there, too," said one of the men—in his fifties, Kett guessed, prematurely grey and wearing a chequered jacket that looked like it belonged in the 1970s. He aimed his dictaphone at Kett like it was a weapon. "According to our source you harassed and beat a suspect in an attempt to make him confess, even though there was video evidence of his innocence. *Police* video. Care to comment, DCI Kett?"

Stillwater, he thought. The bastard must have gone straight to the papers.

"You want a statement, talk to CID," he growled. "Now get the hell out of my way so my children don't have to see what a bunch of rotting arseholes looks like."

He opened Evie's door, lifting her out and ushering her onto the pavement. Alice was out like a flash, wrapping her arms around Kett so hard she pulled his shirt out of his belt. He slammed the door and walked to Moira's side, the reporters closing in.

"DCI Kett, how do you respond to claims that you're unfit for duty following the abduction of your wife?" asked the woman.

"Daddy?" said Alice, speaking the words into his stomach.

"You were forced to leave the Met," she went on. "And

you are currently meddling in an ongoing case in which you have no official jurisdiction. Is that right?"

"Daddy!" Alice was screaming now, and Evie wasn't far off joining in. The fury that churned inside Kett was greater even than that he'd felt sitting opposite Stillwater. It almost blinded him, the world burning like the surface of the sun. He pulled Moira from her seat, trying to steer past the reporters without tripping over Alice.

"No comment," he said.

The other man—young, suited and booted—stepped forward, his phone actually glancing off Kett's lips.

"If you couldn't find your wife," he said, almost smiling. "What makes you think you can find three missing girls?"

If Kett hadn't been holding Moira in one hand, the other resting on Alice's head to calm her, he would have punched the man in his face, no question. He would have knocked the bastard to the floor and broken his teeth and been damned with the consequences. But he couldn't, so he didn't. He put his head down and walked insistently through the melee until he reached the front door. Only when he'd opened it and ushered the children inside did he look back.

"You could be out there searching for them too, you know," he said. "Never mind me, you could be out there trying to find those girls. But look at you."

He did look at them, *really* look at them, in a way that made all three lower their gadgets. The two men muttered as they walked away, and the woman stared back at Kett with a genuine expression of remorse.

"Look, off the record," she said. "Do you think you'll find them?"

Yes, Kett wanted to say. *They're out there, they're okay, wherever they are, whoever took them, we'll bring them all home.* He wanted to say that more than anything.

But it wasn't true.

He sighed, hanging his head.

"I don't know," he said.

Then he shut the door.

CHAPTER TWENTY-THREE

HE WASN'T JUST A SHIT COPPER THAT NIGHT.

He was a shit dad too.

He couldn't focus, his mind packed full of the case. There were three young girls in the house waiting for him to appear, waiting for him to emerge from the cocoon of his work, but the three girls he couldn't stop thinking about were Connie and Maisie and Delia. He saw them in every worst-case scenario, and in most of those they were dead—doll-stiff corpses who stared at the sky with glassy eyes as their killer shovelled soil over them. Days had passed since they'd been taken, and with the world now looking for their kidnapper it was unlikely anyone would ever set eyes on them again.

They'd missed their window. They'd messed up.

He had messed up.

He put the iPad on for the girls then he sat at the table while he waited for the kettle to boil. All he wanted to do was call Bingo down in London and ask the same damned question he always asked—*any news?*—but he managed to stop himself. The day was bad enough without another crushing blow.

Billie's gone, part of his mind told him, but he shook his head, refusing to believe it. Even now, even after all this time, he still expected to hear the jingle of her keys as she came through the door, the little 'phew!' she always breathed when she got home; he still expected to feel her arms wrapping themselves around him and her lips pressed against his.

How have they been? she would ask. *Little monsters?*

"Yeah, like always," he said. "Moira had her first day at the childminder, she did really well. Alice is settling in, slowly but surely. And Evie helped me with a case. She's going to be a detective for sure."

And you? How are you?

"Better, now you're home," he said. He could almost smell her perfume. "Always better."

"Dad? Who are you talking to?"

He realised his eyes were shut and he opened them to see Alice hovering in the doorway.

"Nobody, sweetie," he said. "I'm just tired. You ready to tell me how school went?"

She didn't reply, just hung onto the door and swung to and fro.

"You hungry?"

She nodded, and Kett stood up, grabbing a mug and throwing a teabag into it.

"Takeaway?"

"Or you could cook?" she said. "I miss normal food."

Mum food.

"I'll see what I can do," he said. "Go watch something, I'll be through in a minute."

She didn't move.

"Alice," he said, a warning now. She scowled at him, then turned and slouched back to the living room.

He sighed as he prodded the teabag with a spoon. He was being an arsehole to her, he knew. None of this was her fault, and she needed him now more than ever. But there was an invisible barrier between him and the kids tonight, he didn't feel connected to this world. He was deep inside the dark, cold ocean of the case and he was sinking fast. This was his lot, this was the company he was destined to keep—the missing, and the dead. Until he, too, was so lost that his kids would never find him again.

Christ, he said, rubbing his eyes. *Just go spend some time with them. Just be with them.*

Spending time with them wasn't a problem. He carried his tea through to the sparse living room, squeezing onto the sofa and letting Moira and Evie climb onto his lap. Reluctantly, Alice held the iPad where they could all see it, some Netflix show he half recognised.

But he wasn't *with* them. Not really.

Where were the paper girls? What connected them? What did they have in common? *Who* did they have in common? Connie, snatched on her route and dragged into a dead person's house. Maisie too, less than twenty-four hours later. And Delia, taken from her own house even as her mother lay dying on the kitchen floor. She was the first, and Kett was almost certain her kidnapper had botched the job. He hadn't meant to murder Evelyn Crossan. That's why he'd altered his MO, targeting the girls as they delivered to dead houses on their rounds where they were unlikely to be interrupted. Why else had his pattern changed so drastically?

But how did he get the girls from the houses to wherever he was keeping them? They were all slight, but even an eleven-year-old could pack a punch if she wanted to—Alice gave him problems sometimes, when she was having a serious meltdown, and she was only seven. They could scream the world to pieces if they needed to. The kidnapper had to have had a car, which meant—unless he'd killed them outright, which there was no evidence to support—he'd carried the girls kicking and screaming to the kerb, fumbled for his keys, dumped them in the boot, all in broad daylight. And yet they'd canvassed every street, every house. No witnesses.

There was the question, too, of why the kidnapper would need *three* girls. It didn't make any sense.

"Dad!" Evie grabbed his mouth, twisting his lips. He wrenched free.

"*What?*"

"Moira's chewing the cable again," said Alice, trying to pull the iPad charger from the baby's mouth. Kett grabbed it and yanked it free—a little too hard. Moira's eyes welled, her bottom lip jutting out.

"Sorry," he told her, but it was too late. She threw herself back, almost tumbling off his knee, and when he lunged for her he knocked Evie onto her older sister's lap. And then they were all screaming.

"Sorry!" Kett yelled. "Just be calm."

He picked Moira up, clamping her to his chest.

"Keep the noise down, okay," he said as he stood up. "I'm going to try to get her to sleep."

He left the room, the anxiety like a lead weight in his gut. What he wouldn't give to have his wife here, their mother. What he wouldn't do for an extra pair of hands. It was impossible, he simply couldn't do it.

He used his phone to search for nearby delivery places as he carried the baby up the stairs, settling on a Chinese that was one street over from the Walker shop. He made an order for chicken balls, spring rolls, and chips—although whether the guy on the phone could hear him over Moira's screams was anyone's guess.

Ignoring the fact that there were still no curtains in the master bedroom, he laid the baby on the bed. Trying to change her nappy was like trying to wrestle a bronco, and at one point he thought her kicking heel might have shattered his nose. He bit down on the anger as he lay next to her and held her tight, plastering her sweaty head with kisses until, at long last, she calmed down. She lay there, sniffing, every breath hitching in her throat. She lay there, and he sang to her.

"You are my sunshine, my only sunshine, you make me happy, when skies are grey."

It was Billie's song, the one she'd sung to each child in turn every single night before they went to sleep. He'd carried on the tradition, even though it was the hardest thing imaginable, even though every verse was torture.

"You'll never know dear, how much I love you. Please don't take my sunshine away."

Billie's magic worked, though, even though it was conducted through him. Moira settled, pawing at his face with her chubby fingers. She lay that way for a while, almost asleep, almost awake, but she didn't go off entirely. Neither did he, although in the heavy silence he easily could have done.

"Addy," she said after a while. "Shoes."

"I thought you were tired?" he replied.

"No, shoes," she said, then something that sounded like 'open peanut butter horse.'

"I don't have a peanut butter horse," he said, stroking a finger down her cheek. "Sorry."

She sighed again, then sat up, scrubbing her eyes with her fists.

"Shall we try again after dinner?" he asked.

"Nana."

"I'll take that as a yes."

The doorbell rang as he was halfway down the stairs, Alice and Evie charging out of the living room like the house was under attack. He fought his way past them and grabbed the food, thanking the bemused driver.

"Who wants chicken balls?"

"Me!" screeched Evie, then once again all three of them were screaming like banshees as they ran into the living room. Kett grabbed a few plates from the kitchen before joining them, opening up the various containers on the floor and letting them help themselves.

"Just be careful, it will be hot," he said, although his words were lost in the Hungry Hippos-style feeding fest that followed. He found himself smiling as he watched them, marvelling that these strange, beautiful creatures could in any way have come from him. With a deep, shuddering breath he tried to see them, *really* see them, in a way that finally allowed him to push the three paper girls from his thoughts.

"That was my chip, moo-moo!" yelled Evie as Moira raided her plate. "Daddy, that was my chip!"

"There are literally about a hundred chips left in the container," he replied. Evie ignored them, grabbing a chip from Alice's plate instead and earning an outburst of pure fury.

"No! Give it back!"

"Dad!"

"Daddy!"

Kett lifted a chip from his own plate and lobbed it at

Evie. It was a good shot, slapping her gently in the forehead before plopping to the plate beneath. She froze, her eyes wide with shock. Kett picked up another chip, holding it above his head.

"Anyone else want to make a fuss?" he asked.

"But dad," Alice started, and Kett threw the chip at her. It bounced off her shoulder and she picked it up and lobbed it right back.

It was a stupid thing to do, he knew. A terrible waste of food. But right now it was exactly what they needed.

"Food fight!" he yelled, and suddenly the air was full of flying chips. Alice was an exceptionally good shot, one chip bouncing off his chin and another hitting him on the bridge of his nose. "Evie! Moira! Defend me!"

Evie obeyed, throwing a chip at Alice. Moira was just grabbing handfuls of whatever she could and throwing them anywhere. Alice was laughing, really laughing, in a way he hadn't heard for far too long. And he was too, he realised, it spilled out of him like a burst of sunshine on an overcast day.

"No!" screamed Alice through the laughter. "Get dad! Get dad!"

They all turned on him, a hail of chips battering off his face and chest. He ducked onto the floor, retreating on all fours to the door, blindly throwing the last of his ammunition at the three girls.

"That's not fair!" he yelled. "You're not allowed to gang up on me, you're not allowed to tag team!"

A hefty chicken ball thumped him right in the eye and he held his hand up, ready to tell them to stop. But he didn't speak, he *couldn't*, because something had exploded inside his head.

You're not allowed to tag team.

He stood up, walking out of the room so that he could think straight.

Holy shit.

Chips flew out of the door like arrows but he ignored them, running into the kitchen and digging his phone from his pocket. He dialled Porter's personal number, listening to it ring.

"Dad! Better get ready because we're coming for you!" Alice yelled, her head peeking out of the living room.

Come on, come on.

"DI Porter."

"Pete, it's Robbie," Kett said. "I think I know why Stillwater and Percival had alibis. I know why there was CCTV footage of them both that seemed too good to be true."

"Yeah?" Porter said. "Because they're innocent?"

"No, they're guilty," Kett said. "I think they're both guilty. They're a tag team. They're working *together*."

CHAPTER TWENTY-FOUR

THE PAIN WAS UNBEARABLE. IT WAS UNLIKE ANYTHING she'd ever felt, even the time she'd fractured her finger after a basketball hit it in PE.

It was the worst pain ever.

But she couldn't stop.

Maisie flexed her wrists, twisting them one way, then the other. Over and over. Her hands were sticky and even though they were hidden behind her back she knew it was blood. But the wire that bound her was definitely looser. If she tugged her arms in opposite directions she could feel the space opening up between her wrists.

But it was agony. It was making her head pound, it was making her feel like she was going to be sick.

Don't be sick, *she ordered herself. Because if she was sick then the monster would come, he'd pick her up and take her away just like he had the other girl, the one called Connie. Maisie didn't know how long ago that was. It might have been an hour, it might have been a month. The room's only window had been boarded up, but at least the light was on now—a single bulb hanging directly above her—and the world was quiet, as if time had moved on without her. All she knew was that the monster had heard the other girl calling out and he'd taken her away.*

"You won't cry without your tongue," he'd said as he'd dragged her through the door. "You'll try, but you won't be able to do it."

And then there had been two.

Maisie rested for a moment, the fringes of her vision pulsing with darkness. She looked to her side to see the third girl there. She'd been here already when Maisie had been dragged in and tied up. Back then—Days ago? Weeks?—the girl had been wide-eyed and alert. Now, though, she was slumped on her chair, her eyes closed, her breaths so shallow and so fast that they reminded Maisie of a mouse she'd found once in her grandad's garage, its back half pinned in a trap. She wasn't well, her skin so pale it was almost translucent.

Maisie wondered if she looked the same. Nobody had fed her since she'd got here, and she'd only been given a few sips of water. The monster had come in that morning, and he'd smelled so disgusting she almost hadn't been able to drink from the cup he'd offered her.

The other girl hadn't drunk at all.

Maisie took a deep breath and set to work again, twisting her arms, working the wire free. It creaked every time she moved, the noise impossibly loud against the silence. She knew that any minute now the monster would charge into the room, his knife glinting, ready to remove her tongue or her fingers or her eyes. And then what? He'd kill her, of course. Wasn't that how these things always ended? She hated the news because it was full of death, murders, terrorist attacks, and far worse too. She was only eleven, but she knew enough about the world to understand that you didn't kidnap three girls without having an end game. And since she was fairly sure she wasn't here for a ransom, the only other outcome was death.

It wasn't fair. It wasn't fair. It wasn't—

She felt it give, the wire pinging loose and spilling to the floor. Her joints were locked so tight that at first she thought she was still tied up. Then, with a cry of pain that she had to trap behind her lips, a cry she thought would shatter her, she moved her hands to her lap.

Don't stop, *she willed herself.* Don't stop now.

It was like somebody had sewn razors into her spine and her hips, but somehow she managed to bend down and get her fingers to the wire that bound her ankles. This one was easier, even though her hands were sticky, and it took her less than a minute to unwind it.

She was about to stand up when she heard footsteps.

No.

They were coming from beneath her, and they were getting louder.

Maisie tried to stand, her leg cramping. She cried out as she crashed back onto her chair, her hand slapping across her mouth. The sounds from below stopped.

Had he heard?

Was he coming?

Maisie rubbed the pain from her swollen calf, tried again. She didn't stand this time, she lowered herself onto all fours and crawled across the bare boards. She didn't head for the door, she moved to the other girl, trying to undo the knot of wire around her legs. It was too hard, her fingers numb and slick with blood.

I'm sorry, *she thought.* I'll get help, I promise.

More footsteps from below. Was that a voice, too?

Little girls should do as they're told, *it would be saying.* Little girls who run away don't need their toes.

She reached the door and used the handle to pull herself to her feet. It would be locked, she knew. Only it wasn't. The handle squeaked, the door creaked, and she hobbled into a dark, bare corridor.

Maisie paused, feeling her way along the wall, seeing a staircase emerge out of the shadows ahead. It was a noisy one. It was how she'd known the monster was coming—the creak of boards, the thump of his boots. She dropped onto the top step, staying as close to the wall as she could, her fingers leaving bloody smudges on the crumbling plaster. There was a smell out here, the same one she'd caught before—so rancid and so cloying that it made her stomach churn.

She ignored it, moving as quickly as she dared. Two steps. Three. Four five six until she reached the bend. The voice came from beneath her, hushed but urgent. The monster sounded like he was having an argument with himself—or maybe with the girl he'd taken from the room.

"... not well, we need to get..."

She couldn't figure out what he was saying. But it was good. He was distracted.

Maisie kept moving, almost stumbling when her foot connected with a loose step. The noise it made might as well have been a gunshot.

The voice fell quiet.

Maisie moved fast, her bare feet trampling down the last few stairs before hitting cold flagstones. She was in a large corridor, two doors up ahead, one on each side. There was a light coming from one, so she doubled back and made for the other end of the house.

"Did you hear that?" a voice behind her. The monster's voice. It turned from a whisper into a shout. "Little girls who spoil our plans don't deserve to have their hands."

There, a kitchen. Maisie threw herself inside its

welcome darkness, pressing herself to the wall just as somebody stepped out of the door at the other end of the corridor. She did her best not to breathe, her heart a wrecking ball that was surely loud enough to bring the entire building down.

"You sure they're tied up good?" came the monster's voice, quiet again.

"I'm sure," came another voice, softer, more hesitant. "I did everything you told me to. I did everything right. You have to—"

"You couldn't tie your fucking shoelaces right," the monster said.

"I did," whined the first voice. "Please, I'll go and check."

"I'll do it. I'll cut them both to shreds."

The monster laughed.

"No, don't, please!" said the other voice.

The thump of boots on stairs. He was going up, which meant she had seconds before he discovered she was free. She walked into the pitch-black kitchen, waving her hands in front of her. Was that a glimmer of light ahead? A door? It had to be. It had *to be.*

It was. It looked like a pantry, lit by a dust-caked bulb. The door was only open a crack, but that was enough. It didn't need to be open any more for her to see the bundle of old rags soaked in blood, to see the hand that stretched from beneath them, perfectly pale and perfectly still, as if pleading for her to help.

She couldn't help. It was too late.

Maisie backed away and her leg cracked off a chair, shunting it across the floor. Then she was running, heading for a door on the far side of the room, grabbing the handle and pulling hard, praying that it would be open, praying—

It swung inwards and there was the night, the air. She

ran, stumbled, ran, so wild with joy that she didn't see the shape loom up in front of her, a hessian sack for its face.

The monster grabbed her, hoisting her off the ground.

"No! No!" Maisie screamed, lashing out. It was pointless, he was too strong. A gloved hand clamped down on her lips, his other arm crushing her chest as he carried her back to the house. The kitchen door looked like an upright coffin, full of darkness, until another monster ran out. He, too, wore a mask, staring at her through the crosses of his eyes, and he held an evil blade in his hand.

"Fuck," said the second monster.

Then there was a third, like the house was vomiting bad men. This one was still trying to pull the mask over his head, struggling with it. The monster with the knife turned to him.

"You fucking idiot."

"Enough," said the monster who held her. He leant in, feeding his whisper into her ear. "Where are you running to? Don't you know, everyone loves me. Come back to me, the fun's just about to start."

"No!" Maisie cried through his fingers. "No!"

She punched, she fought, she bit, she kicked. But it was no good. There were three of them, after all, a forest of hands that grabbed her and pulled her, screaming, into the dark.

CHAPTER TWENTY-FIVE

Saturday

It was after midnight by the time Kett made it to police HQ, and it was thanks to Superintendent Colin Clare's wife that he found himself there at all.

"You sure she's okay to babysit?" Kett asked as he walked into the incident room. "She didn't look too happy about it."

Fiona Clare QC had shown up at Kett's front door fifty minutes ago with a face like thunder. The girls had been asleep, thankfully, and she'd sat herself down on the sofa without more than a handful of words—three of which were, "Bugger off, then."

"She's fine," Clare said. "That's just her face."

The boss punched both fists down onto the desk, fixing Kett with eyes that were more red than white. He hadn't exactly looked great when Kett had first met him, but now he looked positively ghoulish.

"You'd better have something for me," he said.

"I do," Kett replied, nodding to the rest of the team. Porter was half asleep on a chair. Dunst and Spalding sat on the other side of the desk. DCI Pearson leaned against the wall, chewing her pen like it was a cigar. Savage was here too, clustered in the corner of the room with another couple of constables. She smiled at Kett and he read her expression like she'd spoken aloud.

It's good to have you back.

"Well?" Clare barked. "Porter said you had a flash of inspiration. I almost dread to think what that might be. They're working *together*?"

"I think so," said Kett, rubbing his temples as if it might alleviate the exhaustion. "We've been under the impression that we're dealing with a lone serial kidnapper, right? That's the way these cases usually go, unless you're dealing with traffickers. One guy, the same crime, over and over and over until they get caught."

"There's nothing to suggest this is anything different," said Clare. "Unless you're chasing waterfalls again."

"I..." Kett frowned. "*Waterfalls*, sir?"

"Just get on with it."

"Okay, both Stillwater and Percival had perfect alibis," Kett said, walking to the front of the room. "In fact, you couldn't have asked for any better alibi than being filmed inside a police station while the crime was taking place. Stillwater wanted to be here on Tuesday, he wanted his alibi to be cast iron."

"But he didn't make the appointment," Spalding said. "We did."

"I'll bet you anything that wasn't the first appointment time he was given," Kett said. "See if he cancelled any other slots before sticking to that one. He wanted to be here when

Maisie was taken, because he knew we couldn't argue with our own cameras."

"So he knew Maisie was going to be taken at that exact time," said Clare. "By who? Percival? He had an alibi too."

"His cameras at home," Kett said, nodding. "You've been through them?"

"Of course," Porter said, his eyes still closed. "I had that distinct pleasure. That man walks around with his hand down his pants way too often for my liking. But he was at home during all three abductions."

"You're sure?" said Kett. "Show me."

"I'll have to get the phone from evidence," Porter said, groaning as he stood up. "Hang on."

He left the room and Kett took a moment to collect his thoughts.

"A tag team of kidnappers makes sense," he said. "Two men can manage a kidnapped girl far more easily than one."

"This is great speculation," said Clare. "But so far you're tossing into the wind. I need *evidence*, Kett."

"I'm coming to that," he said. "Is there any indication that Stillwater and Percival know each other?"

"None," said Dunst. He took a notepad from his pocket, flicked through a few pages, then replaced it. He examined his nails for a moment before realising everyone was still looking at him. "Oh, sorry, that's it. There's no reason to believe they know each other at all."

"Right," said Kett. "Except they were arrested at roughly the same time, weren't they? Percival was accused of murdering Jenny O'Rourke in, what, November 2013? Stillwater in 2014."

"Stillwater took Emily Coupland from the park in Spring 2014," mumbled Pearson through her pen. She pulled it out, wiping it on her shirt. "Percival had just been released, it was all over the news that he was innocent."

"No, no, we covered all this at the time," Clare said. "We investigated the two men to see if there was a connection, because their crimes were so similar. There was absolutely nothing that indicated they knew each other. Different upbringings, different parts of the county, no contact at all on social media, no phone records, no CCTV, nothing. It was a wild goose chase then and it's a wild goose chase now."

"That was *before*," said Kett. "I think you're right, they didn't know each other before 2014. Stillwater taking the child from the park, and Percival being falsely accused of murdering that fourteen-year-old tourist, they were completely unconnected. But what about after?"

"After?" said Clare.

"It was something that Percival said," Kett explained. "He spoke about his support group, the one he went to as part of his therapy when his conviction was quashed. Mistreatment by the police or something."

"Yeah," said Porter. "It was a trauma group for people who had suffered miscarriages of justice—real or imagined."

"Was it a requirement that Percival went?"

"To group therapy?" Clare said with a sneer. "Of course not. He chose to go. That whole group was a pain in my arse."

"But we provided it?" Kett asked. "As in, the police."

Clare nodded, then shook his head.

"Well, not really. We provided a room, some biscuits, but the group was an outreach project. Why? What does this have to do with anything?"

"Maybe nothing," Kett said. "Maybe everything. Stillwater spoke about therapy too. He mentioned it. Was it the same group?"

"Wait a minute," said Clare, frowning. "Wait a fucking minute. It *was*. I remember. The bastard went to town claiming that we'd treated him like shit. He said he was a samaritan who had been trying to do the right thing, who'd rescued that girl. He wanted the world on his side, which is why he went to the group. He brought reporters once, it was a complete shitstorm because they took photos of people going in and out and it's supposed to be anonymous. It was all part of his show, all designed to make him look innocent when we all knew he'd just fucked up an abduction."

"So they know each other," said Kett. The feeling he got was half relief, and half horror.

"That doesn't mean anything," said Spalding, drumming her fingers on the table. "There were a dozen people in that group, and dozens more support groups over the years. They might never have crossed paths, let alone spoken to each other."

"It needs to be checked," said Clare. "See if there's anything in the archives."

"On it," said Savage, sitting down at a computer.

Kett was about to carry on but he was cut off as Porter came back into the room. The DI was holding an evidence bag with a phone inside, and he passed it to Kett.

"Battery is low, but we've got a charger if you need it."

"Cheers," said Kett, pulling the phone out of the bag. "Passcode?"

"Have a guess," said Porter, and Kett typed in 1-2-3-4-5-6. The phone unlocked and he navigated to the Nest app.

"Let's start with Monday," he said, exploring the history. He scrubbed through the afternoon, switching cameras every time Percival left a room. "Connie left for her paper round at..."

"Half five," said Savage. "They noticed she was missing in the morning."

"He's there the whole time," said Porter.

He was. Percival in his stinking tracksuit and baseball cap watching the TV. Percival in his stinking tracksuit and baseball cap playing video games. Percival in his stinking tracksuit and baseball cap pouring glass after glass of wine. Percival in his stinking tracksuit and baseball cap going for a piss.

"There's no camera in the bathroom?" Kett asked.

"No," said Porter. "Thank god."

Percival in his stinking tracksuit and baseball cap watching more TV, one hand down the front of his trousers.

"Jesus, this guy plays a *lot* of pocket pool," muttered Kett. He was ready to scrub some more when, on screen, Percival got up and went to the bathroom again. "Twice in ten minutes," he said. "And we know he wasn't washing in there."

"I dread to think what he was doing," Porter said, shuddering.

"Hurry up," barked Clare.

Kett waited, watching as the bathroom door opened again. There was Percival in his stinking tracksuit and baseball cap heading into the kitchen. Percival in his stinking tracksuit and baseball cap making a sandwich. Percival in his stinking tracksuit and baseball cap sitting down on a chair in the living room.

"I can't see his face," said Kett, squinting at the screen. The man was there, but he was keeping his head down, keeping it away from the cameras. He scrubbed through a little more until 19:43, when Percival walked into the kitchen and got himself a drink. He limped to the same chair again, staying there until 21:13 when he went into the bedroom and lay on the bed. At no point did the cameras reveal a glimpse of the face beneath the hat.

"That's him though, right?" said Porter, leaning over Kett's shoulder. "It has to be."

"Who goes to bed wearing a baseball cap?" said Clare who was looming in from the other side, both of the big men sandwiching Kett. "Is it Percival?"

"I don't know," said Kett, all three of them practically cheek to cheek as they watched Percival leaning over to switch off his bedside light.

"There," barked Clare, loud enough to make Kett's ear ring. "Rewind it!"

He did, playing the shot frame by frame as Percival leant over. His hat was pulled low over his eyes, and one hand was in front of his face, fingers splayed. But for a second—a *fraction* of a second—as he neared the light, he angled his head up to see what he was doing.

"Oh fuck," said Clare. "That isn't Lochy Percival."

"And it's not Stillwater either," said Kett. The face was pixelated but familiar, a neatly trimmed beard visible. He couldn't quite place it.

"Sir?" Savage called out from the other side of the room. "I've just found the archive for the therapy group. You're right. For a few months in 2014 both Percival and Stillwater attended together."

"Who else?" Kett asked, not taking his eyes off the screen. He wracked his brain. Who was that? There just wasn't enough of the man's face visible to make sense of.

"There's a whole bunch of people on the list," she said. "And plenty more who didn't give their names. It will take hours to sift through it all. But... hang on... there was somebody in charge of the group, of all the sessions Stillwater and Percival attended. He's police."

It suddenly clicked. Kett stared at the man on Percival's phone and knew exactly what Savage was about to say.

"Holy shit," he said.

"Raymond Figg," Savage reported. "He was a therapist before he was a family liaison officer."

"And now he's a kidnapper," said Kett, pointing at the screen. "That's him. That's Figg. There are *three* of the bastards."

CHAPTER TWENTY-SIX

The cruiser hit a speed bump at forty-eight miles per hour, almost taking off into the night. Kett squealed as his backside came off the seat, his grip on the door bar hard enough to turn his knuckles white. Savage knocked them down a gear as they burned rubber around a corner, then she punched the accelerator, the car roaring like a jet plane as it tore down a residential street.

"*You've* done this before," Kett said, wiping the sweat from his brow with his free hand. "Watch out!"

Savage pumped the brake, expertly steering the car around a fox that stood, startled, in the middle of the street. Kett's head thumped off the window and he winced.

"Sorry," said Savage. "Hang on."

She slowed as they passed one street, checking the sign, then she took the next turn, bumping the car onto the kerb.

"Number six," she said, climbing out. "I'll take the back."

The street was as quiet and still as a photograph, only the flashing blue lights bringing it to life. Overhead the sky was full of stars but the moon was a yellow fingernail that kept its light to itself. Darkness closed in from all corners, so heavy it was claustrophobic. The street was lined with large, modern houses, all glass and steel and surrounded by gardens. Kett ran to Percival's and hammered on the door.

"Lochy Percival, this is the police. Open up."

Nothing, and no lights on inside. He was about to try kicking the door down when a bright yellow shape appeared in the glass. He heard the click of a lock, then the door opened to reveal Savage.

"He's gone," she said. "Back door was wide open."

Kett pushed past her, switching on the lights as he went. The house stank of Percival's unwashed body, the stench so bad he had to put his jacket sleeve to his face. A quick search revealed that Savage hadn't been lying, the place was deserted.

The PC's phone rang and she answered it, putting it on speaker.

"You got him?" came Clare's voice.

"He's bolted, by the look of things," Savage said. "Stillwater?"

Clare's roared response told Kett everything he needed to hear.

"There's no sign of Figg either," Clare said. "How can we have been so *stupid*?"

"We'll find them," said Kett.

"We *had* them," growled Clare over the phone. "We had both kidnappers in the station yesterday, Figg too. They were all in the same goddamned building. *Our* building. And we let them go!"

"And they know we're onto them," said Kett, cursing beneath his breath. That was bad news for the three paper girls. From his experience with kidnappers they would be doing all they could right now to destroy the evidence so that nobody could prove their guilt. The thought of it, of Stillwater and Percival and Figg murdering those three children then grinning their way to freedom, made the fury boil in his veins.

"Get back to the station," Clare ordered. "We've got to find those girls."

"Sure," Kett said, but he was shaking his head.

We're too late, he thought. *We're just too late.*

"TRAFFIC CAMERAS CAUGHT STILLWATER AT 22:17."

Porter was mid flow when Kett walked back into the incident room. Clare and Spalding were here too, but other than that the room was empty, everybody on the hunt for the three suspects. The big DI nodded to Kett, then continued.

"He was heading south around the ringroad on the east side of town, clocked doing thirty-three in a thirty so obviously not in too much of a hurry."

"Was he alone?" Kett asked.

"As far as we can tell. Nobody in the passenger seat. Could be anyone in the back."

"Or the boot," said Savage from Kett's side.

"We need to check every camera on those roads," said Clare. "Wake the whole city up if you need to, we have to find out where he was going. Figg?"

"Nothing," said Porter. "Left after the meeting and never showed for his afternoon appointments."

"He knew we were closing in," said Kett. "That explains what he was saying when I bumped into you both, I thought it was weird. You remember, Pete?"

"Vaguely," Porter replied. "Something about everything becoming clear, and the old case you worked in London. Khan?"

"The Khan boy died," said Kett. "Figg was telling me all I needed to know about the girls. That bastard. But it explains how they seemed to have the jump on us. Like Stillwater and his rabbits. Figg told him we were coming, he wanted Stillwater to make himself look guilty so we'd arrest him, then panic, then let him go. Figg, more than anyone, understands the power a false arrest can give somebody, thanks to his therapy groups."

"I know Figg," Clare said, shaking his head. "I've known him for years. Didn't suspect a thing."

"I've met him too," Kett said. "I don't really remember. He did his training alongside another FLO in the Met, liaison work. He mentioned he worked on the Khan case, and that was brutal."

"Sick bastard must have loved it," said Savage. "He was probably just there to do some research."

"But *why*?" Clare asked. "Why take those girls?"

"Why did Dahmer kill seventeen kids?" Kett said. "Why did Shipman kill 250 people? Raymond Figg's a monster, and I'll bet you anything he was using those therapy groups as a recruiting ground for people like Stillwater. He knew Stillwater wanted to take that girl in 2014, he knew he was a monster too, all he had to do was shake his hand and *bam*, he had himself the start of a little gang. Then he wormed his way into the force and the world was his oyster."

"Percival's different, though," said Savage. "He genuinely was innocent."

"And broken," said Kett. "What was Percival's greatest fear? What did he spend every waking minute being petrified of?"

"Being accused of another crime," Porter said, nodding.

"Which would give Figg and Stillwater some serious leverage over him."

Kett thought for a moment.

"But not as much leverage as a missing niece," he said. "That's why Delia Crossan was taken first. They knew we'd come after Percival. It was how they'd be sure he'd stay quiet. And maybe they promised to keep her alive if he worked with them."

"So Figg took Delia Crossan?" Clare asked.

"Maybe," said Kett. "Or maybe it was Stillwater. He didn't have an airtight alibi for Sunday, but we didn't care because he had alibis for the other two kidnappings."

"So Stillwater took Delia, then Figg posed as Percival inside his house, wearing his clothes, giving Percival the chance to snatch Connie Byrne on Monday." Clare shook his head. "That's insane."

"But it's good," Kett said. "You know, not *good*, but if they were using Delia as leverage to get Percival to commit a crime, then she was still alive. She might still be alive."

"And who took Maisie?" Savage asked. "It had to have been Figg, right?"

"Because Percival and Stillwater had alibis," said Kett, nodding. "Three men, and each of them took a girl. They've been planning this for years. It's almost like they were competing."

"But where do they go from here?" Savage asked. "If

they were challenging each other to kidnap their victims, then what next?"

Everyone in the room knew the answer, but only Kett managed to say it.

"They take it to the next level," he said. "They're going to challenge each other to murder them."

CHAPTER TWENTY-SEVEN

"What have we got?"

Kett took a swig from his tea, hoping it would do something to keep the tiredness at bay. Fortunately Savage had made this one, and it was a damned sight better than Porter's. She sat next to him now, a pile of paper folders on the desk in front of her and her phone in her hand.

"Figg didn't own, he rented a place over near Mousehold and it's empty now." She popped her lips. "When they raided it they found that he'd taken apart two laptops and burned the hard drives along with a load of paperwork."

"Mousehold," said Kett. "So there's a chance he'd have come into contact with our girls. That's probably where he targeted them. Did he have his newspaper delivered?"

"We're looking into it. If he did, it wasn't from Walker's."

"No family in the city?" Kett asked.

"None."

Kett breathed out a sigh of frustration, slamming his fist on the desk. All he wanted to do was get out there and find the three paper girls and the arseholes who took them, but Figg had covered his tracks well. He'd been planning this for a long time.

"Anything from the boss?" Kett asked, and Savage shook her head. Clare had taken Porter, Spalding, Dunst and Pearson out into the city with every uniformed officer available and a promise to knock on door after door after door until they found something. Kett pushed himself up, pacing. "Come on," he said, as much to himself as anyone else. "Come on, come on, come on."

The team had already searched everywhere connected to Stillwater, Percival and Figg. Their houses, their workplaces, their childhood homes, their favourite woodland walks. *Everywhere.* Wherever they'd taken the girls, it was somewhere new.

"Building sand," said Kett.

"Huh?" Savage muttered, still leafing through the files on the desk.

"Stillwater was covered in building sand, his girlfriend told us. We're still looking for a building site, a home renovation."

"Needle in a haystack, sir," Savage said. "Unless we know *whose* building site or renovation it's just impossible."

"Somebody dead," Kett said, rubbing his temples. "Recently dead. And the smell. Stillwater's girlfriend mentioned a smell. Something *off*."

"Maybe he just smelled of Percival?" she said. "I mean the man was rancid. I could smell it on *me* after I'd searched his house."

"Maybe."

Kett paced to the far side of the windowless room, the lights seeming to buzz inside his skull. He wondered if his kids were okay, if they'd wake up to find a bulldog-faced stranger in their house instead of their father. What was he doing back here? He'd promised to leave the case alone and focus on his family, and he'd deserted them yet again.

Sorry Billie, he said.

He'd been offered therapy when Billie had been taken, of course. Bingo had practically stuffed the fliers for bereavement groups into his hand, to the point where he had almost screamed at him.

"She's not fucking dead, Barry!"

But one afternoon, when the darkness had been so powerful that he wasn't sure he even had it in him to pick up Alice from school, he'd driven to Victoria Embankment with Moira in the back seat and watched a dozen or so people walk into a therapy session. It had been like watching a procession of shadow puppets, hollow figures emptied by grief.

I won't be like them, he'd told himself. *I can't give up hope.*

And he'd floored it.

He thought of them now, those poor souls. He wondered how many of them had survived their loss, and how many of them had given up.

"Wait a minute," he said. "The therapy group."

He walked back to Savage.

"Have you got the list of people who attended?"

"Oh, uh, sure," she said, rummaging through her files before handing him a folder greasy with dust and disuse. "Hard copies. Like I said, some people didn't give their names."

But some had, Kett saw. He flicked through the registers until he found Figg's trauma group, scanning the names and seeing both Stillwater and Percival. There were seven other people on the list, two of whom were listed as 'anonymous'. The other five, though, had their full names and phone numbers.

"What are you looking for?" Savage asked.

"Maybe nothing," he replied, sitting next to her. "But Figg was using his therapy sessions as a recruitment drive for psychopaths, right?"

"Yeah," said Savage, leaning in. "You think it might not just be Stillwater and Percival?"

"Can we check these names?" Kett asked, handing her the list. "Flag anything suspicious, anything out of the ordinary."

Savage carried the list to the computer, typing the information into the database. She hit the keys so hard the sound of it echoed around the room.

"Uh, Mayhew's up North," she said. "Gatward's dead."

"Local?"

"Spain," she said. "Sanford... Yeah, Alan Sanford is still in Norwich. Well, just outside. Hang on." She typed a little more and Kett took a moment to rest his eyes. "He attended the group after he was hit by a police car during a chase. They were chasing somebody else, not him. Fractured his femur and his tailbone."

"Ouch," said Kett.

"Let me check his social media," she went on as she drummed the keyboard. "He's uh, fifty-six, works as a copyright lawyer out in the Broadland industrial park, although he's halfway retired. Divorced, wife and kids live in Surrey."

"That's all on his Facebook?" Kett asked.

"If you know where to look."

"Doesn't exactly sound like a serial killer," said Kett. "Who's next."

When Savage didn't answer he turned to her. Her face was so close to the screen he could see the glow reflected in her eyes.

"Savage?"

"It's..." she frowned. "There haven't been any updates on his socials for the last two months, by the look of it."

Kett got up, walking to her side. On screen was a balding, mutton-faced man in glasses smiling for the camera. There was hardly anything on his page except for cricket.

"The Ashes have just finished," said Kett. "Seems like the sort of thing he'd brag about."

"And yet nothing," said Savage.

"Where does he live?"

Savage hammered the keyboard a little more.

"Trowse, sir. It's a village south of the city. Very close."

"I remember," said Kett. "There's a broad there, a big one. Boats and canoes and stuff."

"And an artificial ski slope," Savage said. "Not much else past that apart from woodland."

No, there was something else there, Kett was sure of it. He'd passed it once when he was younger and his mum had taken a wrong turn while driving along the river. Savage seemed to remember as well, because she suddenly twisted around in her chair.

"The sewage treatment plant," she said. "It's down there."

"The smell," said Kett, the revelation blasting the fog from his mind.

"We should tell the boss," Savage said, scraping her chair back as she stood.

"I'll do it," Kett said. "You're driving."

AS FAR AS HUNCHES WENT, it wasn't the best Kett had ever had. He was looking for a house owned by a man who had once attended a therapy group run by their main suspect, a man with no prior convictions who seemed to have lived his entire life by the book.

But a hunch was a hunch, and right now they didn't have much else to go on.

"Check it out," said Clare on the phone. Kett heard the man stifle a yawn. "From a distance. If you see anything that leads you to believe our men are there, or the paper girls, then you call for backup immediately. Clear?"

"Clear, sir," said Kett, ending the call. "He didn't sound impressed."

Savage muttered a reply, her attention on the road as she roared downhill at almost sixty miles per hour. She slowed as they neared a red light, but only to about fifty-five, and Kett had to close his eyes as a taxi screeched to a halt while turning the corner.

"I'm not going to ask where you learned to drive," he said, tasting his pulse on his tongue.

"Dodgems," she replied.

"What?"

"Dodgems, I used to ride them all the time when I was a kid. We lived out at Hemsby and my granddad used to take me on them. Told me I was a natural."

"That doesn't fill me with confidence," Kett said. "Roundabout!"

She didn't even slow this time, just shot straight over it, the fire station a blur as they roared by. The car almost took off when it crested the humpback bridge beyond, then a few seconds later Savage steered them onto another road, this one narrower and surrounded on both sides by woods and fields.

"Is it much further?" Kett asked, feeling the chips and chicken balls trying to climb out of his stomach.

"Couple of miles," she replied.

"Turn the blues off," he said. "Best that nobody sees us coming."

She did as he asked and the lane stopped flashing. Luckily she kept the speed down as they wound their way past the lake—the water as black as ink in the night. The car's headlights turned the trees into a carnival of shape and shadow, weird figures seeming to dance between the trunks and hang from the branches. There wasn't a soul in sight, but owls screeched from the forest like they were sending out a warning, and the eyes of nocturnal creatures glinted from the riverbank.

The smell hit him as they turned a corner, the deep, rich, cloying stench of treated sewage. His eyes began to water instantly, and for a moment he thought it was the final straw, that he was actually going to be sick. He swallowed it down, breathing through his mouth.

"I'd forgotten how bad it got," groaned Savage, one hand to her nose. "It's like the Bog of Eternal Stench. And this is at night. Imagine how awful it is during the day, especially in the summer."

"Bad enough to linger on somebody's clothes? Somebody's hair?"

"If you got close enough to it," she replied. "And for long enough. It's... it's definitely distinctive. How did Stillwater's girlfriend describe it? Sweet? It's not sweet."

She was right, it wasn't sweet. But there *was* a strange sweetness to it, an undertone of something floral—maybe the chemicals they used to treat the waste. Kett's heart was drumming again, and this time it was nothing to do with Savage's driving. They passed beneath a graffiti-strewn concrete flyover which seemed totally out of place here in the wilderness, cars and trucks rumbling over it at motorway speeds.

"The A47," Savage explained.

Ahead, the road ended, becoming nothing more than a strip of gravel and dirt. Kett grunted as the car bounced in a pothole as big as a garden pond. To his right was a barn, complete with a silo and outbuildings. It looked abandoned, the windows either boarded up or broken. Most of the walls had holes in them, one side of the barn almost totally collapsed. There was no sign of life inside.

"That's Alan Sanford's place up ahead," Savage said, nodding through the windscreen. The car's headlights fought against the night, illuminating the front wall of an impressive farmhouse. It, too, looked like it was in a state of neglect, the mortar around the bricks and flint crumbling like rotting gums around teeth. The windows were dark.

"Cut the lights," Kett said. "And back up a little."

Savage switched off the headlights, the track instantly swamped by darkness. She reversed slowly until they were under the bulk of the flyover. The farmhouse was a deeper shadow against the night, looking like a whale breaching the surface of a fathomless ocean. But as the echo of the lights ebbed from his vision Kett made out a weak glow from an upstairs window.

"Somebody's in," said Savage, squinting.

"Let's go find out who," Kett replied, popping his door. The smell from the sewage works instantly flooded his nose and mouth, making him feel like he was drowning. He coughed into the crook of his arm, pushing the door shut behind him. Savage was by his side, one hand on her radio.

"We should call it in," she said.

"There's still nothing worth shouting about," Kett replied as a truck growled overhead. "Let's check it out first. Any sign of trouble, I'll call for backup. I promise. I don't want another Brandon Walker kicking my arse."

"What happened, sir?" Savage asked. Kett looked at her, frowning. "You said you'd tell me one day, why you don't like to wait for the cavalry."

He sighed, then nodded.

"It'll have to be the short version," he said. "I was a brand new detective, right off the carousel. I chased a domestic violence call, up in Elephant and Castle. Uniforms couldn't get there so I took it. There was a guy going crazy, threatening to shoot his wife and kids. Backup was on the way so I waited."

Kett dropped his head, seeing it now, hearing the screams, the thumps, the sobs.

"Ten minutes, that's all it was. By the time the squad arrived and knocked the door down he'd strangled both of them. No gun, just his bare fucking hands. The wife survived, but the little boy didn't. He was three."

The same age as Evie, he thought.

Savage cleared her throat, shaking her head.

"That wasn't your fault," she said.

"All in the past," Kett lied. "But now you know. Ten minutes is all it takes. Come on."

Without the car's headlights the path was treacherous, loose rocks and gravel doing their best to trip them up. Kett stepped onto the dry grass of the verge, brambles tugging at his trousers like a dead man's fingers until they reached a junction ahead. To the left was the access road to the sewage plant. Ahead, the farmhouse loomed over them. This close, the glow from the upstairs window was barely any brighter than before, and Kett saw heavy boards nailed to the frame. He tapped Savage's elbow, pointing to them, and she nodded back, whispering a word.

"Weird."

It got weirder still as they walked along the face of the farmhouse. The front door was original, and only about five foot high. It was also sealed with a monstrous padlock. A handwritten note by the letterbox read: *Deliveries and building materials to rear.*

"Building materials," whispered Kett. His Spidey-sense was going into overdrive.

He peeked around the corner, seeing a silver Mercedes parked in the gravel drive between the main building and a brick and flint workshop. Past that the bloated farmhouse stretched back into the night, made up of a cluster of mismatched pieces. Another faint light burned through a window ahead, thick curtains drawn across it.

"That Stillwater's car?" Kett said quietly, and Savage shook her head.

"It's not Figg's either, and Percival didn't drive."

"Sanford's then," Kett said. "He's home."

They kept walking, skirting around the edge of the property. Other than the sewage works and the crumbling barn there were no other buildings in sight. The farmhouse stood like an island in the night, impossibly still.

Not empty, though. Kett could feel it.

They were walking along the side wall when another clue clicked into place.

"Scaffolding," Kett said, nodding to the back of the farmhouse where a metal scaffold climbed the old wall like ivy. Hulking shapes sat beneath it, making Kett think of immense guard dogs, and it was only when they got closer that he saw they were actually builder's supplies—tonne bags of sand and hardcore.

"Okay," said Kett. "I've seen enough. Call it in."

"Yes, sir," Savage said, and she was reaching for her radio when a scream cut through the night.

CHAPTER TWENTY-EIGHT

For a second, Kett couldn't move.

The scream hit him like a punch to the solar plexus, and he almost doubled up at the force of it.

Then the adrenaline took over and he was running—heading down the side of the farmhouse towards the towering forest of scaffolding. He heard Savage call his name but he ignored her, scanning the house for a way in. The ground floor windows were boarded up, and there wasn't a door in sight.

He reached the scaffolding just as another scream lit up the dark. There was no doubting it, that was the voice of a young girl. Kett swore, looking up. The first-floor windows were all covered with tarpaulin that flapped lazily in the breeze, and he could see well enough that there was no glass in them.

"... and come now!" Savage hissed into her radio as she caught up to him.

He grabbed a scaffold bar and hauled himself up, bracing his boot on the slippery metal. Savage was younger and fitter, and by the time he'd got himself off the ground she had reached the first level. She offered him a hand, pulling him up. From here there was a ladder and Kett took the lead again, climbing to the platform that ran beneath the windows.

He could hear more voices now, shouts—and was that laughter? High-pitched and cruel. The scream had turned to a hysterical sob, one that drove Kett to the nearest window. He pulled back the tarp, seeing absolutely nothing at all.

"Here," Savage said, handing him her torch. He beamed it inside to see a bare room, the door ajar.

He paused, but only for a moment. Running in like this would be the stupidest move. It could cost him his life, and possibly even the lives of three children and a young PC. In ten minutes the entire Norfolk Constabulary would be on site, guns and dogs and a hundred people ready to take down Figg and his little posse.

But he'd waited before. He'd waited ten minutes, and somebody had died.

He clambered through the window, the heavy tarp flapping in his face and doing its best to keep him out. He didn't have a weapon but Savage was right behind him, her telescopic baton gripped in her fist. She caught him looking.

"You want it?" she whispered, offering him the weapon. He shook his head.

"You're a better shot than I am."

More laughter from deep inside the house, muffled but close enough that Kett could tell it wasn't just from one person.

"Please, no, please, no."

The words broke Kett's heart, and they stoked a fury inside him that was almost overpowering. He marched to the door, wincing as the hinges screamed.

The laughter stopped.

Kett paused, his heart pulsing inside his throat, inside his fingertips.

"Let me go," came that voice. "I won't say anything, I promise, you don't have to kill me. Please. I don't want you to."

Beyond the door was a corridor, its floor bare, its walls crumbling plaster. The voice was coming from up ahead and Kett headed that way as quietly as he dared. There was no more laughter, but he could hear heavy footsteps from somewhere beneath him.

A junction, the left-hand turn leading to the front of the house, the right-hand one ending at a door. Kett looked at Savage, gesturing to the door with the torch. He set off to the left, the ancient floor playing a string concerto beneath him. This stretch of corridor didn't last long, branching to the right. Kett stopped, barely breathing.

There was another door ahead, light spilling out of it.

He glanced back, seeing Savage enter the room behind him. He left her to it, advancing in a crouch towards the door, seeing a wooden chair draped with wire. He walked a little further—a second chair, more wire, the floor here drenched with fresh blood.

We're too late.

Taking a deep breath, he peeked around the door to see the rest of the room.

One more chair.

And this one had somebody in it.

Fuck.

Kett ran into the room and dropped to his knees beside the occupied chair, the torch rolling across the boards. There was a girl in it, her hands bound behind her, her feet held tight by wire. She was still, her lank hair plastered over her face, her fingertips black from the lack of blood. The room stank of piss and shit, vomit and blood—and rot, too.

Too late, he thought again, pushing her hair out of the way then pressing his hand to her neck.

The girl was warm—and there, a pulse, as weak as the flap of a butterfly's wings.

She groaned, her mouth opening. Her lips were as dry as sandpaper, her tongue swollen. Even though her face was streaked with blood and dirt and tears Kett knew who she was.

"Delia," he said. "Delia, I'm a policeman, you're safe."

The girl groaned again. Kett heard Savage enter the room quietly behind him.

"It's Delia Crossan," he said. "She's okay, but she needs—"

Something cracked across the back of Kett's skull, and for a second he felt his conscious mind break away. The world flashed white, then black, then white again, the pain flooding his head like boiling water. He was on the floor, he realised, and by the time he'd rolled onto his back, his limbs as stubborn as a puppet's, there was a man standing above him. His vision swam so much he couldn't make out who it was—it was as if the man's face was plain, except for two x's for eyes—but there was no mistaking what he held in his hand.

A crowbar.

The man lifted it, and it was his laugh—as cold as you can get—that gave him away.

"Christian," Kett said, tasting blood. Just speaking made the room cartwheel around his head. "Christian, you don't have to do this. It's not too late."

Stillwater stood there, the mask bulging then retreating

with every breath, his crowbar raised like an executioner's blade.

"We know Figg made you do it," Kett said, panting. "You want a get out of jail free card like last time then you know what you have to do. Help us bring him in."

"You're nothing," said Stillwater. "A man like you could never understand."

Stillwater's whole body tensed and then released, the crowbar beginning its descent.

Savage entered the room, her baton a blur as she swung it at the back of Stillwater's leg. It was like watching an old tree snap beneath a lightning strike, a brutal crack echoing from wall to wall as the man folded in two. He fell onto his back, the crowbar spinning out of his hand. He gasped wetly, trying to get a breath in, and when he did he unleashed an awful, howling shriek.

"You okay, sir?" Savage asked, holding out her free hand. Kett took it, letting her pull him up. The room was still moving, and he was almost certain he was going to puke, but he managed to nod.

"Secure him," he said. "Stay with the girl."

"No offence," she replied as she dug out her cuffs. "Maybe you should stay with her. I'll go after the others."

Kett shook his head, walking past Savage to get to the door. He stopped on the way to scoop up the crowbar, then he turned to her, squinting through the pain.

"Thanks," he said.

"Go get those fuckers," she replied. She reached into her pocket and pulled out her little silver police whistle, handing it to him. "If you need me, just blow."

He nodded, walking out of the room. To the left the corridor stretched towards a flight of stairs that descended into darkness. There were streaks of blood on the walls, dry but not old. Kett gripped the crowbar as he dropped onto the first step, the old wood crying out in alarm. Together with Stillwater's shriek, it meant that any hope of surprising the other kidnappers was shot.

"Figg," he called out, his voice cracking. "Percival. We know you're here. The house is surrounded. Come out now and I won't cave your fucking heads in."

Nothing. He couldn't hear laughter, or the screams of the girls—just the ringing in his ears and the thunderstroke of blood as it washed through his aching skull.

"Your choice," he grunted as he reached the bottom step. There was another hallway down here, two doors ahead and a third behind him which looked like it led into a kitchen. There was a definite draft coming from that direction, so he marched to the kitchen door and peered inside.

"Figg?" he shouted. "We know everything. We know about the group, we know you recruited Stillwater and Percival, Sanford too. We know you planned this whole operation. You don't have a hope in hell of getting out of this, unless you hand the girls over right now."

The kitchen was dark, except for a light that streamed from under a pantry door. Kett slapped the wall until he found a switch, flicking it. Reluctantly, a bank of bare bulbs in the ceiling blinked on, revealing a farmhouse kitchen that looked perfectly ordinary.

Except for the blood.

It was everywhere, pooling on the flagstones, splashed over the counters, welded to the AGA. It was dark, congealed, old. Whoever it had belonged to was long dead.

"Percival," Kett yelled as he walked to the pantry. "We know they forced you. We know this isn't your doing. Come out now, help us save those girls, and I'll do my best to get you out of this."

He used the crowbar to open the pantry door, screwing his face up when the smell hit him. Not sewage, this time. Not unwashed flesh.

This was the smell of the dead.

No.

There was a body in here, buried beneath a pile of blankets. All Kett could see was an arm, almost entirely drained of blood, its fingers contorted into talons. He snatched in a breath, his lungs empty.

Was it Maisie?

Was it Connie?

Or did both girls lie there, entwined beneath that stinking shroud?

He checked behind him then ducked down, grabbing the top blanket and pulling it away. A face came into view, waxy and mask-like in death.

A *man's* face.

He recognised it from the picture he'd seen less than an hour ago. Alan Sanford, the owner of the house. His throat was a jagged mess where somebody had sliced it open, everything from the neck down drenched in an apron of cold, dried blood.

Kett breathed again, pulling the rest of the blankets off to make sure Sanford was alone. Then he stood up, fighting the vertigo as he walked out of the pantry.

They'd just been here, he'd just heard them—laughing, screaming, pleading.

Where had they gone?

"Maisie?" he called out. "Connie? If you can hear me, if you're free to move, then follow the sound of my voice. I'm here to help you. I'm going to get you out."

"No, you're not."

The voice came from the hallway, and Kett stumbled towards it, exiting the kitchen with his crowbar raised.

Figg stood in the doorway at the other end of the corridor, past the stairs, grinning at Kett through his goatee. His eyes held nothing of the warmth they'd had when Kett had first met him, they were dark, and small, and full of something primal, something *dangerous*.

Clamped in one hand, held by her scalp, was Maisie Malone.

In his other hand, pressed to her neck, was a knife.

"You're too late, Robbie," said Figg, digging the blade into Maisie's throat hard enough to release a bead of blood. She opened her mouth but no scream came out, just bubbles of silent terror. Figg was smiling, but he was furious. Kett could see the rage boiling in his every movement. "I know the house isn't surrounded, so why don't you do us all a favour and *fuck off*."

"Maisie," said Kett, speaking to the girl. "Just stay calm, you're going to be okay."

"You say that like it's true," Figg said. "But here's the thing. I'm leaving now. You take one step in my direction and I'll empty her like I did that pussy Sanford, like I did the other little bitch."

Connie, Kett thought, a wave of dark anger pulsing through him.

Figg retreated into the room. Maisie walked clumsily with him, whispering *nonononononono* with every breath.

"One step, Robbie, and you end her."

Figg smiled again, then he lunged to the side and they vanished into the shadows.

CHAPTER TWENTY-NINE

ONE STEP WOULD END HER.

But one step could save her, too.

Kett counted to five, listening to the thump of movement from the other room. There was a soft scream, a grunt, then nothing.

He moved as fast as he dared, the crowbar still locked in his sweaty grip as he charged through the door. One look told him everything he needed to know: it was a living room, empty, and the bay window on the far side was open.

Kett ran through the dark, reaching the window in time to see Figg struggling away from the house. He pushed Maisie in front of him, hard enough that she spilled to the ground, sobbing. Then he looked back.

Kett ducked, trying to make sense of the tornado of his thoughts. Figg was insane, he'd kill the girl the moment he knew she wasn't useful any more. If he saw Kett coming through the window, Maisie was dead.

He had to be smart.

He doubled back, running through the kitchen and out

the door. He was at the back of the house, but even from here he could hear the distant cavalry-horn of sirens.

He set off across a builder's yard of sand and brick, stumbling blindly. At one point he fell, the crowbar ringing off the ground like a church bell. He scooped it up, taking great, gulping breaths of sewage air as he climbed over the crumbling remains of a wall to see nothing but the night.

Stupid! He'd lost them. If Figg got away then—

No, there, two silhouettes against the trees, heading in the direction of the sewage plant. Kett pulled the night over him like a cloak, chasing after them. He could hear the percussive thump of a helicopter coming this way, and more sirens now.

They weren't going to get here in time.

Kett pushed onwards, tripping over knots of bramble and grass before hitting the dirt road that led to the treatment works. He could hear Figg up ahead, he was practically screaming at Maisie to hurry up.

Then another voice replied—not Maisie at all. It was a man, his voice whimpering, pathetic.

"No, Raymond, no!"

Lochy Percival.

The road curved to the right, a cluster of buildings ahead. The smell here was so thick it was almost liquid, Kett practically swimming through it as he chased the two men and their prey. He could just about see them climbing over a chainlink fence, Maisie screaming as she landed hard. Mercifully there were lights ahead, Figg and Maisie coming into view like they'd stepped onto a theatre stage, Percival limping after them.

They were all running out of steam, and so was Kett, but he put his head down and closed the distance between them. He scaled the fence and stumbled through a low hedge onto grass, seeing the giant, circular aeration basins ahead. Figg had stopped by the edge of the nearest one, his wheezing breaths like a siren going off. He looked back and saw Kett, then he grabbed Maisie around the neck and held her tight. Percival was right next to them, his hands on his knees as he sucked in air.

"This is how you want it to end?" Figg shouted, the tip of his blade pressed against Maisie's cheek. "You're a fucking idiot, Kett. You never knew when to listen."

"Hey," Kett said, slowing to a walk. He tightened his grip on the crowbar, wishing he was fast enough to cover the twenty yards between him and Figg in a single stride. His head was pounding, every heartbeat like a flare going off behind his eyes. "Just put the knife down, Figg. It's over."

"Over for her," Figg replied. Behind him the arm swung in a lazy circle around the giant basin, churning the stench of sewage into the air. The chopper was closing in, and the trees behind Kett were full of flashing blue lights. Figg glanced at them, licking his lips, but Kett turned his attention to Percival.

"It's not too late for you either, Lochy," he said. "None of this is your fault."

"It is." Percival spoke the words through a heaving sob. "It is. She's dead and it's my fault."

"Delia?" said Kett. "She's alive. Your niece is okay."

Percival looked up, making a sound like he was choking.

"She's okay?" he asked. "Stillwater said—"

"Stillwater's in handcuffs," Kett said. "Delia's dehydrated, and in shock, but she'll live."

"Christian failed," sneered Figg, wrestling with Maisie as she struggled to free herself. "What a surprise. All talk and no trousers that one. But you're too late for Connie. Lochy made sure of that."

Figg's grin made Kett want to stave his face in. But Percival was shaking his head.

"I couldn't," he said. "I couldn't do it. She was so... so young. I'm sorry. I'm sorry. I'm sorry."

"Connie Byrne's *alive*?" Kett asked. Percival nodded.

"I hid her in the basement. I told her to be quiet."

"You fucking coward," said Figg. He pulled the knife away from Maisie's face and jabbed it at Percival—almost close enough to skewer his eyeball. Percival reeled back, covering his face and whining. "You fucking coward! I knew you couldn't do it."

Kett wasn't watching Percival. His eyes were locked on Maisie—and hers on Kett.

"I should finish you off right now, you *cunt*," Figg growled at Percival, loosening his grip on the young girl.

Kett nodded to Maisie, and she knew exactly what to do. With a scream of defiance she broke free of Figg's grip and bolted across the grass.

"Go!" Kett roared, running towards her. "Go! Go! Go!"

Figg's face was a carnival mask of delirium—a sick grin sliced from ear to ear. He lunged at Percival, the blade sinking into the other man's throat like he was made of butter. Percival clamped a hand to the wound, his eyes bulging, his mouth opening into a perfect O as the blood began to pour between his fingers. Figg wasn't watching, he was sprinting after the girl, his arms and legs like pistons.

"Run!" shouted Kett.

Maisie was halfway between them now, glancing back after every other step. Kett put his head down, ready to smash Figg's face to the other side of his head. He expected the girl to run past him but she didn't, she threw herself into his arms, wrapping herself around him, blinding him.

"Please!" she screamed in his ear, her grip on him suffocating. "Please!"

He spun, angled his head to see Figg just feet away.

Kett shoved Maisie hard, sending her flying. Then Figg's blade punched into his left shoulder.

"Fucker!" Figg screamed, spraying spit into his face. He pulled the knife out with a gout of blood and an explosion of ice cold agony. Then he rammed it forward again. Kett angled his body out of the way, bringing up his other arm—the one that held the crowbar. He swung wildly, missing Figg and spinning around in a circle. Figg was lunging again, the blade slicing across Kett's chest.

Kett tried to punch with his left hand but his injured shoulder wouldn't let him. Instead, he lifted his boot and slammed it into Figg's knee. The pop it made was like a gunshot and the man staggered away before falling onto his backside.

The world had slipped off its axis, careening into the void of space. Figg was retreating on his arse, jabbing the blade into thin air like a scorpion's tail. There was absolutely no doubt that his leg was broken, bent at an impossible angle at the knee.

"Fucker," he grunted as he went. "Fucker. Fucker."

Kett dropped the crowbar, pushing his hand against the wound in his shoulder. The blood that poured from him was as hot as boiling water—and there was a lot of it. He looked at Maisie, the girl somehow still standing after everything she'd been through.

"See those lights," he croaked, nodding to the trees. There had to have been half a dozen police cars over there now, the chopper hovering overhead with its searchlight blazing. "Run to them, and don't stop. Tell them where we are."

Maisie didn't move. She looked at Figg, her eyes narrowing. It was the expression of somebody beaten and bent by a harrowing trauma, somebody who would never be the same again.

"I want to see it," she said. "I want to see him dead."

"He's not going to die," Kett said, picking up the crowbar again—the metal almost sliding out of his blood-slick fingers. "He's going to prison for a long, long time."

"You think?" said Figg, still backing away. The basin of sewage sat right behind him, that arm rotating. "You haven't won this one yet. How'd you even know it was me?"

"Come with me now and I'll tell you everything," said Kett, advancing.

"But you're so fucking stupid," said Figg. "You failed."

"Failed?" asked Kett. "You're the one lying down there, I'm the one about to reel you in. Three girls back in their beds, three arseholes behind bars." He glanced at Percival, who was crumpled on the grass, as still as a boulder. "Well, behind bars or dead. Either works for me. I'd say I was the winner here."

Figg laughed, but it was brittle. He had nowhere left to go.

"You failed your wife," he said. "You failed Billie."

If Maisie hadn't been watching, he'd have happily finished Figg off right here and now and claimed self-defence. Hell, he got the feeling he could do it anyway and the young girl would back him up. He swallowed, holding the crowbar so tightly that his hand ached. Somehow, Figg was clambering to his feet, all his weight on his good leg.

"Don't," Kett said. "Drop the knife."

"You're so stupid," Figg said again, swaying like a drunk. "How could you not know what happened to her? It's so fucking simple. Even I figured it out."

"What?" said Kett. "What are you talking about?"

"You really don't know, do you?" said Figg, his face twisting in pain as he tried to move his leg. He almost fell again, sheer force of will keeping him up. "See, at first I thought you were in on it, because I didn't believe anyone could be so dense. But you really don't know what happened to your wife."

He laughed again, a sound of pure delight.

"If you know something, I'll happily beat it out of you in the nick," Kett said. "But I'm guessing you're full of shit."

"If I'm full of shit, then ask me about *him*," Figg said, grinning. "Ask me how Billie knew the Pig Man. Ask me what it has to do with that Khan boy. You coppers, you think we're all Jack the Rippers, working alone. You think we don't talk to each other. But we do, we all share, we all compete, we all follow each other on fucking Facebook. You think I don't know, but I do, I know where she—"

Percival thumped into Figg so fast that at first Kett couldn't figure out what was going on. Lochy was drenched in blood and halfway to death, but somehow he managed to wrap his arms around Figg and knock him backwards. Figg screamed, his face contorting with pain as he tried to stop Percival from grabbing the knife. The pair of them performed a grotesque, limping ballet across the spotlit grass, grunting like pigs.

"No!" Kett shouted, running for the men.

He was too late. Percival took the knife, almost fumbled it, then drove it down into Figg's neck. Figg threw a punch, grappling with his attacker even as he sprayed a fountain of blood from his mouth.

"No!" Kett yelled again, almost on them.

Percival stabbed again, and again, the two men stumbling wildly until, with gargled shrieks, they fell into the basin of sewage. Kett skidded to a halt beside them, reaching for them, then the rotating arm swung by again and they were gone.

"No!" he said as he dropped onto all fours. He rested his head on the grass and felt blood pour down his neck from the wound in his shoulder, filling his ear. "Please."

A hand on his arm, a young voice.

"Mister? Hey, are you okay?"

He wasn't okay. He was bleeding out. Already he felt empty, the husk of his body as light as air, ready to be cast away by the slightest breeze. He wasn't even sure if his eyes were closed, or if they simply didn't work any more. All he could see against the black were the faces of his daughters, the three girls he would never see again.

He slapped his pocket, trying to work the whistle loose. Maisie must have helped him, because he suddenly heard it —a shrill call that would bring help.

Savage's lucky whistle.

But not lucky for him, not today.

Not lucky for Billie, either. Or for his girls.

He lay on the ground and felt Maisie's arms around him, he heard the whistle blow, and he heard shouts as people ran this way.

Not lucky enough, he thought.

And that was that.

CHAPTER THIRTY

It was the smell of tea that woke him. Hot, aromatic, deliciously strong.

Kett tried to sit up, then immediately stopped. Pain radiated from his shoulder into his chest, his neck, his arm. It was muted—tempered by some serious painkillers, if his suspicions were right—but it was still agony. His head, too, was pounding.

But that smell was definitely making him feel better.

He settled for opening his eyes, managing one and then the other. The response was a round of shrill cheers that was almost deafening. He recognised them instantly, breaking into a painful smile. By the time his vision had cleared Alice and Evie were on the bed, clambering up his torso in order to plant a hail of kisses on his face.

"Whoa! Whoa!" yelled DI Porter. The big man was wrestling with Moira, and by the look of it he was losing. The baby was doing her special move where she lifted her arms over her head, allowing herself to slip out of any grip like she'd been greased. Porter almost dropped her, his face a mask of panic as he lowered her to the floor.

Kett laughed, instantly regretting it.

"Easy," he wheezed to the two older girls as they continued their loving assault. "Let your old man breathe."

"Daddy! I didn't think you were ever going to wake up," said Alice, genuinely upset.

"How long have I been out?" said Kett, gently pushing them away with his good hand while searching the fog of his memories.

"Not long," said Porter. "They're not even serving breakfast yet. The girls have just got here. Like, five minutes ago. Clare's wife dropped them off."

"But it was a really scary five minutes," said Alice, burrowing her head into his good shoulder.

"Okay, that's quite enough," said a nurse, walking into the room and whisking both girls off the bed in a single motion. "Your father is a very brave man, but he needs to rest. I'm sure your friend here will take you to visit the vending machine."

Porter's eyes widened.

"*All* of them?" he said. "At the same time?"

"Yeah, and you'd better be quick," said Kett, nodding at Moira who was already waddling out the door. Alice and Evie chased after her, all three of them laughing their heads off—their dad already forgotten.

"Oh shit! Uh, I mean shittlesticks, no, *shizzle*sticks," Porter spluttered as he followed. He turned back before he left. "Oh, I made you tea."

"*Seriously*?" Kett said, the disappointment almost unbearable. He looked to the table beside the bed and sighed at the cup of milky nothingness that sat there feeling sorry for itself. It wasn't hot, aromatic, or deliciously strong.

"I used three teabags!" Porter's voice echoed down the hall.

"Did he empty the tea out of them first?" the nurse asked, raising an eyebrow. She smiled at Kett. "You took a bad puncture wound to the shoulder, but he missed your brachial artery by some way. The wound on your chest is just a slash, but it needed stitches and it will leave a scar. It will be a while before you're carrying your girls again."

There was a knock on the door, and an angry, hairy-nosed face loomed in.

"I hope it was worth it," Kett said to the nurse. He turned to Superintendent Colin Clare. "Sir."

Clare walked to the bed, and Kett was happy to see Savage right behind him. Neither of them had had any sleep, by the look of it, although Clare looked a lot worse for it than the young PC. Both of them smiled. At least, Kett *thought* Clare was smiling. It was hard to be sure because he still looked angry.

"The paper girls?" Kett asked.

"Alive," said Clare. "All three of them, thank Christ. They're being treated for dehydration. Those bastards didn't feed them, and from the sound of it only Percival was giving them anything to drink—and hardly a drop at that. Delia Crossan had it worst, she was in that room for almost a week. I don't know how she survived."

"Girls are tougher than you think," said Savage, perching on the end of the bed. Clare nodded.

"We found Connie in the basement with a bottle of Coke and some garlic bread," he said. "You know what that was about?"

Kett tried to sit up and Clare helped, fluffing his pillows.

"I think each man was supposed to snatch and then kill one of the girls," Kett said. "Figg picked Maisie, Stillwater was supposed to murder Delia. Connie was Percival's, but he couldn't do it. He hid her and lied to Figg. It was happening as we arrived. Any later and they'd be dead, I think."

"That's messed up," said Clare. "Utterly. In all my years, I don't think I've ever known anything like this."

"It was all Figg," said Kett. "He masterminded the whole thing. Did he survive?"

"Figg?" Clare laughed, but there wasn't a lot of humour there. "No. We fished them both out of the tank. Figg died with shit in his lungs, he drowned in it."

It was Kett's turn to spit out a bitter laugh.

"The last thing I said to him was you're full of shit," he said.

"Well, I don't believe in poetic justice," Clare went on. "But hey, you can't deny it in his case. Percival died of blood loss. I don't even know how he did what he did. Maisie told us he jumped Figg, pushed him in?"

Kett sighed, then nodded.

You think I don't know, but I do, I know where she—

Where she *what*? Had Figg been about to tell Kett where Billie had been taken? He would never know. But he had mentioned somebody, hadn't he? The Pig Man? Or had Kett dreamed it after passing out?

No, he hadn't dreamed it. It was a clue. It was a lead. It was *hope.*

I'll find you.

He screwed his eyes shut, then opened them again to see Clare staring at the tea beside his bed with disgust.

"Porter's been in then," the boss said.

"He's taken my girls for snacks," Kett replied.

"Poor sod," said Clare.

"Stillwater?" asked Kett. "What happened to him?"

"He's alive," said Savage. "Although he won't be walking straight again. He's in custody, looking at a long time in prison—not just for the abductions, but for the murder of Evelyn Crossan, too. Delia's mother. No lawyer on earth will get him out of this one."

"Good," said Kett. "It's over, then."

"It's over," said Clare. "You did good. Both of you. Savage, I'm putting you on the carousel. The sooner you're out of yellow and dressed in a suit, the better."

"Thank you, sir," Savage replied, beaming.

"I have no doubt that in ten years or so you'll be running the place," Clare went on.

"And me, sir?" Kett asked.

He was answered by a chorus of laughter as Moira waddled into the room, Alice and Evie on either side of her. Each of them was carrying a chocolate bar. Porter was close behind, panic-stricken.

"Are they all here? Where's the baby? This is so fudging stressful!"

This time, even Clare laughed. He turned to Kett.

"Take some time," he said. "Some *real* time. Spend it with the girls. You've earned it. And when you're better, let's talk."

"About a new case?" Kett asked, and Clare pulled a face.

"Christ no! Let's talk about getting your meddling arse back to London."

The boss laughed, and so did Kett, clutching his shoulder as the pain burned out of it.

"Now, I've got to go fill in the paperwork to cover the gaping holes you two left in your wake," Clare said, leaving the room. "But thank you, Robbie. Thank you, *both* of you. You saved those girls."

Kett nodded to him, then closed his eyes again to give his brain a rest.

"Daddy, did you save them?" Evie asked through a mouthful of chocolate.

"He did," Porter replied. "He's a proper hero, your old man."

"Give it up," muttered Kett. "We all saved those girls."

"Well I think you're quite cool," said Alice.

"Gee, thanks," Kett replied, looking at his girls. God, how he loved them. "Quite cool works for me. Come here. I missed you all."

They sat on the edge of the bed, and Porter dropped Moira into Kett's lap. He hugged the baby, who was too interested in her Wispa to even notice.

"I won't leave you again, okay?" he said. "I promise. From now on in, no more police work. Just family time."

"Yay!" said Alice, leaning in for a cuddle.

"Ay!" echoed Moira.

"Yay," added Evie. She frowned. "Daddy, I need a poo."

"Of course you do," he said.

"I'll take her," said Savage, holding out a hand and helping Evie to the floor.

"Thank you," said Kett. "And I don't just mean for this. Thank you for what you did back in the house. You saved *me*."

She smiled, then led Evie to the door—looking back as she walked through it.

"See you in a minute," she said. "And don't worry, I'll grab you a proper cup of tea on the way back."

SOME LEGENDS CAN KILL YOU

A DCI ROBERT KETT NOVEL

ALEX SMITH

THE INTERNATIONALLY BESTSELLING SERIES

Some legends can kill you.

When a young woman is brutally murdered in the Norfolk countryside, the locals blame Black Shuck—a legendary wild dog.

There's only one problem: the wounds weren't made by an animal.

DCI Robert Kett is battling a black dog of his own. With his wife still missing, and the injuries from his last case leaving him in constant pain, everything seems impossible—not least looking after his three young children.

When a second body appears, even bloodier than the last, Kett finds himself on a hunt for one of the most ruthless serial killers the country has ever seen.

A killer who may be hunting him, too.

You won't be able to put down this fast-paced British crime thriller from million-selling author Alex Smith.

PROLOGUE

Thursday

IT JUST WASN'T THE SAME WITHOUT THE DOG.

Maurice had been a little bastard, sure. Half pug, half god-only-knew-what-else, he had never *not* been neck-deep in cow shit on their daily walks across the fields. He'd spent most of his life trying to hump every fence post, grassy hillock, or bemused ewe he crossed paths with, even when he was pushing fourteen and his fur was more grey than black. Roger Carver had spent the best part of each walk either yelling at the dog, rescuing the dog, or carrying the dog home because his little legs were tired. Maurice had been a royal pain in the arse.

But what he wouldn't give now to have him back.

Roger sighed, a little more dramatically than he'd intended. The evening air was thick with dust, and the recently harvested corn-stubble crunched beneath his boots. To his left the fields stretched for miles, bright and open, sighing with relief now that the weight had been lifted from them. To his right was the woodland, dark and ancient, the trees already burnished with oranges and browns. Autumn was well and truly here, and it was going to be a cold one. He'd lived in this part of the world long enough to be able to judge the seasons, even in the notoriously unpredictable East Anglian climate.

"Not enjoying yourself, then," said Sally from half a dozen paces behind him. It sounded like an accusation, and when he glanced over his shoulder at her sour expression he knew that's exactly how she'd intended it. He felt a sudden rush of anger—maybe even hatred—and he swallowed it back down. He looked instinctively for the dog, that same awful hammer blow to his heart when he remembered Maurice wasn't there. That he'd never be there again.

Stupid little bastard.

"I'm fine," he said, hearing the passive aggression in his voice.

"Yes, you're *fine*," she shot back, thick with sarcasm. "You're always *fine*."

How had they got here, he and Sally? They'd only been together seven years. Surely that wasn't long enough for the foundations of their relationship to rot away. They were both young, he a couple of months north of thirty-five, she a few weeks south of it, with good jobs and no kids—no desire for kids, either. The world was theirs, and they'd been so keen to take it. Maurice had been their one commitment, the old dog the only thing keeping them on the leash. With him gone, anything was possible.

According to Sally, at least.

"Look," she said. "You admitted it yourself, he was in pain. It was his time."

They were approaching the end of the field, the ridges

of hard soil threatening to turn their ankles. Ahead, where the land met the woods, was a battered stile, and Roger knew that somewhere on it was a carving—*Rog + Sal + Maurice 4 eva*—that they'd made with Sal's apartment key when they'd first started dating.

"I know," Roger said. "It's fine. I said it's fine. What else do you want me to say? You killed my dog?"

The words were out of his mouth before he could stop them, but there was no taking them back. He heard Sally suck in a breath, braced himself for what was about to come. But she didn't reply, and when he looked back he saw that she'd stopped walking. There was enough sun left overhead for it to reflect in the tears that clustered in her eyes, that carved trails down her dusty cheeks.

"That's what you think?" she said.

Roger shrugged, cleared his throat. He reached out and took hold of the stile, the wood damp to the touch.

"No," he said. "But you insisted. You wouldn't let it go. He could've had surgery. He might have had years left."

Sally shook her head, her hands wrapped around her chest so tight that her white coat looked like a straitjacket.

"He was dying," she said. "The vet said so. I thought... I didn't march you in there. I thought this was what you wanted?"

"It's what *you* wanted," Roger said. "It's what you always wanted. You just wanted rid of him."

He waited for the pleas, for the apologies, for the excuses. But instead the sadness etched into her expression became something else.

"Go fuck yourself, Roger," she said.

She turned and walked away, stumbling in her welly boots.

"*What?*" Roger said, almost choking on the word. "No, fuck *you*. Bitch."

He left her to it, clambering over the stile and pushing through the hawthorn bushes that grew on the far side. He made it three steps into the next field—the anger pulsing inside his head with every heartbeat, making the sky dance—before forcing himself to stop.

"Fuck," he muttered.

He was angry at Sally because she was right. Maurice had been on death's door. Yes, they could have cut him open and sliced out enough of his cancer to keep him going, but he'd have been in constant pain, and he would have needed daily medication—and that's if he'd survived the operation and recovery period. The poor sod couldn't even see any more, could barely shuffle more than a few feet. He'd had the most amazing life, and she was right—it had been the right time for him to go.

In the distance, he heard Sally scream in frustration. And this time he didn't blame her. He was being an arsehole.

"Fuck," he said again, turning and fighting his way back to the stile. "Sally!" he yelled. "Sal, wait up, I'm sorry."

There was no sign of her in the field, which meant she had to have broken into a run. Roger set off after her, the ground crumbling beneath each step and making him feel like he was running in a dream, not getting anywhere. He kept his eyes down to navigate his route, staring so intently at the earth that he almost missed it—a flash of white in the trees to the left.

He stopped, his heartbeat the only sound in the world. For a second he thought he'd imagined it, but he squinted into the woods that edged the field and saw it again. Something white, moving fast.

"Sally!" he yelled. Why the hell was she going that way? It wasn't exactly a forest, just a strip of ancient woodland that stretched from their village down towards Beccles, but the trees were old, and they kept the last of the day at bay. Night had arrived early in the woods, and shadows crawled between their gnarled trunks. Roger shivered in his Barbour jacket.

Just leave her, he thought. *She'll come around.*

But he'd been in the wrong, and the longer he left it without an apology, the worse it would be.

"Sally!" he called, scrabbling up the low embankment and grabbing a branch. He hauled himself into the shade of a monstrous yew tree, the air instantly ten degrees cooler. Where had she gone?

He stepped carefully over the roots, blinking the harvest dust from his eyes and trying to make sense of the shifting darkness. There, a glimpse of something white, gone in an instant.

"I know you loved him," Roger said, his words swallowed whole by the trees. "He loved you too. I'm sorry for what I said, I'm still upset."

Her reply was a whisper, or maybe her voice too was rendered inaudible by the crushing weight of branches and leaves overhead. Roger hesitated, looking back. The field seemed further away than it should be, the day too dark. He'd never liked the woods, not since he was a kid and he'd got lost in Thetford Forest on a school trip—for less than an hour, but that was long enough when you were nine. Nothing made you feel smaller than the trees, nothing made you feel more vulnerable.

"I'll tell you what," he said, venturing forward again. "Let's get away for a bit. Let's just take some time and go somewhere."

A twig snapped beneath his foot with a sound like a gun going off. His heart just about exploded and he clamped a hand to his chest.

"Sally?"

There was another noise ahead, but this one didn't sound like Sally. It didn't sound human at all. It was a low growl, almost dog-like but louder. Maybe somebody was walking their dog through the woods. It wasn't a common route—they'd hardly met anyone in all the years they'd been crossing the fields—but new people were moving this way all the time thanks to the big estates they were building.

He pressed on, using the huge trunks to steady himself as the ground got rougher. Every now and again he'd catch a glimpse of Sally's coat, closer with every step. She was sitting down. *Lying* down, maybe. Waiting for him, he hoped. Maybe they'd hug, tell each other they were sorry, then head home. Maybe this really could be the start of something new between them, a kind of freedom. Roger stepped into a puddle of sunlight as he had the thought, feeling a powerful surge of relief—one that almost bordered on joy.

It didn't last.

He climbed down from the torso-thick root of another tree, and suddenly she was there.

At least, part of her was.

One arm, clad in white, stuck out from behind a clump of bracken. It twitched, the hand bouncing on the ground like it was beckoning him. Now that he'd stopped walking he was aware of a sound—something wet, something *crunching*.

He opened his mouth to speak Sally's name but found nothing in his lungs except dust. Keeping one hand on the tree he took a step to the side, then another, and every time he did, more of his girlfriend slid into view—her elbow, her bicep, her shoulder, her neck.

At first, he couldn't figure out what was all over her skin, because in the darkness of the forest it looked like ink. It was only when he took another step that he saw the blood on the lapel of her coat, so bright and so red that it looked fake. And that's the first thing that came into his head, that this wasn't real, that it was a trick, a *prank*. Even when he stumbled towards her and saw her face, her eyes open and pleading and desperate, he couldn't believe it.

Because what he was seeing was impossible.

There was something sitting on her. Something big, hunched, its body covered in clumps of matted hair, so dark that it looked like it was made of nothing but smoke and shadow. The deformed lump of its head lifted for a moment and it sniffed the air through the ragged holes of its nostrils. Then its muzzle plunged down into Sally's chest, making her grunt.

No.

The fear was unlike anything Roger had felt in his life, it was a living thing inside him, cold and dark. Sally stared at him, her mouth opened, and even in the gloom of the forest Roger could make out the word on her bloody lips.

Please.

She lifted her arm and the creature pinned it back down with its paw. She tried again, as if expecting Roger to grab her hand and pull her away.

He didn't. He couldn't.

The creature—a dog, surely, a *hound*—lifted its head again and looked back through the trees. Its eyes were two silver pennies, full of nothing but hunger and death.

But beneath them, its grinning lips were almost human.

It sniffed the air. It stared at Roger. And beneath it, Sally reached for him with the very last of herself.

I'm sorry, he said. He screamed it inside his head, hoping that she would hear him even though he was silent, even though his back was to her, even though all he could do was run. *I'm sorry! I'm sorry! I'm sorry!*

ABOUT THE AUTHOR

Alex Smith wrote his first book when he was six. It wasn't particularly good, but it did have some supernatural monsters in it. His DCI Robert Kett thrillers have monsters in them too, although these monsters are very human, and all the more terrifying for it. In between these books he has published twelve novels for children and teenagers under his full name, Alexander Gordon Smith—including the number one bestselling series Escape From Furnace, which is loved by millions of readers worldwide and which is soon to become a motion picture. He lives in Norwich with his wife and three young daughters.

Find out more at alexsmithbooks.com

R
RELENTLESS
MEDIA

In Drawer

Printed in Great Britain
by Amazon

56394659R00173